THRONE *of* SERPENTS

Published by Renegade Publishing

Dust Jacket Design by Sanja Balan

Case Artwork by Santa Balan

Proofreading by Red Ninja Edits

ASIN: B0BLQRF5MMISBN

ISBN (hardcover): 979-8-89238-997-6

Created with Vellum

To Kylo:

Thank you for starting my obsession with villains.

THE DRAGON ISLES
BIENN
Biengel
Dragon Nests
Pearl Grove
NEAMH
Dune
Radiem
VADON

Tythe
Wyrn
Bathez
Black
Diamond
Mines
Perish
ISLES OF
LORNE
SEKMIS
Ode
Hallows
Siren
Cove
MEITH

SYNOPSIS

He's the villain of her dreams and she's the traitor of his nightmares.

Wren's world shattered the day Arrik became king and he broke every promise he'd made to her. Fueled by rage and betrayal, she must double-cross her husband to save the realm from war. But with every passing day, as her devilish king tries to entice Wren to stand by his side, she finds herself struggling not to fall for his charms and seduction.

After years of scheming, Arrik finally held the world in his hands. But it wasn't enough. Secretly, he'd always wanted someone to share it with, but his queen was hiding something from him. On the brink of civil unrest, he must secure his power at all costs. Even if it means losing the woman he loves.

PROLOGUE

THE LINE BETWEEN VILLAIN AND HERO WAS THIN.

Wren thought she had honor.
That life was black and white.
But it wasn't and she didn't.
The Dark Court had changed her.
Or she liked to tell herself that.
The darkness had always been there.
Now she welcomed it.
Like the serpent she'd been all along.
She could shred her skin,
But that didn't change who she was.
A villain. A liar. A monster.
All hail the Dragon Queen.

CHAPTER 1

WREN

She hardly knew the woman in the mirror.

A year ago she was carefree, with the promise of a happy marriage and long life.

Sure, the scarlet hair she was currently styling back from her face in several braids was the same, as was the line of her jaw and cheekbones, and her pale green eyes were still blue... except now they held a world weariness that infused her soul.

Everything was different.

After witnessing the ransacking of the Dragon Isles, the murder of her parents, and being kidnapped by the barbarian elf prince of Verlanti, anyone would change. But that had only been the beginning.

She'd been wed against her will. She'd discovered her childhood sweetheart was not, in fact, dead, but had been a spy from Vadon all along. Her dragon had been murdered before her very eyes, only for her to be saved—in more ways than one—by another dragon.

Wren had discovered who her real father was and hated him. She'd gained a brother through blood, and another through love and trust. She'd found friends and made enemies.

Someone is being morbid today...

Wren sighed and dropped her braids.

Her biggest problem was Arrik, her dark elf husband, the man who swayed her heart, set her body to burning, and asked for her to trust him, only for him to prove time and time again that he could not be trusted.

Help me, and the Dragon Isles will be yours once again, Arrik had said, before humiliating her instead of including her in his plan, binding her to his side as his queen consort instead of letting her go.

HE WAS THE ROOT OF HER TROUBLE, AND YET SHE couldn't seem to let him go.

Because you're weak.

Wren squared her shoulders and stared her reflection in the eye. She'd made mistakes in the past, and it was true that there was something about Arrik that drew her in like a moth to a flame. But she was done playing his game. She was over dancing to someone else's tune. It was time for her to take matters into her own hands. She'd play the part of Arrik's perfect little queen because *she* wanted to, all the while orchestrating her own plans.

Free the slaves.

Release the Dragon Isles from the hold of Verlanti, Vadon, and any other force hoping to utilize it for their own gain.

Keep Britta safe.

Undo the hold Arrik has on her heart, body, and soul.

Wren shivered, though her dressing room was warm and balmy as was typical in Verlanti. Despite what her mind said, her heart would make it more difficult than she anticipated, she was sure.

She blew out a breath, slowly finished her braids, then began adorning them with tiny black diamonds—taken from the mask Arrik had created for her for the masquerade ball using stolen Dragon Isle gems. Her lady's maids had been scandalized when she sent them away with the plan of dressing herself. As if she hadn't been doing simple tasks most of her life.

With resignation, she slipped into the black dress they'd chosen for her. The wisps of silk and gauze caressed her body as she adjusted the silk so all of her important bits were covered.

Wren looked once more upon her countenance in the mirror.

Yes, the woman staring back at her was definitely a stranger.

A liar.

A rebel.

A dark elf queen.

Verlanti's undoing.

The compromises you've made to get here.

Wren brushed a braid behind her right ear and touched the tiny scars on the edge that had hidden the reality of her parentage. A secret that had been in plain sight Wren's whole life.

Half elf. And her sire was the worst of the worst.

She dropped her hand and fisted her thin skirts as she thought of Idril. He was a blight on the world. Was it depraved that she wanted to kill him? *Yes*. Did she feel bad at the thought? *No*.

She had other worries though.

Just how low would she have to go to end Lord Idril's life forever? What further compromises would she have to make to give Queen Astrid her comeuppance, or get through to her Aunt Vienne that consorting with slave-owners for the *sake* of freeing slaves was only going to end in disaster?

How many more transgressions would she sweep under the rug to justify the way her heart throbbed whenever she saw her wretched husband?

But Wren couldn't stop the changes occurring within her any more than she could stop the sun from shining.

Britta, think of Britta.

A thread of happiness wrapped around her heart. Soon she'd be reunited with her sister, that much she was certain of. So long as she focused on Britta, everything would be all right.

At least that was what she kept telling herself.

An oddly familiar whistle floated in from the palace gardens. Wren stiffened and glanced toward the white gossamer curtains that gently waved in the breeze. It couldn't be. Perhaps it was because she was thinking of Britta, and home, but the whistle sounded decidedly like...

A dragon song?

The whistle came again.

Snapping to attention, Wren lifted her skirts and ran on silent feet to the door. She twisted the lock and backed away before turning on her heel and striding to the gardens. Worry and fear bubbled under her skin with every step she took toward the whistle. For she *did* know it, and it *was* a dragon song.

Namely, her late dragon's favorite song.

And also Rowen's.

That bastard.

Only he'd be so bold.

She eyed the courtyard, looking for any spies and found none, then pushed through the tall plants that surrounded the pond toward the sound of the whistle, planning to wring his bloody neck.

"You shouldn't be here," Wren hissed, the moment she caught sight of the dark-skinned former love of her life.

Rowen grimaced from his position leaning against a wide-trunked palm tree, though he made no effort to retreat from the gardens. He rolled his dark eyes. "Hello to you too."

"What are you doing here?" she demanded, as she closed the gap between them to stand beneath the palm leaves. "This is dangerous."

Rowen snorted. "Says the woman sleeping with the enemy."

Wren blushed, but didn't refute his assumption. He didn't deserve to know anything about her life. Plus, he'd just take it right back to Vienne and Vadon.

"Why are you here?"

Rowen sighed. "Fine, have it your way. You shouldn't go

through with the coronation. You're already in trouble with the rebellion. Why are you going out of your way to anger them further?"

"Who said I did this because of the rebellion?" Wren countered, jutting out her chin and crossing her arms as she squared up against Rowen. But the man remained unperturbed.

"I hardly think you'd betray them, Wren." And then, softly: "That isn't the kind of woman you are."

Wren hated that Rowen could still speak to her like that. Gently. Fondly. As if he knew her. The girl he knew died back on the Dragon Isles.

Give him a little something so that he'll leave you alone.

"I have a plan," Wren finally relented.

"Which is...?"

"Not something I care to divulge to you *or* the rebellion. Given how often I've been left out of every other plan thus far, I'm sure you understand why."

A small smile quirked Rowen's mouth. "That is your right, of course. But you should know: if you don't report into the rebellion soon, they'll take this coronation as an act of war against them."

"And they would be foolish to act on such a stupid conclusion," Wren spat out. She eyed Rowen warily. "Do *you* believe me? Do *you* trust me?"

He raised his hand as if to stroke Wren's cheek and she flinched. She couldn't help it. His smile faltered and he pulled back slowly. "I always have, Wren," he said, very quietly. A secret for only the two of them to hear. "You say you don't know me, and never have. That the person I was back on the isles was a lie. But I swear that isn't true. You *know* me, Wren, so if I say I believe you—that I trust you—I hope you can afford me the same courtesy. I've loved you all my life. That was never a lie."

Her heart clenched as she stared at her childhood friend.

All at once, Wren's stony façade melted away. She was no longer in love with Rowen—that feeling had drowned when she'd mourned his apparent murder—but that didn't mean a large part of her didn't still care for him, didn't long to have him on her side, defending her corner, respecting her wishes. They'd always had each other's backs.

She could really use that right now. But she wouldn't count on it.

Letting out a massive sigh, her hands dropped to her sides as her shoulders slumped. "Then stop contradicting me at rebellion meetings. Stop trying to ice me out. Quit all the lying."

"It isn't you I don't trust. It's your...husband."

She quirked an eyebrow. "You think I don't know how to handle Arrik?"

"I think you *think* you can, which is different."

"Now you're just being obtuse."

"And you're being childish." When Rowen's smile returned, Wren didn't dare mirror it. Rowen was so disarming—so easy for her to fall into step with—that if she wasn't careful she'd end up falling into sway with *his* suggestions rather than her own.

She shook out the slackness in her body and lifted her chin. "I'll talk to the rebellion when I'm good and ready. I have things to do here, and I'm not their slave. If anything, they serve *me*, not the other way around."

"Now that sound like my queen," Rowen murmured, his dark eyes glinting with pride as his smile widened into a bright, toothy grin. An achingly familiar sight.

When those eyes flickered to Wren's lips and Rowen leaned forward in a way that was achingly familiar, her hand moved without thought. Wren's slap across his left cheek was vicious, startling and reflexive. The crackof her hand across his skin echoed in the garden. They stared at each other in the resulting quiet.

"Don't do that again," Wren warned, breaths coming hot and heavy as the unspoken threat behind her words were absorbed by Rowen.

The man's gaze narrowed as he rubbed his cheek and he opened his mouth to speak.

She held up her hand and took a step back. Wren didn't want to hang around to hear another word he said. Whether he was intentionally doing it or not, Rowen was still trying to manipulate her. He wanted her to be the princess he knew. The princess he purported to love.

But she wasn't that young woman anymore.

For better or worse, she was an entirely different person than the Princess Wren who once wanted nothing more than to marry the future captain of the Dragon Isles navy.

They weren't those people anymore.

"You should watch your back, Wren!" Rowen called out after her, as Wren stalked away from him toward her chambers. "Neither of us wants you as the enemy."

The enemy.

Was that all she was now? An enemy to the rebellion? To Lord Idril?

To Arrik?

She stormed through the curtains to her suite and back to the mirror.

Her hair was a little ruffled, cheeks flushed, and determination filled her eyes.

"If it's an enemy they want, it's an enemy they'll get," Wren muttered to her reflection, no longer hating what she saw quite so much. She had goals she wanted to achieve, and people she wanted to save.

If being the enemy was the only way to do that, then an enemy was exactly what the dragon princess would be.

CHAPTER 2

WREN

STILL SHAKEN BY HER ENCOUNTER WITH ROWEN, WREN ran her trembling hands over her dress and adjusted her hair. Time to show no fear.

She nodded to her reflection and left her chambers to attend the coronation ceremony. Two guards peeled away from the walls and fell into step behind her.

Soon Arrik would be king.

And in a few short minutes Wren, the dragon princess, would be queen and consort to the king of Verlanti.

It seemed unfathomable to her.

Her steps were silent as she wove through the white marble hallways, her silent shadows trailing behind her. Her prince had been downright paranoid since his father's death. She was allowed nowhere without an escort.

It was annoying but necessary. Just the day before, an assassin had tried to poison her.

It still hadn't sunk in yet—but that could be because she tried not to think too much upon it. Any time she did, it felt like someone was trying to slowly choke the air from her lungs.

Keep your composure. Rowen himself said it. You're already acting like a queen, so just keep it up. Don't let anyone know how unsettled you are on the inside.

She swallowed hard when she spotted Arrik's second-in-command, Shane, impatiently waiting for her inside a nearby hallway.

There was no going back now.

Wren plastered a polite smile on her face when she fell into stride with Shane. The heavily scarred man glanced at her, his mouth twisting into an unpleasant grimace. What had she done now?

"Arrik doesn't take kindly to dalliances," he murmured, low and threatening as they strode through the cool, shadowed hallways of the Verlantian palace. But despite the cold air, Wren felt like she was boiling. Was Shane suggesting what she thought he was suggesting?

"Just what do you think you're implying?" Wren asked him, careful to keep her tone measured and emotionless. She trained her eyes directly in front of her, determined not to give the man even a hint of a reaction.

Shane let out a grunt. "You think I didn't see him in the gardens? The Vadonese man?"

"Is he alive?"

"For now."

“Is he in the dungeons?”

“No.” It was said grudgingly.

“Just how much did you see?”

“Enough.”

“If you saw us, then you know I wasn’t *dallying*. Perhaps you should examine your overactive imagination before accusing me of such things.”

Wren was inordinately satisfied to see that she’d gotten under the man’s skin. Shane stopped abruptly, so she did too. When she tilted her chin up to meet his eyes, she realized just how much she’d rankled him.

“Just who is he to you?”

Now she had to tread carefully. “Did you really think that I wouldn’t have my own allies in Verlanti? I’m the Dragon Isle heir.”

“So he’s one of your men?”

Was he? “Yes. Make sure you don’t kill him, or I’ll have your head.”

“Arrik might not be suspicious of you,” he growled, eyes narrowing, “but I am. And trust me, *Princess*, that’s something you don’t want. I have no qualms about destroying his chosen queen in order to protect the king.”

Wren didn’t doubt it. If her heart hadn’t been turned to steel over the last year, then Shane’s intimidation might well have worked. He was a terrifying man to behold, after all. But as it was, she knew she could handle Shane’s threat with ease.

“It pleases me to know Arrik has such a man in his corner,” she said, inclining her head graciously before continuing on her way to the ceremonial hall. "I would expect nothing less from you."

Summarily dismissed, Shane had no choice but to continue down the corridor with her, then open one of two gigantic, ornately carved doors to allow her entrance to the impending ceremony.

Arrik was already standing on a decadent raised dais at the head of the massive room, surrounded by loyal supporters, simpering court nobles, and no doubt furious men of Soren's alike. Even Wren could appreciate that Arrik cut a commanding, handsome figure in his king's garb. Everything he wore was a shade of black, as was his preference, from his cloak, to his shirt, to his supple knee-high boots. But it was the waistcoat he wore over the billowing shirt that caught Wren's attention most.

It was embroidered with silver thread and inlaid with the tiniest of Dragon Isle black diamonds. Those same diamonds were woven into the elaborate braids he had his silver hair styled in—which Wren had emulated in a looser style upon her own head. She fought the urge to bristle at seeing him covered in the diamonds he'd stolen from her homeland.

A land which he had sworn to give back to her, only to snatch that promise away the moment it was safe to do so.

Well, safe was the last thing Arrik was, if Wren had anything to do about it. But for now she had to play her part. With a winsome smile upon her face, Wren allowed Shane to part the crowd for her, granting her a clear and uninterrupted path toward the dais and her waiting husband. When he caught sight of her, Arrik's eyes went wide with appraisal, taking her in from her head to her toes and then back again. The lazy, satisfied smile of a contented man lifted his lips.

"You look like a queen," he murmured, when Wren took his hand and let him help her up the stairs onto the dais. He pressed a lingering kiss to her knuckles, heat filling his eyes as he gazed upon her.

He tucked her left hand into the crook of his arm and led her to the thrones.

Just off to the left stood Queen Astrid and Arrik's two brothers, Ares and Kalles—Kalles for once actually looking sober. He offered Wren a wicked grin and a quick wave when she looked his way.

"Thank you, my lord," Wren told Arrik, before dutifully sitting down on the throne prepared for her on the right-hand side of king's throne. These, too, had been adorned with Dragon Isle black diamonds, and his headrest was carved into the maw of a serpent, and hers a dragon. They looked like something out of a villain's lair.

They couldn't have been more fitting.

Arrik kept hold of Wren's hand as they sat, readying themselves for the master of ceremonies to begin the coronation. She was aware that he kept glancing at her out of the corner of his eye, a moment away from whispering something to her. Wren tried her best to ignore him—and the way her heart pounded even harder with every glance.

Heart of steel indeed.

But after the master of ceremonies had finished his preamble, Queen Astrid strode onto the center of the dais, in front of Arrik and Wren, and addressed the crowd. Arrik's hand tightened around Wren's so badly she winced. Was this not part of the plan?

"My wonderful court," the viper queen announced, her voice loud and euphonious as it boomed around the hall, "I fear that if I do not speak out on behalf of everyone, then nobody will. But we all know this is a sham! Prince Arrik"—Astrid pointed a sharp-taloned finger at Arrik—"has no claim to the throne! He is a bastard, as well we all know. So why are we allowing him to go through with this coronation?"

Wren kept her mask in place. She had been wondering when Astrid would try something.

All around the hall voices began murmuring, then shouting their assent. The problem was that, as far as Wren knew, Astrid was correct. Arrik had not told her any further prescient information about why he was so certain his claim for the throne would be accepted.

To Wren's left, Ares, the true heir to the throne after the murder of his elder brother, Cathal, and Astrid's son, looked somewhat uncomfortable as his mother continued garnering support. Aside from him being a playboy, Wren hardly knew a thing about Ares, though in contrast to Cathal, who had been wicked to the bone, he seemed more serious and introspective. He certainly lacked the drive and lust for battle that Arrik possessed.

Kalles, of course, seemed amused by the whole affair. Wren had known from the beginning that the youngest son of Soren would never sit upon the throne, and nor did he want to. He liked to play games and lose himself to his drugs too much.

In fact, he could be very useful to her. He had wanted Wren to kill Arrik on their wedding night, and yet he seemed to have a fondness for his brother. She flicked a bored glance between Kalles and Arrik. What was his endgame? Did he really care if Arrik was king? What was his part in all of this?

So many games.

"What are you going to do?" Wren finally asked the barbarian prince in an undertone, when the noise from the crowd swelled into a clamor. Arrik's devoted followers were screaming at the dissidents to be quiet, while those on the side of Astrid and former King Soren refused to back down.

It was therefore to Wren's surprise when her husband returned her question with a tiny smile. He finally let go of her hand—it had started cramping, he had been holding on to it so hard—and stood to address the room.

He always has a plan.

When he swept Astrid to the side, the woman huffed in displeasure. Wren had to wonder how she'd ever been fooled by her kind words and actions toward her.

She thought she would be consort to Arrik should he take the throne, but I have taken her place. I should not expect any love, nor favors from her now.

"While it is true that I am one of Soren's bastard children"—Arrik emphasized the *one*—"there is something very few of you are aware of. Cathal was not older than me. No. I was born first." An uproar quickly followed.

"Being the firstborn changes nothing when you're a bastard," Astrid said, her upper lip curling unpleasantly.

"That may be true, but my father being the...shall we say, *interesting* figure that he was, thought it would be amusing to put in writing that I was recognized as his true son and heir to the throne proper." His stony face broke into a disarmingly charming smile directed at Astrid. "Perhaps if Cathal hadn't been such a useless waste of space, he'd have been disinclined to do such a thing."

Wren barely kept her expression schooled. Could it be true?

Astrid's nostrils flared and her hands shook at her sides. "You dare speak such lies—"

"His Royal Highness speaks the truth," the master of ceremonies cut in, his sonorous voice demanding everyone's attention. From his cream-colored robes he pulled out a scroll and unrolled it. The unmistakably elegant slant of High King Soren's handwriting could be seen upon the parchment. "I have here the written confirmation in question." A soft cough. "Forgive me, Queen Astrid, but I would not have permitted this ceremony to go ahead if I had not witnessed the existence of this document personally."

Wren's heart pounded furiously as silence spread over the room like a heavy blanket.

Arrik would be king, and there was nothing anybody could legally say against it. Not even Astrid's or Soren's staunchest supporters.

It was done.

He would rule the northern half of the world.

The queen mother turned and stormed from the ceremonial hall without another word. Arrik exchanged a look with Wren when he turned, and indicated she should stand by his side. Wren understood exactly what the look meant.

Astrid means trouble. This is not the last time she will attempt to interfere.

But Wren was ready for Astrid. The master of ceremonies continued with the coronation, first placing an elaborate crown upon Arrik's head, then on Wren's. The flames of determination and rage flared inside she'd felt as she approached the hall.

Of course she could handle the previous queen. She could handle anything. All she needed was time, a little help from her friends...

And the power of a queen.

CHAPTER 3

ARRIK

TODAY SHOULD HAVE BEEN A HAPPY DAY, BUT HE WAS IN A foul mood.

Wren was dancing with Kalles.

His wife dancing with the brother who had quite happily sought to have her murder him on their wedding night.

Kalles had never truly explained why he'd done that save to say that it was fun. True, their family was known for games and assassination, but something around his explanation rang false, even for Kalles.

Was his brother really so broken that he'd tried to have Arrik murdered at the hands of his wife just for the fun of it? Or was it a desperate cry for attention? For help?

He brushed a braid from his cheek and took a deep sip of his wine while he watched his wife smile at his brother. It caused something dark and ugly to wriggle in his chest. She shouldn't smile at any man like that except for him.

Arrik sighed. His wife no doubt would wring his neck if she discovered his barbaric thoughts. A small smile tugged at his lips. Maybe he would tell her just to get a reaction out of her. She was something to behold when angry.

Kalles tossed his head back and laughed, pulling Wren closer.

Now that was just uncalled for. It was like his brother was taunting him.

Calm down. You know Kalles likes to needle you. Let it go.

Before Arrik met the dragon princess, he'd never have given it a second thought. Indeed, he'd have found a way to prove that Kalles had been behind the assassinations of his previous brides,and have him executed. But now...now things were different. Arrik was able to see the bigger, twisted picture much more clearly, and Kalles was more than he seemed.

The question remained: was Kalles friend or foe?

His brother in question caught his eye and winked, before spinning Wren around.

The bastard *was* taunting him.

Kalles was taking up too much of Wren's time. More infuriatingly, she almost appeared as if she was having fun. *His* wife, lookinglike the female mirror image of Arrik in her onxy gown, gleaming black diamonds, braided hair, and fierce expression.

The perfect woman for him, and him only.

But she was laughing at something Kalles said.

She's rarely ever laughed with me.

Jealousy, hot and molten and dangerous, filled Arrik's veins as he stood from his throne and prowled through the crowd toward the dancing pair. Enough of this farce. It was time *he* held his own wife in his arms.

A hand on his shoulder gave Arrik pause. A snarl hovered on his lips as he whirled around to confront whoever had thought it wise to interrupt him. But in a moment Arrik plastered a neutral expression onhis face. No need for everyone to see how blatantly in love he was with his own bloody wife.

"Yes?" he replied crisply, staring down Oriza, who had been one of King Soren's advisers before he had dispatched with his father and the supporters in his circle most likely to try to assassinate him in his sleep. The wispy-haired, heavily lined man in front of him had been no staunch supporter of Soren, preferring simply to help whoever held the most power, and so it followed that Oriza was still alive—still useful.

Oriza glanced around Arrik's shoulder toward Wren and smiled slyly. "I'm sorry. I must have been interrupting you trying to reach your wife." Arrik was too stunned by the shockingly accurate observation to respond, so the man continued: "After all, you must be impatient to begin the bedding ceremony and complete your coronation. Securing the throne with so many heirs and enemies around is imperative."

Ah. That's what he meant. Nothing to do with my actual feelings for Wren.

A bitter taste filled Arrik's mouth, though he couldn't pinpoint why. With a tight nod, he acknowledged the old man's comment. "Indeed. If you would please excuse me, then."

Somewhat blindly, Arrik strode across the dance floor to stand imposingly beside Kalles and Wren until his infuriatingly confusing brother stopped spinning the dragon princess around.

Queen consort now. His queen.

The thought satisfied him.

Kalles had the audacity to grin sloppily at him, clearly drunk. But when was he not?

"Brother," Kalles hiccupped, "or should I say, my king? Did you know—*hic*—that your wife is a *glorious* dancer? So light on her feet!"

"I'm well aware," Arrik said, his voice like chips of ice even to his own ears. "I've danced *and* fought with her. Nobody is as graceful as she is."

It was this comment that brought Kalles and Wren to a complete stop. Wren glanced at Arrik—the first time since they'd been crowned—with a look of pure suspicion, as if his compliment was laced with poison or daggers or some other danger that she should be wary of. But it was his brother's expression that bothered him more.

It was piercing—*knowing*.

Kalles could see that Arrik's compliment was genuine. More than genuine: it was made about someone he clearly very much cared for. It was knowledge he didn't want his brother to have. He needed to be more careful. If anyone really perceived his obsession and adoration for his wife it could ruin him.

With a soft cough, Kalles let go of Wren's waist and

bowed graciously despite his drunkenness. "I can see where I'm not wanted," he said, before ambling through the dancers whilst pulling a silver hip flask from his waistcoat.

Fool.

With all eyes on them, Arrik wasted no time in gently touching Wren's elbow and careening her toward the exit of the ceremonial hall. He was tired of sharing his wife with everyone. He'd hardly even seen her in the last few days.

Wren clucked her tongue in distaste. "Who said I was ready to leave?"

"Me. I'm done with the noise."

As more and more people noticed the king and queen leaving, a low round of hollering, whooping, and cheering filled the air.

He hid his smile as his wife's cheeks grew as crimson as her hair, though she kept her head held high. He loved that she was still innocent in some ways.

"I can see your point," she relented as they entered the hallway, guards materializing behind them like wraiths as they moved through the lantern-lit corridors. "Where are we going?"

"My chambers." He smiled. "*Our* chambers."

Wren's face grew even more scarlet, though her gait turned stiff and slow as they neared Arrik's chambers. He knew why, but he chose not to comment on it. Instead he asked, "What did Kalles say that made you laugh so much?"

A snort. "Tell me, Arrik"—his heart throbbed to hear his name on Wren's tongue—"did you spend any time this evening *not* watching me?"

"So you knew I was watching you?"

"Of course. Your eyes followed me everywhere I went. There was a portrait back in Lorne—I hated it, but my mother thought it was wonderful—of a man and a dragon. Both of their eyes were painted in such a way that they followed you down the corridor. It gave me nightmares as a child."

Arrik let out a burst of unexpected laughter. Wren had never told him anything of her life before he took it as his own. Nothing important. Nothing trivial. Nothing happy. Nothing upsetting.

Simply nothing.

To hear her talk about something from her past with such fondness was a gift Arrik never knew he'd been longing for.

"We had a similar one, actually," he said, as they turned the corner toward his chambers. "It was of my father. Awful painting. Perhaps it was the same artist?"

Wren offered him the smallest of smiles, which made him feel like he'd just won a great battle. What was this woman doing to him?

"Wouldn't that make this such a small world. And Kalles was just relaying some filthy jokes he'd once heard from some Dragon Isle sailors. It was...comforting...to listen to something that felt like *home*."

Curse him.

Arrik glared at the far wall, spying two more guards standing in front of his door waiting expectantly for them. Of course his brother would be the one to bring her comfort.

Calm down. Be happy that someone brought her joy.

He exhaled heavily, noticing how Wren clutched the

sleeves of his shirt, nails digging in. "You shall not come inside with us," Arrik ordered the two men.

The blond soldier glanced at his companion uneasily. "Your Majesty, there must be witnesses to prove that the ceremony took place."

"I'm well aware of that fact. My own men will bear witness." At this, Wren's eyes flitted to Arrik's, a look of absolute betrayal on her face. Behind them, Ronan and Shane filed down the corridor, having been dutifully following from a safe distance. Ronan winked at Wren, but she ignored him.

In fact, Wren ignored everyone, making no effort to move nor protest, nor say a single word. So Arrik lifted her into his arms—disappointed when she continued to do nothing—and carried her over the threshold into his chambers. Shane closed the door in the faces of the guards.

When Arrik felt a blade pressed into his gut, he let out a low chuckle. "Disappointed but not surprised," he said, rolling his eyes when he took in the tiny silver blade Wren had held between herself and his stomach. "I thought we were over this part, *wife*." He hadn't planned on touching her this night, but a small part of himself that he'd locked away hoped Wren would let him undress her and worship her like the goddess she was.

Even thinking about it make heat course through his body.

Her lips curled into a snarl. "If you think I'm letting you touch me—"

"Then you would be thinking wrong."

CHAPTER 4

WREN

"WHAT DID YOU JUST SAY?" SHE GROWLED, THE SMOOTH metal feeling slippery in her sweaty palm.

This was not how she'd envisioned this happening.

"I said I wouldn't touch you. Not unless you want me to, which going by the knife you're holding against me is unlikely. So sheathe the blade, savage wife. I have no designs on you despite how much I want you."

A shock of surprise and desire ran through her body at his blunt confession, but she didn't focus on them.

For a long moment Wren didn't move, choosing instead to glare up at the confusing man holding her close against his chest. Her husband did not seem fazed in the slightest to have a knife pressed against his gut. Even if it *was* laughably small—it was the only weapon Wren could conceal within her dress—it was, after all, still a blade, and she could wield it with fatal results. How easy it would be to kill him right now.

You're a liar. You've allowed him to wriggle into your heart.

That was the horrible, shameful truth.

It made her want to kill him though. It was preferable to conceding to her throbbing heart and flushed skin to overrule her brain and allow Arrik to take her to bed.

It would be so easy to give in.

Slowly, though every instinct told her not to, Wren pulled the knife away and allowed Arrik to gently place her down on the floor. She had expected him to look amused by her protest. Instead, a strange sort of sadness twisted the wry smile on his lips.

Her heart withered the tiniest bit, but Wren didn't want to think about what that meant, or how it made her feel.

"There won't be a bedding ceremony," he said quietly, so the guards on the other side of the door could not hear, "so don't fret your beautiful head about it." He gently crooked a finger beneath her chin and lifted so she met his gaze. "When you let me have you, it won't be because duty demands it. It will be because you burn for me as much as I burn for you."

A shiver ran down her spine as he held her gaze once more.

Denial was on the tip of her tongue, but she couldn't utter the words.

Looking satisfied, Arrik nodded and then released her.

A strange sense of déjà vu overcame Wren as Arrik padded away from her toward his wardrobe, carelessly shedding articles of clothing as he did so. It was like their original wedding night all over again. Wren and Arrik's twisted relationship had come a long way since then, but in many ways it remained exactly the same: Wren didn't trust him; he underestimated her; and their marriage was a sham.

Why did that make her feel the same sense of sadness she'd only just witnessed upon her husband's face? She liked to think there was a future for them, but deep down she was worried he wouldn't let go of his poisonous dream of ruling the world.

When Arrik finished removing his waistcoat, shirt, belt, and began unlacing his trousers, Wren found herself flushing and turning to face the bathing gardens. The rustle of clothing caused her breath to hitch. She found herself focusing so hard on a fountain in the gardens that the features of the stone elf set within it became blurry.

It's completely acceptable that watching Arrik undress makes your heart feel like it's going to come crashing through your ribcage. You're just human. There's no shame in that.

"Something the matter, Your Highness?" Ronan called from her left, his voice growing louder as he approached. "I didn't peg you for being so shy! You're in front of friends now. No need to be such a pru—"

Wren whirled around and tossed her knife in the redhead's direction, deliberately only just missing his head and lodging the blade deep into the wooden lamppost behind him. He glanced at the blade and then back to her. Much to her dismay, Ronan smiled indulgently like he was fond of her, and it didn't seem to deter him in the slightest.

What was with these dark elf men? It was like their love language was violence.

Pot, meet kettle...

"I bet Arrik enjoys that fire in you *very* much," he teased.

Wren couldn't stand how easily the man got under her skin. She knew why he was doing it, and knew he meant no harm, but it rankled nonetheless. What annoyed her even more was that, had she known Ronan back in Lorne—if he were a sailor or a merchant or even a simple visitor—Wren would have found his bawdy charm and sense of humor agreeable. She'd have liked him.

She was being a prejudiced twit. And they both knew it.

"What's the plan, then..." she said, completely ignoring Ronan's comment and keeping her line of sight decidedly away from her devilishly handsome husband who was taking ages to get dressed. Maybe the barbarian was doing it on purpose to torture her. She waved a hand. "...if those guards outside are waiting to listen to us having...having...?"

"Having sex?" Arrik said, striding back into Wren's vision looking even more bloody handsome than ever in a loose pair of trousers and shirt with a long, fluttering robe worn open down the front. He'd removed the diamonds from his hair but kept the braids tied back. Wren didn't want to admit that she was disappointed he hadn't let his hair loose. She'd come to discover that, as striking as Arrik was dressed in all his black armor and finery, Wren preferred him like this. Casual. Relaxed.

Looking like a real person rather than the terrifying warmongering prince the songs and stories made him out to be.

Not a prince. A king.

Her gaze trailed his form. So why was part of her wishing no clothes adorned Arrik's body at all?

Get a hold of yourself.

He caught her lingering glance and the air seemed to crackle. Arrik closed the distance between them to place a soft, claret-colored swathe of material in her hands, cotton by the feel of it, as opposed to gauze and silk and chiffon. She smiled. Arrik did really know her, and she appreciated his gesture more than she'd ever admit.

"So..." she drawled, "what are we to do?"

With a feral grin, Arrik indicated toward Shane and Ronan with a thumb. "The two of them will be, ah, *consummating* on our behalf," he chuckled. "So get changed and don't worry about it."

She blinked slowly and stared at the two soldiers. How had she missed that...?

Ronan rolled his eyes. "It's not what you think. We'll be *pretending* to be you."

Wren blushed and nodded. Both men turned and moved back into the bedroom. Yet Arrik made no move to leave or to look away, his gaze following the line of Wren's neck, along her clavicle and down her breastbone with a burning hunger he made no attempt to hide.

Wren's breath caught in her throat. Swallowing hard, she just barely managed, "Do you mind?"

A wolfish smile. "Of course not. I enjoy looking at you."

The cad.

"You know what I mean!" Wren spat out, horrified at how easily her heart fluttered at the flirtation. Arrik's cackle of laughter followed her to the bathroom, where she changed into the flowing dress and matching robe her husband had given her. Everything fit like a glove, clinging to her in all the right places while still remaining cool and airy and maintaining her modesty.

It's as if he has the shape of my body committed to memory.

Wren ran the fabric of the robe between her thumb and forefinger before deciding to undo all of the braids in her hair. It left her hair set in soft, shining waves. Alongside the deep red dress and robe, she had to admit that she was a sight to behold. She looked lush and tumbled.

"But it's for *him*," she whispered, hating that she didn't in fact hate that at all.

A horribly feminine moan coming from the bedroom proper pulled Wren out of her anguished reverie. Bolting out of the bathroom, she caught Shane and Ronan standing on Arrik's bed, Shane letting out a grunt before kicking the headboard when Ronan loosed another moan.

She gaped.

There were no words.

This was what Arrik meant by them "consummating" things.

Shane kicked the headboard again and released a moan that sounded like a dying goat.

Wren slapped a hand over her mouth to keep from giggling and scurried for the gardens in dire need of an escape. Her husband was nowhere to be seen. Wondering where Arrik had gone, she circled the fountain, heading toward the outdoor bath, but paused when she heard a low whistle from above her.

"Up here," Arrik said. Wren tilted her chin toward the

sloping roof over Arrik's bedroom. He knelt by the edge of the dusk-colored tiles and let down a length of rope. He quirked an eyebrow when Wren made no effort to move. "Unless you want to listen to *them* all night." As if emphasizing his point, Ronan let out another of his pretending-to-be-her moans that sounded like a cat in heat.

Oh stars. There was no way she could deal with that racket all night.

Wren clambered up the rope without a second thought. Anything to get away from the pair of men making nightmare fuel for her brain. Arrik held out his hand and she hesitated, straining to keep hold of the rope. She'd missed too many training sessions and had started to get a little soft.

"Darling?"

Butterflies took flight in her belly at the endearment, and she found herself reaching for him. Arrik helped her to her feet when she reached the roof, his warm fingertips lingering across her palm long after he should have let go.

The moment was electric—an understanding passing between them that her mind hadn't agreed to. She let it happen, but just as equally didn't say anything when Arrik finally pulled his hand away entirely.

"Come with me," Arrik said, eyes shining with excitement as he led her across the roof. "I have a surprise for you."

"Not more of your men pretending to be in the lusty throes of passion, I hope."

"I just as equally never wish to hear that again. No, this is a surprise you'll like. I'm sure of it."

"That's awfully cocky of you." But Wren was intrigued;

she couldn't help it. Just what did Arrik want to show her that he was so certain she would enjoy?

There was only one way to find out.

And she was too weak to say no.

CHAPTER 5

ARRIK

SHE'D TAKEN HIS HAND.

It was all he could think about as they snuck along the roof, the starlit sky stretched out above them.

He saw her moment of hesitation but she'd chosen to trust him, and that was *everything*.

His heart pounded as they reached the gardens on the opposite side of the palace from his own chambers. Arrik climbed down, landing on the balls of his feet, and held his hands up to his wife. She stared down at him with fathomless eyes and swung her legs over the edge before hopping down. His muscles tensed as he caught her around the back of her thighs—her very naked thighs; her nightgown had slipped up in her descent. His hands longed to rove Wren's soft skin, but he curbed the desire. That was not what tonight was about.

Ever so slowly, he lowered his wife to her dainty feet, her body sliding sensuously against his.

Arrik gritted his teeth. It was the most exquisite torture.

"Come with me," he murmured. Stepping away from his wife, he held his hand out.

A thrill ran up his spine as she slipped her hand into his, this time without hesitation. Could this really be happening? How was he so lucky? He'd expected her to refuse to come with him, and he could hardly blame her given how he'd double-crossed her regarding the way King Soren died. It was a difficult decision to make, and he hated keeping the truth from her. But hopefully in time she'd forgive him. He was determined to make it up to her, to prove to Wren that she was right to remain by his side. As his partner. As his wife.

As his queen.

His ears picked up the ruckus of a rowdy group of the coronation guests. Quickly, he pulled Wren behind a copse of palm trees when the small group stumbled along the wide stone path that snaked through the gardens. They were taking their sweet time.

"Stars be good, how long are they going to be out there?" Wren muttered, shifting uncomfortably in the tiny hiding space they were both huddled in behind the trees. The revelers were taking their time traversing the gardens, preventing them from reaching his intended destination lest they be caught and their bedroom ruse discovered.

But Arrik hardly minded. This close to Wren, his nose

was full of her scent. Wild and sweet. Intoxicating. Like nothing he'd ever smelled from Verlanti, because the dragon princess was just about the most un-Verlantian woman Arrik was likely to ever meet.

His gaze flitted from the partygoers to Wren, then back again, then back to her. In their shadowy hiding place the claret nightdress and robe he'd gifted her back in his chambers looked almost black. Wren's long, lustrous hair waved softly around her face in the gentle breeze. When a lock of it just barely grazed her lips, Arrik smoothed it away and tucked it behind her ear without thinking.

His wife froze beneath his touch, but she didn't tell Arrik to unhand her. Just as she hadn't complained when his hands had lingered on her bare skin. Despite their past and his mistakes, he knew that she still felt *something* for him, even if she didn't want to. Yet he just as equally didn't want to push things too far, too quickly. That was the surest way he could think of to cause Wren to run for the hills.

He pulled his hand away and glanced toward the retreating group.

"The coast is clear," he breathed, forcing himself out of the same breathing space as Wren only with extreme difficulty. Cursing his inability to keep his thoughts clear, Arrik led the way on silent feet. With every step he became more and more aware of Wren following behind him, at least for now trusting his intentions.

He could work with that.

"Where are we going?" Wren finally whispered, breaking the silence that had stretched out between the two of them as if she had shouted. The two of them had re-entered the palace, their backs pressed against the wall behind a thick, enormous tapestry detailing Arrik's great-great-great grandfather's victory over Verlantian dissidents generations ago. The fabric scratched against Arrik's nose, but he ignored it.

Spying the way was clear, he slid his hand into Wren's and gently pulled her out of their hiding place, around a corner and, finally, through the door that led to their destination.

"Here," he said, once the door was firmly closed behind them and there was no further danger of being caught out. Wren sidestepped him and swept into the room, looking around when Arrik lit the sconces to illuminate the place.

"This is a...weapons storage?" Wren wondered aloud, taking in a wall covered floor-to-ceiling in dozens and dozens of blades: longswords, short swords, broadswords, rapiers, daggers, knives, and several curved blades that originated from way out to the east.

Each of them bought, chosen, commissioned, or plundered by Arrik himself.

"It's my personal weapons chamber," he said, feeling somewhat jittery when Wren moved from investigating the blades to the bows on the far wall. He realized then that it mattered to him what Wren thought of his collection—if she deemed any of the pieces unworthy, or too flashy, or just plain bad. If Arrik saw her display even the slightest annoyance toward any of the weapons, then he'd toss them into a furnace immediately and with no hesitation.

"You certainly have an...impressive collection," Wren mused, walking at a stately pace around the sparring ring that took up much of the center of the floor. She regarded the rows and rows of arrows all with different tips—silver, gold, steel, black diamond. Some even had a hidden chamber within the point which released a potent toxin into the target when a connection was made. Wren regarded all of them with a practiced eye.

Then, with a nod, she turned to face Arrik, intrigue coloring her expression. He'd captured her attention. Most ladies wanted flowers, jewelry, and trinkets. His bloodthirsty little wife liked weapons. A fact that he loved.

"Which is your favorite?" she softly asked.

"My...favorite?"

She nodded again.

"Out of everything in here?"

Another nod.

Arrik considered his answer for a moment, then with a slow grin realized that he already knew his reply. Waving Wren back over to the wall of blades, Arrik scanned the gleaming metal daggers until he found exactly what he was looking for.

A silver butterfly knife. Small, unadorned, plain. Burnished, even. But it was Arrik's favorite weapon nonetheless.

When he handed it to Wren, she gingerly took the blade. Then, with far more confidence, she flipped out the blade from the handle and performed a series of twists and tosses with the knife that demonstrated that the dragon princess was just as good with a dagger as she was with a bow.

Arrik couldn't tear his eyes away as his wife continued twirling the blade this way and that, the darkened silver of the knife glimmering in the low light of the room.

"Tell me what's special about it," Wren said. "Please."

It took Arrik far too long to work out what Wren was referring to.

The blade. She means the blade, you idiot.

He inhaled deeply and steeled himself. Arrik couldn't expect Wren to open up if he wasn't willing to do the same. "When I was young—maybe six or seven—my mother was all I had. She was fiercely protective of me. Looking back on it all, I knew she had good reason to be. She was—"

"A good woman," Wren finished for him. Her gaze was steady and unrelenting on Arrik's—the most eye contact she'd given him all evening. It made him feel vulnerable, but in a good way, like he wanted to continue slowly but surely peeling back the layers that made him who he was so that she could truly get to know him.

"She was," he continued hoarsely. "The best. Even when Soren killed her husband and forced himself on her, she didn't hate what became of it. She didn't hate *me*. She loved me fiercely, as if I was the most precious thing in the world to her."

A lump formed in the back of his throat. He still missed her.

Arrik was drawn from his thought when Wren placed a gentle hand on his elbow. He looked down at it, then back at her face. Was she really touching him of her own volition?

"That's because you were," she said. "Of course you were." The look in her eyes told Arrik that Wren understood exactly how he felt. Knew exactly what it was to have a person love you as completely as his mother did.

He wished his story had a better ending.

With a flourish he took the switchblade from Wren's

hand and snapped the blade back into the handle. "She gave me this blade so I might always be protected when she couldn't be there. She didn't want me to be weak the way she saw herself. Funny, I never once viewed her as weak. But Soren was too much for her. Life...well...she was so miserable but she always hid it from me. I should have seen it." He shuddered, full of guilt and grief. "She took her own life to escape Soren, and then all I had left between me and my bastard father was this blade."

Wren's hand stiffened on his elbow. "I'm sorry that happened to you. To her. I hope you'll believe me when I say she wasn't weak. She didn't die to escape you or leave you alone. There are some things people simply cannot heal from."

Something dark and painful gripped hold of Arrik's heart. Something that he was responsible for. "It's reassuring to hear you say as much," he said, because it was true. Arrik placed the switchblade back on the wall, then headed for a small storage room built into the back of the chamber, Wren's hand slipping from his elbow. He missed her touch immediately. She gave him comfort that he'd been missing for years.

"It wasn't your fault, you know."

Arrik froze by the door. "Why?"

"Why what?"

He spun around to face her. "Why comfort me?"

"Because a child should never bear the burden of what was put on his shoulders. It was Soren's fault alone. Not yours."

Heat pressed at the back of his eyes, and he blinked hard.

He did not deserve this woman. He'd taken everything from her and yet she still gave to him. It shamed Arrik to his very core. "The fact you still think that—and that you still wish to comfort me—speaks volumes about your character, Wren, as well as your mother's. And your father. But I took them from you. I took them from you the way Soren took my mother from me," he bit out gutturally. "Indirectly, but still responsible. The *only* one responsible. I can't do anything about that now. Maybe I never can. But..." Arrik squared his shoulders and gestured to the storage room. "I have to at least try to start somewhere."

Wren didn't move, but she cast a confused gaze into the open storage room, then back to Arrik's face. "I don't understand what you're trying to say. Just where is this...what are you doing?"

"Something I should have done a long time ago," he replied, before retrieving a bow and quiver that were *not* his own from the room. She gasped as he held them out to his wife.

Wren took them by reflex, but her hands were shaking. "...you kept these." It wasn't a question.

"I did," Arrik said softly. "It didn't feel right to leave them behind when I took you."

Wren stared down at her mother's trusted weapons in her hands. To Arrik it looked as if she could scarcely believe they were real. "But they—they shouldn't have mattered to you. *I* shouldn't have mattered to you. So why keep them?" A demand.

"Sometimes people do things they cannot understand," Arrik mumbled, more to himself than to Wren as he procured another, much heavier, item from the storage room, "only to understand it later."

Her fingers tightened on the bow. "Excuse me?"

"Never mind." He was getting too soft. "This is also for you," he said gruffly.

The dragon saddle he'd had commissioned for Wren the moment the deep blue sea dragon had attacked him was made of black, supple, shiny leather. It smelled of excellent craftsmanship and the finest materials.

Arrik hefted it from the storage room and set in gently on the floor before his queen with a smile. "We never exchanged wedding gifts. This is mine to you."

His smile disappeared when she retreated from the saddle as if it were made of vipers. Arrik frowned. What the devil had he done wrong this time? "What's wrong, darling?"

Wren's lower lip quivered and his heart sank. He'd hurt her and he didn't understand how.

She sucked in a shuddering breath. "I can't...I can't accept that, Arrik. You must have known I wouldn't accept it."

But why? "But you need one. For your new dra—"

"If I am to use a saddle with Trove, then it cannot come from you," Wren said, the words cutting like knives even though they'd been spoken softly. She shook her head miserably, clutching her mother's bow and quiver to her chest as she did so. "I'm sorry. It's beautiful. But I just can't."

"I don't understand." Wren's rejection stung. He was trying to welcome her beast into his home. They came as a pair, and Arrik wanted her to know that he accepted all parts of her.

"It is part of the bonding experience. Trove must accept a saddle made by my own hands. I'm sorry. This was truly thoughtful, my lord."

Some of her formality came back. A barrier she was trying to erect between them. He wouldn't allow it. "I understand," he said, heaving the saddle back into the storage room, "but it will always be here if you end up having need of it."

"Thank you for these," Wren said, voice wavering as she indicated toward the weapons in her hands. "Truly, thank you. I had thought I'd forever lost any and all connection I had to my mother."

All at once Arrik's heart felt like it was breaking in two. He'd done this to her. He'd taken away her family like Soren had taken his.

He was the villain.

His instincts overtook him and he closed the distance between himself and Wren. When he curled a finger under his wife's chin to tilt her face up to his, she let him do so. Her eyes were wet with tears Arrik knew fine well she would never shed in front of him, even though he wished she would.

Let me care for you. Let me be your strength.

"I cannot erase the pain I've caused you, Wren," he murmured, his fingers trailing from her chin, along her jaw and behind her ear. Arrik almost imagined Wren leaned into his touch. "But I'm going to try my best to atone for what I've done."

He sank to his knees and wrapped his arms around her waist, his face pressed to her soft belly. "I'll make you happy.

I *know* I can make you happy. But, I've never wanted to do that for anyone but my mother. I'll beg, borrow, and steal to bring you the world."

"...I think it's a good thing," Wren said, running her hand through his braids. "To want to make other people happy. To want to atone. But it means nothing if you don't put in the work, Arrik. Otherwise it's just words."

He knew exactly what his little dragon was insinuating here. Everything he'd said so far to her—every promise, every plan—had been subject to being twisted and broken whenever it suited him. She wouldn't believe that anything he said was more than words.

But he was determined to change that.

He'd burn the world for her.

CHAPTER 6

WREN

It was amazing how a piece of wood and sinew could change everything.

Her hands shook as she ran her fingers over the smooth lines of the bow. She never thought she'd see her mother's gift again, let alone lay her hands on it. Wren clutched it to her chest and closed her eyes. The last year had been horrific and surreal at best. At times she doubted she'd ever make it home, but if her bow could survive such a harsh place, so could she. She opened her eyes and placed the bow on her lap.

It was in perfect condition.

Her gaze darted to her sleeping husband. Not only had Arrik kept the bow after capturing Wren, he had maintained it, cleaned it, and stored it as if it was precious to him.

Like he claims you are to him.

Her stomach lurched at the same time her heart took flight. Wren squeezed the bow to ground herself.

How could she feel so grateful to the monster who'd taken everything from her? It was all so confusing. Logically, she knew they had both been caught up in the age-old games of their fathers, but the man had killed her parents, taken her prisoner, wed her against her will...and yet, she *yearned* for him, and had softened toward him.

All because he'd saved her mother's bow from being lost to her forever.

She was a sodding idiot.

Her attention once again wandered to her husband.

He slept on top of the covers covered by nothing but a sheet for the night had been too warm for anything more. Her stomach tightened as she remembered the look he'd given her right before asking her to come to bed. She'd refused him gently and opted to claim the chaise lounge near the cold hearth. Too much had been on her mind. Plus, it didn't help to have Ronan and Shane standing guard in the room. Even now she could feel their gazes on her from time to time.

Arrik sighed and rolled, the sheet shifting down and exposing all of his muscled back and the top of his buttocks. The heat in her belly increased. Since when had she begun to think backs were attractive?

Since Arrik stormed into your life, you wanton woman.

Wren stood from the chaise, leaned the bow against it, and padded to the bed. She stared down at the prince.

King.

He was now her king.

The thought caused a shiver to run down her spine and she leaned closer, conscious of the guards watching her every move. Just who was this man that he could instill in her such lust and longing? That she could feel gratitude for him, and feel sorry for him, and want to comfort him over the atrocities committed against his mother?

Wren brushed her fingertips over his bicep and down his arm, sitting on the edge of the bed. His hand rested near his face on the pillow. She traced a path back up his arm to the pulse in his neck.

It would be easy to kill him, but her heart wasn't in it.

Unbidden, she stroked a piece of hair out of his face. He'd done the same to her the night before, as if he'd viewed her as a person worth being gentle with rather than just his hostage and bargaining chip.

Arrik's pale eyes snapped open.

"Are you here to kill me, wife?" he asked, his voice still rough with sleep.

Wren gulped slowly; it didn't escape her notice that her husband watched her throat as she did. "Not yet."

"Then just torture, then?"

Without her say-so, she smiled. "Something like that."

Before she had the wits to stop it, Arrik used the full weight of his body to tumble Wren beneath him, pinning her arms above her head using the span of a single hand. She gasped, embarrassed by how easily he'd gotten the best of her.

"Did you sleep well, dearest?" he teased, a slow grin forming on his face as she tried to wiggle out of his grip. It was a pitiful display. With every brush of their bodies, she became more aware of how much she liked his weight against her.

She was a wicked, wicked woman.

Wren could not win against Arrik in a battle of brute strength, but maybe she could surprise him. Her husband slid a leg between hers and she struck. She snapped her legs around his waist, hiking her nightgown up, and bucked her hips to flip him, but he didn't budge. It only pressed them more intimately together.

She choked on her surprise when Arrik's entire body tensed against hers, hard and prone wherever his skin touched hers. His pupils dilated and his other hand clutched her naked thigh, fingers pressing into her sensitive skin.

The air was charged with tension; sound ceased to exist as she stared up into his eyes, his silver hair haloing their faces. It was like the second before a viper struck.

He shifted and she read intention, desire, and *need* a moment before he claimed her lips.

Wren let it happen.

They hadn't kissed recently, save for one obligatory kiss during the ceremony—and yet now, away from bedding expectations and the weight of their entwined past, they burned for each other.

"That's it, darling. Let me taste my queen properly," he murmured between drugging kisses.

Her senses spun and she sank her fingers into his soft hair, pulling him even closer. He released her wrist and laced their fingers together, nipping her bottom lip and then soothing it with his tongue.

She shivered and pressed her chest against his, causing him to growl and bear more of his weight down on her.

It was divine.

It was sin.

It was truth.

Someone cleared their throat and she flinched.

Ronan and Shane.

Arrik growled and stared down at her with a raging inferno in his gaze.

"We have company, little dragon." His words were soft but tinged with regret and want.

Wren yanked her hands away from him and forced her legs to release him as he rolled away with a groan. Face flaming, she practically vaulted from the bed, tugging down her nightgown. Ronan chuckled and she glared at the redhead, her face probably as bright as his hair.

"Don't you make fun of me after what I heard last night," she snarled, smoothing her tousled hair back from her face as Arrik climbed from the bed with the sheet around his waist. Her mouth watered at the muscular V that disappeared beneath the cloth.

She spun her back so that she couldn't see any of the men and stared blankly out at the gardens. She registered the rustle of clothing. At least he was getting dressed. All his naked skin was causing havoc on her mind and body. And she didn't like it one bit.

Why did he tempt her so?

"I'm dressed, love," Arrik rumbled, humor coloring his tone.

Wren swallowed and forced herself to face the men. She

wasn't a coward, nor would she be ashamed of her actions. She was married and they were natural.

Head held high, she managed to meet Ronan, Shane, and Arrik's eyes.

Her husband still eyed her like he wanted to toss her over his shoulder and ravage her against the nearest wall.

Wren blinked. Where the devil had that thought come from?

"Someone looks a little dazed," Ronan teased.

Shane scowled and slapped him on the back of the head. "Mind your manners. That's your queen."

The redhead rolled his eyes, never losing his smile. "My apologies, my lady."

"Don't worry about it," she muttered, crossing her arms over her chest. Time to change the subject. "What is on the agenda for the day?"

"It's time to train," Arrik replied, splashing his face with warm water from a stone basin that sat in a beam of morning sunlight.

"...so let's train," Wren replied, unsure about the fact she was actually being included *in* training.

Anything to distract herself from what just happened.

She swept passed the guards and washed her face just like Arrik had. He finished lacing his boots while she dried her skin. Her mouth popped open when he pressed a kiss to her temple.

"Meet us outside once you're finished."

He was going to be the death of her.

Training felt like coming home.

In the past, she'd never faced off against her husband during training, choosing instead to pick out specific men from his guard to try out her skills, men she'd identified here or there as being worthy of fighting.

Men who did best her.

But each time was a learning experience. She found their weaknesses and exploited them. Wren began to win. She gained respect.

It was a start.

But there was one man she could not beat—Shane. The scarred and knotted man absolutely obliterated Wren. It didn't matter if he was her first or seventh bout, he soundly thrashed her in the ring. He attacked with such focused, vicious energy. At first Wren thought it was because he didn't trust her—but he treated everyone that way, so it was something.

This morning was no different.

He soundly trounced Wren like she was a mere child playing soldier with a stick. She groaned from the ground and tossed her arm over her eyes to keep the sweat from burning them. At least she could take a break and catch her breath.

But that rest was short-lived.

"What do you think you're doing?" Ronan called. "Get off your royal arse and fight."

Wren lifted her arm and sat up, rolling her neck. "Alright, alright. Slave driver."

He laughed but lowered his voice, sidling up beside Wren with surprising grace and silence for the size of him. "You really think I'd let you off easy after I pretended to be you last night? Especially after that dagger thrown my way. Lucky you missed, eh?"

"Funny that you believe I missed," Wren countered, staring up at the tall redhead.

Ronan regarded her, then burst out into bawdy laughter, holding his hand out to her. "Such a bloodthirsty queen. Our king has his hands full with you."

Wren didn't correct him. She was going to cause so much trouble for Arrik. She accepted the offering and let Ronan help her up.

He slapped her on the shoulder. "You look bushed. Take five minutes, then meet me in the ring."

"Lovely," she replied, dryly.

Wren staggered to the fence that surrounded the sparring ring and wiped the sweat from her brow as she stretched out a cramp in her calf. As she was hopping from leg to leg, a dark-haired man from outside the ring caught her eye.

Ares.

She steeled herself as he strode around the perimeter of the circle, his attention focused on her. He paused just on the other side of the fence, dark eyes sweeping her from head to toe and back.

"My lord, what an unexpected pleasure. How can I help you?" she asked carefully. They'd nary said a word to each other. The prince seemed to like the shadows.

All in all, Wren had no idea what to expect from Ares.

He looked like his mother: dark hair, sable eyes, beautiful bone structure that was seen nowhere in Verlanti. But he lacked the proud, haughty air of his fallen older brother, and the useless foppishness of Kalles.

Ares finally said, "A queen that serves a prince? Unheard of."

Wren shrugged. "I've been told that the purpose of a monarch is to serve."

"How delightful," he murmured. He stared at her for a beat longer before beginning to copy her stretches. "Arrik would never tell you," the young man said in a low voice, "but among Soren's children *I'm* the one most skilled in combat."

"How very interesting."

"You doubt me?"

"No." Wren gave him a side-eye. "But I am curious as to why you weren't appointed to be your father's warlord if that is the case."

He shrugged. "I have no aspirations to be that responsible. And I'm, quite frankly, not clever enough for the throne."

Blunt, humble words from a man who came from a family of snakes. "That's awfully self-aware."

"I know, my mother hates it but...it's what makes me popular amongst the fairer sex." He flipped a lock of hair out of his eyes.

That was not very humble. "I've not heard such rumors," Wren ventured, hoping to needle him but not prick his pride.

"Indeed. I like to keep my private affairs discreet. Those known with gossiping lips are never invited into my circle or my bed."

"How very...sensible of you." She didn't know what else to say.

"We all have our failings," he replied dryly.

Wren snorted out a laugh despite herself. Of all the things she'd expected Ares to be, *funny* was not one of them. But Kalles was funny, in his own way, and if Wren stopped hating Arrik for half a second she'd easily admit that she liked his filthy, rowdy sense of humor. Maybe the royal children developed it to protect themselves?

It was only Cathal who'd been cruel and humorless. But that wasn't completely true. The old king had found humor in pain and suffering.

I hope he rots.

She regarded Ares in silence as he did the same to her.

When she'd recovered as best she could from her short bout with Shane, she finally relented and asked, "Do you think to seduce me?"

He smiled. "No."

"Then what do you get out of telling me these things?"

At this, Ares offered her a small, cagey smile. "By virtue of being the best at hand-to-hand combat in my family, I have more than a few tips you might be interested in hearing about. Should you wish to beat Ronan or Shane."

That surprised Wren. "What do you get out of this? Nothing is free."

"True. But my reward is nothing to you. I only gain the satisfaction of watching that two-bit rake fall into the dirt." His tone sharpened at the end.

She sensed an undercurrent of competition. "Ah, so he's your rival for the affection of all the women in court?"

At this Ares' smile widened into something much more genuine. "You could say that."

"You aren't at all the kind of person I expected you to be."

"Not like my father and elder brother, you mean?" he asked, and Wren nodded. "I just want to live a good, easy life," Ares explained, as the two of them made their way over to the sparring ring. "I didn't ask for this life. I'm just trying to survive it and live to the best of my ability before I die."

"You make it sound like that could happen any time."

Ares cast her a surprised look. "Each day is a blessing. You never know when you might end up with a blade in your back."

Wren pursed her lips and glanced toward Ronan. He was busy flattering a passing maid, entirely oblivious to anyone else. "I don't plan on dying any time soon."

"Good. I will make sure of it."

She frowned and stared at the younger prince. "Why?"

Another secret smile. "With Arrik and yourself on the throne, it means little responsibility for me, but all the benefits of being a prince and brother to the king. I will fight and bleed to keep it that way. So this is my way of saying welcome to our family, sister. Don't die."

"I'll try."

"Excellent. Keep doing what you're doing and let me keep doing what I'm doing." A pause. "And have an heir as soon as possible. Shouldn't be difficult with how much I've heard my brother has been bedding you." Wren blanched and Ares shrugged. "Everyone is a gossip."

"Seems like that is a trait of every royal court." How

many people had heard Ronan and Shane's farce last night? It was embarrassing to even think about.

Ares hopped the fence and landed beside her, leaning in to whisper in her ear. "Go for Ronan's right knee. It's a war wound. He hides it well."

Her gaze landed on Arrik one sparring ring over, thankful his back was to her. Wren took a step away from Ares. They were way too close. One Verlanti royal was enough. The last thing she needed was for Arrik to think she was messing around with another prince and get jealous.

A wicked thrill ran through her at the thought of the king being jealous over someone showing her attention. A very dangerous thrill that she had to stamp down immediately.

Nothing better than a fight to ward off intrusive thoughts.

She ignored Shane's pointed stare as she moved to the center of the ring, Ares' advice running through her head. Ronan swaggered toward her and squared off. The redhead waved and laughed charmingly for his audience, who whooped for his clearly certain victory before bowing deeply to Wren.

"My lady, do try to last longer than thirty seconds."

She smirked. "Isn't that what your last lover said?"

Ronan's smile slid from his face. "Defend yourself." Then he attacked.

She couldn't beat him with strength, but she was faster. She slid beneath his guard, he swung, and she slammed her foot against his knee. Ares had been right. Ronan collapsed like a sack of grain. She leaped upon him and placed her sword at his throat as Arrik turned to face the ring.

"Yield," she demanded.

Ronan glared up at her and lifted his chin. "That was cheap."

"You were slow. Now yield or I give you a shave and we see what's beneath the beard."

Hearing Arrik's uproarious laughter upon his friend's defeat, a warm glow spread throughout Wren's body that had entirely nothing to do with the physical exertion she'd put herself through. Ronan swallowed when she pressed the sword closer to his beard.

"I yield," he growled.

"And that is how you do it, ladies," Arrik yelled, gaily leaping the fence and sauntering over Ronan's heaving, disbelieving form crumpled in the dirt to yank Wren into his arms. He tilted his head down to regard her with a fiercely proud expression and planted a messy kiss on her lips. Then he lifted her up and spun her around. Wren couldn't help laughing as he continued spinning her around in his grasp. The win against Ronan had been inordinately satisfying.

Arrik dipped his head low and caught Wren's lips in another kiss. "You are enchanting. I cannot get enough of you."

Dimly she could hear Arrik's men whooping and cheering and making crude jokes at her expense, but she didn't care. All that mattered was his lip on hers.

Tongue over teeth and then deeper, deeper, deeper, until Wren was panting and gasping and reciprocating. Her arms and legs wound themselves round his body. She *needed* this kiss. It felt like a release. Arrik's hand ran through her hair, tangling it around his fingers whilst his other supported her weight under her arse.

But it wasn't enough. Wren needed more.

"More" was dangerous.

She wasn't sure who broke the kiss first, but when her and Arrik's lips were finally their own again, both parties were breathing heavily against the other. Arrik's eyes were hooded, dark with desire, and trained entirely on hers.

"I'll—be busy for the rest of the day," he said, for only Wren to hear. Then, remembering himself, he boomed, "Remember to take it easy after the night we've had!"

All around her men were laughing and jeering, but Wren didn't care. Never mind the fact that most of them meant their jibes in good faith, but it also did her well for everyone to believe that she would spend the rest of her day relaxing in her chambers, or in the garden baths.

"I'll see you later, then," she told Arrik. Wren was painfully aware of his gaze on her back as she walked away.

It burned through her.

She glanced toward Ares, who'd faded into the men encircling the sparring ring. He winked at her and disappeared into the crowd. It was unsettling.

The journey to their rooms was a blur as she relieved their kiss. Once inside the suite, Wren dismissed each and every servant, claiming to be tired. After all, she and Arrik had apparently being "going at it" all night, if the gossip in the palace was anything to go by.

But the lies worked to her advantage.

The moment she was alone, Wren packed a bag, slung her mother's bow over her back—welcoming the weight and feel of it as if it had been a limb she'd been missing—then slipped out into the gardens and up onto the roof. Thanks to Arrik, she knew where the guards were posted.

It was downright easy to escape the palace and venture into the city.

CHAPTER 7

WREN

FREEDOM WAS THE SUN ON HER FACE, THE WIND IN HER hair, the scent of brine in her nose, the crash of waves and cry of gulls filling her ears and the rocking of a ship beneath her.

And a dragon floating in the water a stone's throw away.

Wren sunned herself on the deck of Gunn's ship, though the pirate was nowhere to be seen. She and Trove had been humming and trilling at each other for the past hour while waiting for Gunn, but the lack of sleep the night before had caught up to her. She closed her eyes for some rest after Trove slipped just beneath the water, his reptilian eyes closing while he napped in the gentle waters. When was the last time she'd felt this much peace? Just knowing her dragon was nearby reassured her beyond measure.

She drifted in a sea of diabolical planning, but her mind kept coming back to the night before.

To the king's gift. She'd lied to him. While it was customary for a rider to craft the first saddle for their dragon, there was no such rule that no one else could create the saddle or gift one. Guilt wriggled in her belly at the deception. Arrik had truly thought about what she loved. The saddle was beautiful and well made. If Wren were being honest she would not have been able to find better craftsmanship even back in Lorne. Truth be told, refusing the gift had hurt a little bit because of how much she wanted it.

But it was a present from a warlord. A wily king.

Gifts from kings came with strings.

Footsteps thumped across the deck and up the stairs toward the helm where she was sprawled out like a lazy cat.

"And don't forget to—how did you get on here?" a gruff voice exclaimed from her left. Wren held a hand over her eyes and peeked over to see Gunn staring at her in disbelief, sweat and oil smeared across his bare chest. A rag was in his hand; he used it to clean off his skin before collapsing down beside Wren.

She raised an eyebrow. "What were you doing? I've been here almost twenty minutes."

"We had some machine trouble," he grumbled, leaning back on his hands, looking ever the roguish pirate.

"I had no idea you moonlighted as an engineer."

Gunn let out a bark of a laugh as Wren eased herself onto her elbows. "You don't own a ship without knowing a bit about engines. In truth, I just wanted to make sure nobody was messing up the engine *more*. You never know who has spies working for them these days."

"You think you have a spy amongst your ranks?"

"Not really." Gunn stretched his arms above his head, cracking his neck and yawning luxuriantly as he did so. "But it never hurts to be too careful, especially given my line of work."

That was something she could appreciate. Gunn had turned out to be a whole lot more responsible and trustworthy than she could have ever hoped he'd be. In fact, he might be the only person she trusted other than Leif.

"How is my cousin?" Wren asked. Clara had been on her mind for the last several weeks.

"Safely back at the isles, you'll be happy to hear."

"Really?" Wren could hardly contain her relief. She almost hugged Gunn when he offered her a reassuring smile and nodded his head.

"I'm a man of my word." He arched a brow at her, suddenly serious. "Although speaking of keeping to one's word, I've heard news that the rebellion isn't very happy with you, Dragon Princess. Or is it Dragon *Queen* now?"

Wren sat up and brushed her hands on her trousers. "I'm not beholden to their rules nor their plans. I'm not a pawn and I never agreed with Vienne partnering with that—with that..." Disgust rolled through her at the thought of Idril.

"Pesky sire of ours?" She said nothing. It was hard to wrap her mind around knowing how awful her sire was. Gunn ran a hand through his hand and stared her down. "Come on, Wren. Stop ignoring the massive elephant in the room. Or the ship, as it were." He let out a humorless chuckle. "You're my half-sister. I'm your brother. We can't avoid this forever."

"You'd be surprised at what I can avoid and for how long," Wren muttered, swinging up to a sitting position so she could wrap her arms around her knees and shake away the chill that spread through her bones.

"Gee, thanks."

She shook her head. "I didn't mean that the way it came out. I'm disappointed with who created me. I'm not disappointed with my brother."

Gunn swallowed and then cleared his throat, the first to look away. "Glad to hear it. It's been interesting...having a sister. At least Idril gave me a partner in crime."

Wren smiled weakly. "That we are, but I don't want to ever have to think or talk about Idril again, even knowing how unrealistic that is."

"Something we happen to have in common. We're best friends already."

Wren rolled her eyes at Gunn's stalwart refusal to leave things be.

He held up his hand and counted on his fingers. "We both hate our father, we're both *dashingly* pretty"—Wren choked on a laugh before she could stop herself—"and we both care about freeing slaves. Anything else?"

After a pause, Wren waved toward the endless horizon. "The sea," she said quietly. "We both love the ocean."

She glanced back at her brother. His smile was no longer mischievous or calculating. No, it was warm and familiar and almost felt like home. "I suppose I should be glad that you and I turned out rather well considering who our...sire was."

She couldn't say *father*. She simply couldn't. He'd never been that.

"And that's how to look on the bright side! Come on," Gunn said, leaping to his feet with surprising grace, "I have someone who can't wait to see you."

Wren groaned. "I hope this isn't some kind of trap."

"Not at all. Don't you trust me?"

"Not as far as I can throw you."

Gunn sized Wren up with a long sweep of his gaze. "I have a feeling you could throw me pretty far."

Wren giggled and rolled her eyes as she got to her feet and made to follow Gunn, though when a rumbling began in the water she shifted over to the railing to whistle down at Trove.

The pirate startled beside her. "How long has he been down there?" he asked, thoroughly discomfited that he hadn't noticed the massive creature snaking its way through the surface of the waves below them.

Wren shrugged. "He's remained in port pretty much ever since I got here. Clearly he knows I need eyes on your ship," she teased.

"Hmm. You should have him watch the palace instead." His tone was too serious.

"I'm fairly sure they'd spot a gigantic dragon spying on them."

"Maybe that would be the advantage the rebellion needs to finally get some people inside the palace."

At this Wren snorted. "I'd like to see anyone get though Arrik's detail. He's far too thorough."

"Arrik?"

She blanched. "The king."

"Careful," Gunn said, as they turned from Trove to exit the ship, "that almost sounds like you're complimenting your husband."

"Take that ba—"

But any insult or exclamation Wren might have spat out was lost in the face of an achingly familiar figure standing on the jetty, waiting for her.

Leif.

Leif, unharmed and grinning, with a seafarer's tan across his cheeks. "It's been a while," he said, before Wren launched herself down the ramp and threw her arms around her friend. Leif chuckled into her ear as he stroked her hair. "I've missed you too."

"Never go away for so long without letting me know you're safe again," Wren cried, not caring that her throat was full of tears that she had to swallow back. She'd been so lonely without him.

Almost lost.

"I promise."

Her brother coughed politely. "Not that I'm one to break up a happy reunion, but I thought you might want to know that the rebellion is meeting above the west-quarter smithy in half an hour."

With some effort, Wren pulled away from Leif, though she kept hold of his right hand. "And what would you have me do at this meeting?"

"Exert your dominance. Show them that *you're* the one in control, not them."

Wren blew out a breath. "I said as much to Rowen when

he showed up in the palace gardens."

Gunn whistled. "That crazy blighter came to you?"

"My thoughts exactly," she replied. "He's an idiot."

"Not going to argue with you on that, but this meeting could be the perfect opportunity for you to seize control. It's been mess since you disappeared with the prince."

"It's not as if I ran off with him," Wren growled. "He changed the game."

"And you were surprised."

She opened her mouth to speak, but paused. In all honesty, she had been, and that's what rankled the most. Wren *had* trusted him. That had been her mistake.

"I'll come as backup," Leif broke in, squeezing her hand as he changed the subject. "Not that you need it."

"Then I guess the rebellion won't know what's hit them." Wren nodded at Gunn. "Thank you for the chat."

"Anytime, sis."

She grimaced. "That's going to take getting used to."

"Clearly we have a lot to catch up on," Leif drawled, glancing first at the pirate and then at Wren.

"And we'll have plenty of time to do so."

"When you're not surrounded by a host of guards, a dangerous court, and a jealous husband."

Her friend wasn't wrong. A slow, devious smile spread across her face as a reckless idea took shape in her mind. "How would you feel about coming back to the palace as my own personal bodyguard?"

The look Leif gave her was positively feral, his eyes glinting with all the fun he no doubt knew he'd get up to in the Verlantian palace. "I've always wanted to go back. Minus the chains and the dungeon, of course."

"Minus the chains and the dungeon."

"You both are going to die," Gunn quipped, shaking his head.

"Never. We'll live forever!" Leif cried.

Gunn pinned Wren with his gaze. "Be safe. I want to see you later this week."

"I will."

"And make sure your dragon won't eat me or any of my men."

She chuckled. "He's been here for weeks and left you alone. Don't be such a baby." She waved goodbye and Leif led her down the jetty.

Time to visit her aunt.

CHAPTER 8

WREN

"YOU'RE DIFFERENT."

Wren paused in her humming to regard Leif with a quizzical raised eyebrow. "What do you mean?"

"You seem sharper than when I left, but also…happier?"

"You're not making sense."

Leif cocked his head. "No, you're not making sense, love. Just what has happened?"

"Many things, but today I am appreciating every moment outside the palace." She squeezed his arm affectionately. "I've been reunited with my best friend"—Leif beamed—"and Trove is safe at sea, ready to antagonize Gunn. Considering all I've been through…I'd consider today to be a major improvement over the coronation and 'bedding ceremony' yesterday."

"Not many women would say that, but I see your point."

They fell into silence and Wren began humming as they strolled through the back alleys of the city. Leif joined in with a harmony that made the melody sing. It was a dragon song—Wren's own variation on an old lullaby—that she was hoping to finish before she next saw Trove. Hearing Leif's harmony gave her the final burst of inspiration she needed to complete it.

Yes, today was a good day. Since all Wren could do right now was plan for the future whilst living in the moment, she could allow herself the feeling of contentment that spread across her skin like the late afternoon sun's rays. Happiness was fleeting. She'd hold on to every little bit that came her way.

Besides, the moment she stepped into that smithy, all peace and contentment would disappear.

Wren had no doubt about it. Considering Rowen's warning before the coronation, she knew fine well the rebellion was not pleased with her. But, despite that, Wren was still surprised when she and Leif ascended a staircase above the smithy, opened a door, and barely avoided being stabbed on the end of Ever's sword.

"Hold on!" Leif exclaimed from behind Wren, who narrowly avoided the blade by twisting her abdomen so hard it hurt from all of her training that morning. She caught Ever's eye, exchanged a nod, and then the older woman sheathed her blade.

That was a close one.

"And here I thought you sought to use me, not to kill me."

The hostility in the meeting room was palpable. Wren

gritted her teeth; she knew to expect this. At least with Leif on hand as backup, she had a fighting chance of making it out of the room alive. Josenu was leaning by a narrow window. He gave her a small nod. She was fairly certain he'd help them escape if need be. And Rowen was standing all the way at the back of the room, with Bram standing in a defensive stance in front of Vienne—as if she had any designs on her aunt's life. It was laughable.

Her aunt waved Bram down to confront Wren on her own, the features she shared with Wren's mother contorted in fury. But Wren did not flinch away from her obvious anger.

"That's some welcome you gave us," Wren said, ensuring her voice remained calm despite the fact her blood was roaring past her ears. Leif gently touched her back before subtly placing himself on her lefthand side. It made her feel less alone.

"You didn't follow our plan," Vienne all but spat.

"You didn't divulge your complete plan to me." She nodded toward Bram, who still held a sword in Wren's direction. "Are we now enemies?"

"Should we welcome you with open arms? We sent Rowen to speak with you—to give you the chance to see sense and come when called. But you ignored even him. Why should we face you with anything *but* a blade in the gut?"

"*I* didn't follow your plan?" Wren bit back, her ire rising. "Since when did your plan involve killing innocent people? You told me nobody was going to be hurt, but the docks weren't evacuated before you put your *plan* in motion."

Her aunt's eyes were steely. "Sometimes sacrifices have to be made."

"You were careless and callous. It was not a sacrifice."

Wren turned her attention to Rowen, hoping he didn't agree with Vienne. He lifted his chin as if to challenge her. All she could do was stare at him in disappointment.

Wren held his gaze. "Children."

His resolve flickered for a moment before his mask slipped back into place. There was no saving him if he didn't want to be saved. Rowen had made his decision and she had to make her own. For a moment she considered taking the graceful way out and keep her mouth shut, but silence was getting her nowhere. Staying silent was as good as being complicit in some ways.

Who was she being quiet for? Her aunt? Rowen? What about their victims? Who would speak for them?

"Innocent lives aren't a sacrifice," she said resolutely. "Killing them when you could have evacuated the docks is murder, plain and simple."

"Watch your tongue," Bram warned.

Beside her, Leif snickered. "I'd watch yours, personally. You are speaking to your queen."

Bram spat on the ground. "I just knew you were going to betray us to work with her. You were always weak."

"I didn't betray you," Leif replied coolly. "Our mission has always been to free slaves from Verlanti rule. Wren and I achieved more in one night than anyone other than Ever here have achieved in years."

"How dare you," Bram snarled, echoed by several other members of the rebellion.

Wren scanned the room, noting that Josenu had subtly made his way from the window to stand a few feet away from her. To her left, Ever exchanged a look with Leif. Peculiar. Wren studied the people who tactfully shifted in her direction. They all had connections to Josenu, Ever, and Leif. They were making a stand.

She stared at her aunt. Working with Idril had cost Vienne her staunchest supporter and best friend. Her aunt didn't know it yet.

Wren straightened her spine, rolled back her shoulders, and stared down Vienne, Bram, and Rowen. "I came to you in good faith for your aid and to offer my help as the dragon princess of Lorne. You took advantage of me, which I do not take kindly to. Before, I may have been just a foreign girl to you, but now I stand before you as the queen consort to the throne of Verlanti. One word from my lips would destroy you."

"You wouldn't dare," Vienne hissed. "You'd incriminate yourself."

"Oh, but I would. Do you really think that the king hasn't been aware of my exploits with you?"

Her aunt paled. "You lie."

"No, you have lied. I have spoken truth."

Bram snorted. "Do you really think you hold so much sway over the king?" His eyes ran over her body. "You must truly be something in bed."

Leif took a step forward but Wren held her hand out.

She smiled, but it was icy. "Would you like to be the first to test out how much sway I have?"

"Are you threatening us?" Vienne demanded.

"No. I make promises." She scanned the group. "I am tired of the games and tricks. Much needs to change in this kingdom and in my own. We can do this together." Her gaze landed once again on her aunt. "You do not keep me out of your plans if you intend for me to follow them. You do not tell me that sacrifices are *necessary* when they could have easily been avoided. And you do not order me to do your bidding only to place a blade at my throat when I object to those orders. You wanted to wield a dragon princess...well, now you have dragon queen on a throne of serpents to lead you."

"You think to lead us?" Vienne laughed but no one else did.

Wren stared down her aunt. "If your plans don't involve freeing slaves rather than working with the monsters who subjugate them, then I'm your enemy. And I don't think you'll like that...nor those it would cost you."

Realization dawned as Vienne looked around the room, finally noticing the change in the air. Josenu was now standing on Wren's right, with Leif on her left, and Ever—sword now partly unsheathed—plainly on her side. For a moment, a tense silence spread across the room. Bram bared teeth, waiting for an order to attack.

But the moment passed.

"It is just as Rowen told us," Vienne remarked, choosing each word slowly and with precision. "You truly are acting like a queen now, Wren. Bravo, niece. I truly did turn you into something spectacular. I just hope you know what you're doing before it's your turn to murder those around you."

Wren swallowed down the venomous retort on the tip of her tongue. Engaging her aunt any more would prove fruitless. The rebellion and Vienne didn't hold any more power over her. True, she could use their help, but they weren't the only way to get back the isles. She didn't need them to rule. Wren could command people. She had been raised a princess, after all, and taught how to fight both on a battlefield and within a royal court.

She didn't need to *act* like a queen: she was always meant to be one.

"Your advice is noted. Now, are you ready to negotiate?"

"Negotiate? I thought this was your rebellion now, *my queen*." Her aunt's voice dripped disdain.

But Wren's thoughts never materialized into words. For at that moment, when she opened her mouth to speak, a scout from the southern section of the rebellion barged into the meeting. Sweat dripped drown their face, their eyes wild as they panted for breath.

"S-soldiers," they gasped, clutching at their chest in frantic dismay. "Soldiers are coming for you. They're de-descending on the smithy. You must get out!"

CHAPTER 9

ARRIK

Arrik hadn't been lying when he told Wren he would be busy today.

Josenu had sent word that the rebellion was meeting that very afternoon. It was up to Arrik and his men to round up the ringleaders who had bombed the port.

Wren better not be there, he thought, bracing himself to kick down the door. *She better not. She cannot be there*. On the other side of the door, he could hear scrabbling and panic, but it didn't matter. He had men waiting out on the street to catch anyone who tried to escape through the window.

Shane had reported that Wren had sent all their servants away to sleep. To anyone else that might seem normal for a royal who'd stayed up all night indulging in bed sport, but Wren wasn't the typical royal. And she'd given his first-in-command the slip.

Neither Shane nor Ronan knew where the queen was.

Arrik prayed she wasn't inside.

One swift kick and he had the door protesting heavily on its iron hinges; another and it came away from the frame entirely. Someone came at him with a sword just as a wall of noise hit his ears. Arrik swiftly parried, dodged the assailant's off-hand dagger attack, then twisted around to slam the pommel of his own sword into the back of their neck. The attacker crumpled to the floor, immediately unconscious.

All around him was pandemonium. The room the rebellion had been meeting in was roughly the same size as the smithy below it—rather large. But there were only three people remaining when he kicked down the door, so Arrik made quick work of scanning the frantic inhabitants. A sense of relief washed over him when he didn't spot a tell-tale sign of crimson hair.

Wren wasn't there.

Shane shackled the man Arrik had knocked out. "My liege, you really should have let me go first."

He rolled his eyes. "I will not become a soft king and hide in my palace."

Arrik examined the space and frowned.

Something was wrong. The room hadn't been nearly so full of people as he had expected. There were only three rebellion members, who had been corralled into a corner by his men. Looking out the window he saw that his men on the streets had captured two more.

Strange. Josenu said that the central force were all meeting today. That's thirty people, at least.

Where had they all gone?

"My lord, up there!" Ronan cried, pointing.

Arrik followed Ronan's raised arm and saw a trapdoor leading to the roof. In a flash, Ronan made his way through it. Arrik wanted to follow but knew he had to deal with the people down here, including his attacker, who was regaining consciousness. At first glance, he thought they were a man, but they were in fact a middle-aged, bald-headed woman with heavy scarring down her neck.

He knelt before her. "Where are they?"

The look in her eyes was fierce as she said, "You won't find the rest."

"I'm sure that thought will grant you peace as you suffer in prison," he threw back. "Did you really think you'd get away with bombing the dock? You are a traitor to your own people. You killed women and children."

The woman gritted her teeth but held her silence. Arrik knew the signs of a trained warrior. There would be no intelligence to be gathered from her here.

He watched with grim satisfaction as Shane pulled her to her feet and lined her up with the other rebels. They would be forced through the streets loudly and with purpose. All the better for the residents of the city to see that their new king was swift and sure in his punishment of those who sought to hurt them.

It was the only course of action available to him. Anything less would make him look weak and vulnerable to those who eagerly sought to tear him down.

When Ronan returned from his excursion across the

roof, he had with him a dark-skinned man. Vadonese. That struck a memory for Arrik. He eyed the man. He looked familiar.

"Do I know you?"

The man stayed silent.

Questioning could wait for later.

"Take them away," Arrik ordered Shane and the rest of his men. But just as Arrik made to exit the smithy, Ronan pulled him to the side. His friend hesitated. "Out with it."

"I saw a red-haired woman escape across the rooftops," he said grimly. "I pursued her but she was too quick."

Arrik clenched his teeth, seething. Could she have gotten out this far? He knew he couldn't afford to have his feelings for his wife taint his judgement. "You believe it to be Wren?"

"I can't say for certain."

"But…?" Arrik bit out.

"Who else do you know with red hair who might be entangled with the rebellion?"

Arrik knew Ronan had a point, but he didn't want to believe it. Though he had brought Wren to his side under duress—had forced her hand, had kept things from her—they *were* still a team. They'd put all of that behind them and moved forward.

She wasn't supposed to be meeting with the rebellion behind his back.

You don't know that she is.

Arrik indicated toward the meeting room. Chairs and barrels and tools alike were scattered across the floor. "Take care of this for me," he ordered, exiting the smithy. "And keep filtering through the city for more members of the rebellion."

Ronan nodded his assent.

Arrik thundered down the stairs, not in the mood to drag the criminals through the city. He swung up onto his war horse and tore through the streets back to the palace, frightening several people on the way.

He vaulted off his horse at the stable and tossed the reins to the nearest stableboy before storming up the steps and into the palace. His angry footsteps echoed around him as guards fell in place behind him.

If she wasn't here...he didn't know what he'd do.

Reaching their quarters, he burst into their rooms and slammed the doors behind him. His stomach dropped. She was nowhere to be seen.

Blast her.

Arrik stalked through the gauzy curtains, his ears catching a soft sigh. He stiffened. Could it be? Was she bathing?

On silent feet, he crept toward the bathing pool in the center of the gardens, parting the plants. To his relief and suspicion, he found his wife soaking in the water, red hair fanned out behind her like flames, eyes closed.

She was relaxed. At ease.

He took a step closer, not able to help himself.

What was it about this woman that made him lose his mind?

Because you truly want her to be yours.

It was a dangerous thought.

He took another careful, quiet step toward the bath, soaking in the picture she made. It seemed like she'd been there for a while, but looks were deceiving.

His little wife was devious—which was why he liked her.

"Are you really going to keep staring?" she asked.

CHAPTER 10

WREN

She knew he was there. Even though she hadn't opened her eyes, nor had he answered her.

It was a half-baked plan to strip down and climb into the bath. She had hoped her body would give him enough pause to not notice Josenu creeping out of the garden. But as she fought with her breathing to pull it down from frantic to relaxed, as befitting sitting in an outdoor bath for hours after an arduous training session, Wren still felt incredibly vulnerable.

She was naked.

And completely at the mercy of Arrik.

She had betrayed the king by continuing to liaise with the rebellion and had almost been caught to boot. It was a lucky thing Josenu had kept her out of Ronan's sight, or she would have been doomed.

Wren felt Arrik approach more than she heard him, though the metallic clink of his armor followed soon after.

Armor. So he really was part of the raid.

Thankful for the steamy water to explain away her flushed complexion, Wren turned her head to glance at Arrik out of the corner of her eye as naturally as she could. But when she caught sight of him she was so struck by the imposing figure of her husband in his full battle gear that she turned, resting her arms on the edge of the bath in order to unabashedly stare at him.

She hadn't seen him dressed like this since he'd first taken her prisoner. The black and silver getup had once inspired nothing but fear and revulsion in her. *Now?* The fear was still there, and so was the revulsion—but not for the same reason. Wren was repulsed by the fact Arrik, with his broad shoulders, platinum hair braided behind his ears, engraved armor and blackened leather, did not repulse her at all.

Her heart caught in her throat as he took purposeful step after step toward her, an increasingly confounded expression on his face as he watched her.

That's right. Keep your eyes on me. Don't find Josenu.

Wren could only pray he remained out of sight until she could signal it was safe for him to come out.

"You're in the bath," Arrik said, breaking the silence between them after what felt like hours but had in fact been seconds.

Wren gulped. "I'm in the bath. This morning took a lot out of me. Can you blame me?"

"No. And yet..."

"And yet...?"

When he reached the edge of the bath, he loomed over Wren like a silver deity, peering down his nose at her as the glowing sun set his armor alight. Wren had to squint in order to see him properly.

"Why are you always shrouded in mystery?" he asked, voice low and gravelly and barely audible over the gentle gust of the wind. "What games are you playing with me this time?"

"I'm no more playing games than you are," Wren said, brain working furiously to think about what she *would* have said had she not just fled the rebel meeting. It frustrated her to realize that biting banter was the answer. *Distract him with what you know he wants*. So she flipped her hair over her shoulder, exposing her neck, and asked, "Which game is it we're playing now, my king?"

He sucked in a sharp breath. "I like it when you call me that."

She was satisfied to see Arrik's gaze drop to her neck and collarbone and down below the edge of the bath. *Distract him. Distract him*. He knelt in front of her; she could see the faintest flush of pink across his cheeks. Someone had torn across the city to check on her. Her dear husband didn't trust her as much as he said.

No one ever said he was dumb.

Her belly quivered as Arrik dipped his finger in the bath, trailing it through the water closer and closer to her without touching her. The ache she felt—the urge to have Arrik's fingertips on her skin—was too much for her to take.

Finally, not breaking eye contact, Arrik traced his fingers up Wren's arm, along her shoulder, her neck, her jaw.

Her lips.

"Tread carefully," he murmured, gaze searing through her hotter than the sun. "Games in the dark elf court always end in blood."

So Wren bit his finger, hard—hard enough to draw tiny beads of blood where her canines cut into his skin. Arrik tensed in front of her, like a cat ready to pounce, but he didn't move.

"I'm tempted to get in, all things considered," he said, low and slow.

Wren only responded when he pulled his finger from her mouth. She missed it, though it frightened her that she did. "All things considered, I'd be curious to see how you think that would pan out."

For a long moment it seemed as though Arrik really *would* join Wren, armor and all, but with one final, scorching look into her eyes, he rolled back onto his feet and stretched out his shoulders. Watching him do so—imagining how every muscle worked beneath the leather and armor—made Wren even *more* curious about the prospect of Arrik getting into the water with her, naked of clothes and barbed comments in equal measure.

But today was not that day.

Nor should she ever want it to come. But the heart wanted what the heart wanted. She'd leave it as morbid curiosity and nothing more.

Time to shake things up.

"Leif is here," she bit out suddenly.

Arrik raised a curious eyebrow. "The...bard? From the dungeon?"

"He's my friend."

"Indeed."

She pursed her lips and rushed out the next part. "And now my bodyguard."

"That slip of a boy? A bodyguard?" Her husband laughed in disbelief. "Have you taken leave of your senses? My men will eat him alive."

"Go on, underestimate him like you did me," she murmured, drawing patterns on the tile with her wet finger. "See how far that gets you."

Arrik had the sense to look abashed. "I don't wager it would get me very far."

"So you won't keep me from him?"

"Does he want you?"

Wren laughed and glanced up, her humor dying at the serious expression on Arrik's face. "No. We're only friends."

A bloodthirsty glint entered his eyes. "If he touches you, I'll kill him. You know that, right?"

"You have nothing to worry about."

"All right, you win. You can keep the bard."

"It wasn't a request, but I accept your graciousness nonetheless."

"You are something spectacular, you know that?" Arrik snickered and shook his head, finally walking toward their rooms. "I have matters of state to attend to. I'll meet you at dinner. Enjoy your bath, wife. And think of me. I'll be thinking of you."

She blushed and leaned her cheek against the tile. What a flirt.

The moment Wren could be certain Arrik was out of sight and earshot, she breathed a shuddering sigh of relief.

That was close. Too close. If Josenu hadn't helped get you back so quickly…

She turned her attention to the copse of trees which shaded the western side of the gardens. Josenu was still in there waiting for Wren's signal that the coast was clear. And though the coast *was* clear, something stayed Wren's tongue from beckoning him over. A feeling of dread. Of being watched.

The baths were private but still…something felt wrong.

Silk whispering across stone caught Wren's attention first.

She braced herself and turned toward the sound.

Astrid materialized seemingly out of nowhere, a disarmingly gracious smile on her face as she sauntered toward the bath, and straight for Wren.

The mother serpent had come to play.

CHAPTER 11

WREN

No thoughts or questions safe to vocalize came to Wren's mind as the viper queen shed her clothes and joined her in the bath. For what could she say? Wren had witnessed Astrid's true colors with her own eyes. The veneer Soren's queen had worn to get Wren to trust her had been exactly that: a veneer. Every word of advice. Every encouragement. Hadn't Wren once believed that Astrid was her only friend inside the Verlantian court?

That thought was laughable now.

Astrid's deep chestnut skin and generous curves glistened as she reclined into the bath, sighing in contentment after she breathed in a waft of scented steam. "It's worth marrying a king just for baths like this, don't you think, daughter?" she asked, a sly smile on her face when she caught Wren's eye.

But Wren knew better than to get riled up by any of the

woman's comments. So she nodded and said, "It certainly has its advantages."

"Although, I must say, said king looked mighty frustrated as he walked away from you..." A probing barb.

Ah, that's where she's going with this.

Wren should have expected it, given that Astrid had anticipated becoming the high and mighty ruling queen alongside Arrik. But he had mercilessly tossed her aside—and had never intended nor told her that she'd rule with him.

So now Astrid was taking out her frustrations by trying to drive a wedge between Wren and her new husband.

Little did the queen mother know that she had no intention of truly getting close to her husband. It was a ploy.

"You know," Astrid continued, stretching lustrously beneath the water to blatantly show off her impressive body, "it's never good to leave a king frustrated. He'll find other ways to satisfy himself—ways that do not include you."

While their marriage wasn't conventional in the least, Wren knew for sure that Arrik was many things but unfaithful was not one of them. It had never even crossed her mind that he had it in him to be disloyal. After hearing the genuine fear and sadness in his voice when he relayed to Wren how his previous wives had been murdered, and about what Soren had done to his mother, she knew in her heart that Arrik was a "one woman for all of time" kind of monster.

And yet, thinking of Arrik sleeping with another woman caused her stomach to roil with jealousy. She hated the idea. Despised it. She knew it shouldn't bother her—and couldn't let anyone *know* it bothered her—but it bothered her nonetheless. For what did any of Arrik's looks and touches and words mean if he could lie with another woman?

Astrid saved Wren from having to respond by saying, "I could always tutor you in the art of being *queen*, so you do not lose my son's favor. Losing it is an easy thing to do, after all. Kings love diversions. They tire easily of their toys."

Wren wanted nothing to do with the woman, but it was true that she needed to keep an eye on her. Then an idea went off in her head. *Someone* can *keep an eye on her*.

Leif.

All Wren had to do was ensure Astrid was not suspicious of her so that her guard was down enough for Leif to do his world-famous spying.

She plastered on a grateful smile and playfully flicked water in the viper queen's direction. "I would appreciate it. I'll admit that I'm far too inexperienced for the Verlantian court. Lorne was far more...conservative. I'll take any help I can get from you, and with thanks."

It was the correct answer, with all the right platitudes and compliments. Visibly pleased, Astrid closed the gap between herself and Wren and placed a kiss on her cheek.

"I look forward to it, daughter," Astrid purred, before rising from the bath, water sloughing off her skin in the process. She grabbed her clothes and sauntered naked back through their rooms. How the devil had she gotten past the guards in the first place?

Wren had to give it to the woman: she might have been rotten down to the core, but she held all the confidence in the world within her body. She used it for evil purposes, but her boldness in and of itself was not a bad quality. Wren would do well to maintain the same level of tenacity and self-possession that Astrid did around other people. She could not afford to let anyone see chinks in her armor.

Finally, after fifteen minutes had passed in silence and Wren's heartrate had slowed to normal, Josenu meandered toward Wren as if he had merely been on grounds patrol. When he neared the bath, he walked backward to give her privacy, a towel and robe in hand. She leaned up and took it gratefully, patting herself dry before tying on the crimson robe Arrik had gifted her the prior night..

"How did you find my robe?"

"I was poking around while your husband was debating on whether or not to ravish you in the pool."

She ignored his comment. "What did you think of Astrid?"

"I'd be very careful around her," Josenu remarked, when Wren was suitably dressed enough to walk back to her chambers, Josenu accompanying her by linking his arm through his. "She is more dangerous than anyone gives her credit for."

Wren quirked an eyebrow. "I thought I had to be careful of *everyone* around here." She expected Josenu to laugh. Instead, the man grew quiet and very still. Wren realized, in that moment, that Josenu had a personal reason to ask for her to be careful. Ensuring nobody was around to hear, she came to a stop a few paces away from her chambers, then turned to face her friend. "There's history between you, isn't there?"

Josenu nodded.

"Did she hurt you?"

He swallowed and looked away. "She's hurt many. I'm not the only one."

"Then it will reassure you to know that I plan to destroy her. I'm going to ask Leif to keep track of her for me. Information is power, after all. She will not get away with her crimes."

"That's a...very good idea," Josenu said appraisingly. "I'd thought you foolish for bringing him back with you, but having the spy around will prove very useful. The king didn't object?"

Wren shook her head. "I think he likes the idea, to be honest. I need friends here—people I can trust. He can't be there to *protect* me at every turn." When she grimaced over the word *protect*, Josenu let out a gentle laugh. She shuffled on her feet. "Will you tell me what happened between you and Astrid? But if you can't—"

"No, I can tell you." He looked to the sky for a moment, hands forming into fists before he released the tension in his arms. "She takes things that do not belong to her. Anything she deems pretty or valuable. I was young when she first came to me..."

Ice formed around Wren's heart.

"I knew it was wrong, but I couldn't stop her. She came to me often."

"I'm so sorry." Wren reached out and held his hand, stomach churning. "I know there is nothing that can erase the past, but she will pay. I promise you; she will suffer. Taking advantage of children is disgusting, and there's a special place in hell for them."

Josenu gave her a tight smile. "I wish there were more

people like you. She wanted to hurt Soren, and no one stopped her."

"What? Why would she use you to—?" Wren cut herself off. "That doesn't matter. I'm sorry I even started to ask. Just know that you have me on your side."

"I know," Josenu said, squeezing her fingers before letting them go. "In any case, it didn't elicit the reaction she wanted, so she turned her attention to Arrik instead. He broke two of her fingers the moment she laid a hand on him." He laughed bitterly. "I wish I'd had the savage confidence to do such a thing to the queen."

Wren was speechless. Of all the things for her to learn, this had never even crossed her mind. For Josenu—and *Arrik* —to have been subjected to this when they were in their youth... she could not fathom it. The longer she spent in Verlanti, the more she appreciated the wonderful upbringing she had experienced thanks to her mother, her father, and the people of Lorne.

But Josenu's heart-wrenching story brought up a burning question for her, one which she had been pondering for a while now but had been fearful to ask. Now, given the fact Josenu had shared such a private story with her, Wren felt that now was the time to ask it.

"I need you to answer me honestly, and I will bear you no ill will no matter how you reply. Who are you loyal to, Josenu? Arrik or...me?" Wren knew which answer to expect. She steeled herself for it, disappointment seeping into her veins like poison even though she knew his alliance to Arrik would be more than warranted.

Josenu got down on one knee, bowed his head, took out

his sword and held it over his wrists. Wren could scarcely believe what she was seeing.

"Once upon a time, serving you was the same as serving Arrik," he said, voice low and steady. "You wished for the same things. But Arrik has lost his way. I believe he can come back—can remember what it is he needs to do, and what compromises absolutely *cannot* be made—but only through you. Through you, Dragon Queen, I believe peace *and* vengeance may finally both be achieved. And if the peace comes at the expense of not getting revenge, then...that is where I side with you, and not Arrik."

It was more than Wren could have ever hoped to hear. Josenu was a man who firmly and resolutely shared in her beliefs. He was fair. He was righteous. He served the people, not the crown.

He was someone she could trust.

"You have no idea how much your support means to me," Wren said, when Josenu glanced up to gauge her reaction. "To say I am grateful is an understatement. I don't know how I can ever repay you for your loyalty."

"Then use me as best you can, free the slaves, take down Idril, destroy Astrid, and release the chains put upon the Dragon Isles. Then we can consider ourselves even."

"That is a tall order. I want to be up to the task."

"I know you can do it."

Wren's laugh was as shaky as her hand when she touched the top of Josenu's head and urged him to get back up. It was only when he joined his own throaty laugh to hers that the tremble was blasted away. Her body felt hot and wired and vital, in a way that shouldn't have been possible given the extreme physical exertion she'd put herself through all day.

She had Leif. She had Gunn. Now she had Josenu.

Every day her strength grew even as the people who opposed her remained in the dark about the fact their power was waning.

CHAPTER 12

ARRIK

Wren had been tight-lipped around the members of the rebellion, and Josenu had only told him what was strictly necessary about the woman Ever. And so it was that Arrik had no clue what to expect from Ever, the prized prisoner he'd taken from their raid on the rebellion. It was clear she was high ranking, and strong, and disciplined, but she was as silent as stone.

Even after three days of questioning she hadn't said a word.

"She isn't budging, Your Highness," one of the guards informed Arrik when he came down that evening to check in on the prisoner. "We've already gotten—ah, *rougher*—but she still isn't speaking a word."

"I'll be the judge of that," Arrik bit back tersely. If you wanted something done right, you had to, at the very least, oversee said thing being done. Especially with such a high-profile prisoner. A twinge of something that felt like discomfort came with pulling information out of a human being, even after all these years. It was a weakness Soren had tried and failed to beat out of him.

The woman, Ever, knew things he needed to know. It was imperative that he knew them. The future of his kingdom depended upon it.

Some things were worth selling part of your soul for.

Your wife wouldn't agree.

He pushed aside that thought. They had different strengths. He could handle this part of ruling. Arrik's father had trained him for it and he wouldn't ask Wren to sully her soul with this kind of business. His was already tainted.

He stood outside the cell and nodded to the soldier in charge of Ever's interrogation. "Ask her again who it was that orchestrated the attack on the docks," he commanded, clasping his hands behind his back as he watched from behind the bars of her cell. The tide was out but it would come in soon, thus forcing the woman to cling to the bars to escape the flesh-hungry fish that prowled in the water, waiting for doomed prisoners.

An invention of his ancestors, crude but effective.

And barbaric.

Just like you.

Another twinge of his heart. Arrik, once more, ignored it.

The bald-headed woman was covered in dirt and blood; a deep purple bruise was beginning to flower over her left eye. He scanned her from head to toe, noting the odd angle of

Ever's right ankle and wrist. His men had gotten rough indeed. It made him sick inside, but when he thought of the children she'd help murder, his guilt evaporated. While Arrik had committed a great many wrongs in his life for king and country, he'd always tried to protect the young. That was a line he would not cross.

Slowly, the woman met his gaze. Though she was battered, bloodied, starving, dehydrated, and sleep-deprived, the light had not left her eyes—the urge to fight back.

The urge to rebel.

Arrik had to respect that.

Many turned into whimpering babies when thrown into the dungeon. But there were the precious few who held their ground to the bitter end. That was the unfortunate dilemma with prisoners who resisted: he respected them. They were just like him, simply fighting on the other side of a pre-determined line. Sometimes that line didn't matter—sometimes it was drawn by spoiled kings who liked to squander their time.

In this case, however, that line *did* matter.

The rebellion had blown up the docks without giving any civilians enough time to evacuate. Dozens of people—families—had died. That was something Arrik could never abide by. It was hardly something he could ignore either, if he expected his people to trust him as their king.

"Your silence will not protect those you love," Arrik murmured to the woman. "You've committed murder and treason. Speak now or it will get worse."

Her lips thinned but she stayed silent.

His men looked to him to see how they should respond to the continued silence. They didn't have anything to trade with the woman, after all. They held no leverage against her —no loved ones, no children, no fame or fortune or any other insipid, transactional thing that lesser men would sell out their best friend for.

"Then so be it."

Grimly he nodded at his men, giving them permission to escalate their interrogation.

They both grabbed one of her arms and shoved her into the low tide water, the blood on her face washing off, turning her into live bait.

Arrik exhaled slowly and slipped into the part of his mind where he could observe without thought or feeling.

Ever didn't struggle. She didn't fight. She didn't even convulse as the oxygen left her lungs, nor when the water began bubbling around her. A sure sign the fish were approaching.

Unbidden, the memory of Wren down here with a look of abject terror on her face as she clung to the bars of the prison flashed through his mind. He snapped out of his impassionate box, feeling too much.

Panic, along with rage, rose up, threatening to swallow him whole.

"Pull her out," he ordered coldly.

His men didn't question their king; they hauled Ever back up, tossing her mercilessly back onto the wet stones of her cell floor. She hauled in ragged breath after breath. Her whole body shook as she sat up, but when her eyes caught hold of Arrik's, fire still glowed in their depths.

She'd never break.

This woman would go to her death silently.

A hiss of displeasure caught behind his teeth as he glared down at her. The raid on the rebellion had been a bust. He'd have to find another way to salvage the mission outside of getting the information he needed from Ever.

"We're done for the day," he growled to his men, and turned from the cell.

Shane leaned against the wall with his arms crossed, studying Arrik.

The king brushed past his friend and stalked up the stairs, Shane quietly in tow.

"Speak," Arrik grumbled. "I can practically hear you shouting at me."

"You pulled her up too early," Shane replied.

"I did not. She wouldn't have given us anything," he replied coolly.

When Shane grabbed his arm to force him to stop, Arrik growled out a warning. But his friend was unperturbed; Arrik had never scared him. That was why they worked so well together.

"The warlord I know would have let the fish eat at her flesh before pulling her out."

"She isn't going to talk. It would be pointless."

"And yet still you would have kept going for far longer to try and break her." Shane swallowed down a preparatory breath.

"What do you mean?"

"Your wife has changed you."

Just what he feared.

Arrik tensed. "Be careful what you say next, Shane."

"I'm not the one who needs to be careful. I'm not the

only one who's noticed that you've grown soft in her presence. I'm simply the only one with the guts to confront you about it. You're supposed to sleep with her, Arrik. To produce an heir. To display your vitality. You aren't supposed to *love* her."

There were many moments during Shane's bitter speech when Arrik could have interrupted. Could have told him to shut up. But, despite the fact it *was* bitter—it would take a fool not to see that—Shane was unfortunately making too many good points for Arrik to dismiss or ignore.

And yet still...

"I don't love her." It tasted like a lie.

Shane scoffed. "You let her bring a *spy* to court, for God's sake! A spy, Arrik. A prisoner you yourself once had toiling in the dungeon. Now he's upstairs eating grapes and drinking honey wine with your bloody wife. She is a means to an end, my lord. Are you really willing to give up everything for Wren?"

"I have it under control."

But do you really?

"I have always been your friend," Shane said softly. "I am bound to protect you, even from yourself. I won't let that dragon princess ruin you."

Not trusting himself to say anything else, Arrik brushed Shane's hand off his arm and turned to walk away.

Shane called out, "Remember what love did to your mother."

Arrik's entire body froze, tense and in abject disbelief. He glared over his shoulder. "How dare you."

His friend had the sense to look ashamed, but he didn't

take it back. Rather he kept his shoulders straight, head held high and gaze unwavering on Arrik. "I am loyal to *you*."

He was right, and they both knew it.

A sick feeling settled in the pit of Arrik's stomach. He had allowed himself to become too vulnerable with Wren. Too understanding. In trying to please her—to find a compromise between his goals and her own—he had, in Shane's words, grown soft.

Being soft was the last thing he could afford to be. He had too many enemies in too many shadowy corners for him to be anything other than black diamond and steel.

Shane was right.

He'd been falling for Wren, and he had the feeling it would be the death of him.

He was finally king, his endeavors just within his grasp.

No one would take that from him.

Not even his little dragon.

CHAPTER 13

WREN

How was this her life?

Wren had never felt less like herself than she did now, lounging on an opulent, velvet couch the size of Arrik's bed, eating miniature Verlantian delicacies whilst allowing several servants to fuss over her and offer her a dozen wine options. All around her, scantily dressed members of the Verlantian court were being tended to in a similar manner.

It had been Kalles' idea to join the court in its lazy afternoon socializing—Kalles, who had of course insisted on joining Wren in her undercover indulgence once it became clear she was going to use his idea. After all, the only way to truly find out what was going on around her was to *listen* to the people around her.

Leif milled between them dressed as a servant, flirting with whoever caught his eye and trading gossip. No doubt by the end of the afternoon he'd have many a story and scandal to share. Just what she needed to navigate the dark elf court.

Wren took another small sip from her goblet and forced down her discomfort at the entire situation for the sake of information gathering. Watching the servants bend over backwards trying to please the court's ridiculous demands was stomach churning at times. If things were going to change, she had a part to play.

"More wine?" Kalles drawled, his voice lazy.

"No, I'm fine." She took another small sip.

The prince smiled at her. "Don't think I haven't noticed that you've been nursing your wine for a while. Just what are you up to, my queen?"

She smiled sharply at Kalles. He never missed a thing. "Just enjoying the hospitality of my court."

"Mmmhmm."

He turned his attention to a trio of women dressed in chiffon the color of pink roses, their faces done up with blush and liner, and their lips stained crimson with wine. Wren observed the prince and the women. They cut a beautiful figure in the room and were indeed being not-so-subtly watched by several members present in the courtyard, the envy of many women.

"And then Roddick caught his wife Posie in bed with not just Dannyl but a slave too!" the brunette in the group stage-whispered. Her two friends, one blonde and one a redhead, gasped into their hands.

"His best friend *and* his servant?" the blonde cried, delighted. "That's humiliating."

"Oh, it gets worse. Now she's leaving him to form a

permanent arrangement with Dannyl. And you know—remember what I was saying last week about it being Posie who has all the money? Yes, through her uncle, poor soul, he never had his own children. Anyway, someone caught Roddick sniffing around in the merchants' quarters looking for *work*."

"So she's left him with nothing!" giggled the redhead.

"Serves him right," the brunette said, sniffing haughtily. "I never liked him. He'd already been unfaithful to Posie for years."

Wren stared into her wine, tuning out the rest of their conversation—it was truly banal gossip, after all, and she had no idea if she was supposed to support Roddick or Posie in this situation anyway. Not that it mattered. Infidelity was wrong in her eyes. How shocked would the court be if she condemned them for leaving their mates for the beds of others?

Bemused, she shared a smile with Kalles when she realized he was gauging her reaction. Did he think she'd be shocked? Even if she had been, Wren would never let those around her see any true emotion. They were all snakes just waiting for the moment to swallow her whole.

"Well, he isn't the only one at court who married into status. At least he was more *honest* about it."

That caught Wren's attention. She glanced in the trio's direction again, their full attention focused on her. Two men who had been listening in with gawkish adoration tittered like gossiping washerwomen.

Wren just smiled at them and saluted them with her wine. The women's eyes widened, and they dropped their gazes like they were ashamed. It was all a show. They wanted Wren to know that they didn't like her in a benign way that wasn't outright insulting.

But she could play that game too.

Kalles nudged Wren, pulling her from her staredown. He pointed at the two men. "That graying one...the one with the potbelly."

"That describes them both."

He wrinkled his nose in agreement. "The one dressed in claret." Wren nodded her acknowledgement. "He's one of my dear late father's advisers. He believes Arrik is unfairly out to get him."

"Is he now?" she mused. Just what was Kalles up to?

"Oh, not unfairly. The man's incompeten."

It was Wren's turn to stifle a smile.

The man Kalles had pointed out made a show of reclining even lower on the sumptuous couch he was lounging on, then sighed, "It seems anyone these days can inject themselves into the ranks of royalty with a few flutters of their lashes and exotic flame-colored hair."

There was absolutely no doubt the comment was about anyone but Wren. A few feet behind the men, serving an obscenely fat man slices of roast goose by hand, knelt Leif, who flashed Wren a visible warning not to let herself get riled up.

But Wren knew exactly what to say. A year ago she wouldn't have, but now she did. The man's words didn't offend her. It wasn't like she'd sought out the king. She'd been *gifted* to the man as a bloody spoil of war.

Ignoring the insipid Verlantian etiquette of talking

behind one's back and never saying what you meant directly, Wren sat up and stared down the man who had spoken with a small smile.

"I have to wonder if you're merely jealous that I possess the skills required to entice your king into my bed and vow his loyalty and love to me," she purred, sounding almost as cultured as Astrid herself. "Perhaps, next time you see him, you should flutter *your* lashes and see where that gets you. A place in the dungeon, no doubt. I heard the fish down there are in need of a good meal." She let her gaze linger over his body. "And you, sir, could provide them that."

Wren had spoken loudly enough for the entire courtyard to hear. Laughter and titters filled the air at the rude man's expense. He puffed up to an even larger size, spluttering nonsense as his face grew red in embarrassment.

Satisfied, she lay back on her couch and allowed Kalles to toss a grape into her mouth. He was laughing harder than anyone else in the room—though Wren knew fine well that Leif would have laughed harder had he not been posing as a servant. Tonight, when they had dinner together, he would no doubt regale her with his version of events.

She looked forward to it.

"I must say I'm impressed," Kalles murmured around a mouthful of wine when he'd finally calmed down enough to drink it. "You're adapting to our court far quicker than I would have imagined. Our dragon queen has claws. Next thing I know you'll be asking me to bring you to a pleasure den. Now *that's* where the real gossip is."

The very thought of such a thing soured Wren's triumphant high, bringing her starkly back to reality. It made her ill to imagine she was adapting so well to the ways of the Verlanti. But, at the end of the day, she had a part to play, and she'd be ruined if she didn't play it well enough to fool her audience.

Still, when the familiar and foreboding figure of Arrik cut through the courtyard like silk, making a direct beeline for her, Wren found herself sighing in relief. At least around him she could be nothing but herself and know that he accepted all that she was.

She hated that this was so.

"My king, good after—" Wren began, though the rest of her greeting dissipated to nothing when Arrik brusquely moved Wren's legs, sat down, then placed her on his lap. She kept her mask in place and wiggled, trying not to startle.

Without a word, he took the bowl of grapes from Kalles and placed them in her lap. Arrik pulled a grape from the bowl and pressed it against her lips. Wren took it from him slowly as his hand ran from her ankle to her knee beneath the hem of her dress.

It was downright domestic. It didn't even feel like he was "playing" at husband and wife with her; it felt natural. But it was still a show for their audience.

A claiming.

"Coin for your thoughts, brother?" Kalles mused, eyes missing nothing as he scanned first Wren and then his brother, noting the possessive way Arrik held her.

"I'm just thinking," he said, tone cold, as if that would put an end to the matter.

But if there was one thing Wren had learned of Kalles so far, it was that he was excellent at needling people. And yet even *she* could not have prepared herself for what Arrik's youngest brother said next.

She picked up a grape to feed Arrik, very aware of all the eyes on her. Maybe a little food would improve his mood.

"I don't suppose any of those rebel traitors that you captured in the raid three days ago have spoken yet?"

Arrik turned to stone beneath her, and Wren paused, grape hovering before his lips as he glared at his brother. And she knew, just *knew*, she wasn't supposed to have known about the captures.

Her blood turned cold, and her hand shook for a moment. Who of her friends had been captured?

Don't betray them or yourself.

With more self-control than Wren knew she possessed; she fed Arrik the grape. His attention moved over to her face as if searching for any cracks, any clues to how she felt. But he'd find none. If she reacted now—surrounded by the Verlantian court, of all places—then that would mark her as what she truly was.

Untrustworthy. A traitor.

Instead, she bit her tongue and played the part of a viper queen—feeding her king grapes.

The adviser Wren had so thoroughly put in his place perked up at this piece of information and, clearly intending to ingratiate himself, said, "You have three of them in custody, I heard. Including a high-level official. You must be close to learning of the whereabouts of the rest of those vermin."

Arrik's lips grew thin. "It isn't something I would speak about freely," he said, before returning his attention to Wren.

He tried to feed her another grape, but she gently pushed his hand away with a coy smile.

"I think I've eaten too much," she murmured, getting to her feet. She stretched and leaned close to place a kiss on Arrik's cheek before pulling back and faking a yawn behind her hand. She glanced around the room, meeting her husband's penetrating stare with a wink. "You kept me up much too late, my king. I feel like I must retire to catch up on my rest. Please excuse me." Wren curtseyed, waiting for Arrik to dismiss her.

Out of the corner of her eye, she saw Leif slip out of the courtyard.

She glanced up from beneath her lashes and it was clear that Arrik wanted to refuse to dismiss her. Kalles was almost beside himself with satisfaction at what had transpired.

"Get your rest, my lady. You'll be needing it," Arrik rumbled, his tone dark.

A shiver ran through her body, and she ignored the giggles around her as she retreated from the room, head held high. Her mask fell away as she stepped into the hallway. She picked up her skirts and swept down the cool marble corridors in a twirl of gauze and silk, her mind whirling with questions.

Kalles did not have to share that information with her; he only did so since Arrik was present. Why? Was it to mess with her, or the king? Maybe both?

Frustration bubbled in her chest. She could no better pinpoint the true motives of Arrik's youngest brother now than she could upon the very first day of meeting him. She didn't trust Kalles; he had his own agenda.

But she truly believed that agenda did not involve hurting her.

At least for the moment.

Kalles had given Wren a vital piece of information—something she would never have known if Arrik had had his way—for a reason.

Now she just needed to figure out why and do something with it.

Her heart sped up. She needed to know who was in the dungeon.

Arrik would be coming for her. It was only a matter of time before he tracked her down. She kicked off her flimsy slippers and ran.

Wren needed to get to the dungeons before her husband found her.

CHAPTER 14

WREN

"I'M SORRY, YOUR MAJESTY, BUT I HAVE ORDERS NOT TO let anyone but your husband through."

"Did my *husband* specifically deny your queen passage?" Wren countered, careful to keep her tone level and almost haughty. Anything to ensure the abject fear and simmering anger she was feeling didn't show on the surface.

She didn't have time for questions. Arrik could arrive any minute.

When the dungeon guard hesitated, Wren knew she had won. He glanced at his companion, who shrugged minutely.

"Are you going to deny your queen's clear command?"

Both men bowed their heads, uncrossed their spears, and allowed Wren entry into the dungeon proper.

Her heart raced as she sedately made her way into the dungeon, walking down the narrow causeway that led onto each of the sloping cells. The tide had begun to come in earnest. Through the gloom Wren could see a few wretched souls clinging to the bars, readying themselves for a long and harrowing night.

She frantically searched the prisoners' faces. No one she recognized.

Had Kalles played her? Were there no rebellion members here? No. Arrik was too angry at his brother for it to be anything but true. Had they been taken somewhere else?

Just as her panic began to rise, she arrived at the very last cell, pulse stuttering.

"Oh my—*Ever*," Wren gasped, so distraught she didn't care if anyone heard her utter the woman's name or not. It hardly mattered if they heard. Arrik knew Wren had dabbled with the rebellion. This wasn't news.

The woman was hanging in chains above the water, her toes mere inches from the surface. She was bruised and bloody and in very bad shape. Wren grabbed the bars and pressed as close as she could, peering at her friend.

"Ever?"

The woman slowly lifted her head and squinted at Wren.

Blast it, her face was a bloody mess.

"What have they done to you?" she whispered.

Ever smiled, but it was pained. "Nothing I wasn't prepared for." She coughed, blood spattering her lips.

"Open the door," Wren yelled down the corridor to the two guards who hovered just out of earshot. One of them looked about to argue, but the other one dutifully complied, unlocking the iron door.

Wren wrenched it open and rushed to Ever's side,

splashing through the ankle-deep water. She eyed her friend. "Where does it hurt the least?"

"Everything hurts," Ever slurred.

"Okay." She wrapped her arms around the older woman's legs and lifted to give her arms some relief from the chains. "Just hang in there, okay?" she said in hushed tones.

Ever chuckled humorlessly. "I think all I *can* do is hang here."

Wren glared over her shoulder and shouted, "Get her down. *Now*."

The pair of them exchanged uncomfortable glances. The one who'd unlocked the door pointed upward with his spear. "Only the king has the keys."

"You're the bloody jailor. Why does he have personal possession of the keys?"

"To stop something like this happening," a voice boomed down the dungeon.

Her husband materialized from the dark. He strode toward the small group, his expression one of cold fury. Wren adjusted her hold on Ever so she could face Arrik. He glared at her, not a hint of compassion in his baleful gaze. She braced herself for what was to come. He couldn't scare her into submission before and he certainly wouldn't now.

The guards scrambled back as Arrik stood in the doorway to the cell. His piercing blue eyes locked on her.

"Get out of the water, wife." A frigid command.

Wren's jaw clenched at his tone, and she shook her head. "Not until you get her down first!"

"Get out," he hissed.

"No."

Arrik looked like he was ready to tear the door from the cell. He inhaled deeply before glaring at the two guards. "Both of you—out."

His men scrambled to do his bidding, nary sparing her a glance as they fled the dungeon. They knew better than to question their king, who had a ruthless reputation. Wren would have felt bad for the retribution they'd face for letting her into the dungeon if not for the fact they were complicit in Ever's treatment.

She stared down her fuming husband. "This is barbaric even for *you*."

"You know nothing about it."

"Clearly. How could you do this?"

"I was about to ask you the same question. You've put everything we've been working toward at risk for a murderer."

"Everything *you've* been working toward, you mean," she spat back.

Arrik's fingers tightened around the doorframe. "Come here, now. I won't ask again."

The water was rising higher. Wren tightened her grip on Ever, holding her ground. "This is it, Arrik. This is my line. You were the one who wanted a partnership. You cannot treat people like this—not now, not ever. You are the one who wants to effect change in Verlanti. That change starts with you. If you don't start showing compassion to anyone other than me, then I will *never* be yours."

He stilled, his face contorting before he snarled at her and pushed away from the door. The king paced in front of the cell, watching her like a caged lion. The water began to bubble behind Wren and she steeled herself. A play of emotions crossed his face as he finally understood that he would not break her resolve.

“Shane!” he bellowed, his voice echoing off the stone walls. “Get in here!”

With a curse, Arrik stormed through the cell door and crashed through the water. He growled underneath his breath as he unlocked Ever’s cuffs and tore her from Wren’s arms without looking her in the eye. For a moment, Wren thought he’d toss Ever to the fish, but he just stormed back out of the cell.

Ever held a weak hand out to Wren, unspoken gratitude in her expression.

Shane jogged down the corridor, his lips twisted down in a frown.

“Sort her out,” Arrik ordered, handing over Ever to Shane. “I have other matters to deal with.”

Shane scowled at Wren but did as his king commanded. Always the loyal servant.

“Come with me,” Arrik muttered, roughly grabbing Wren’s arm and dragging her past Shane and Ever up the stairs and out of the dungeon.

Oh no he did not.

They didn’t get far down the corridor before she yanked herself out of his hold and pulled a blade out from beneath her dirty skirts as he yanked her against his body. She held it up to the crook of Arrik’s armpit.

A dangerous move. A move that meant she was deathly, deathly serious.

"Touch me like that again and see what happens," she seethed, breathing hard.

Arrik smiled and ignored the blade, pressing himself against her. Her back met the cold marble wall as he invaded her space with every inch of his body. "Do you think a little pain scares me? Or death? I *am* death."

Wren stared up into his burning eyes and felt a measure of pity. When had this man ever experienced a kernel of compassion or love? Just what kind of demons turned him into such a monster?

"It doesn't have to be this way," she said softly. "You get to choose who you are."

His expression hardened even more.

"If you ever speak like that again in front of my subjects —if you *ever* question my authority again when we're in public, then you'll find yourself in the dungeon just like your friend. The place should feel like a second home to you by now."

"Back to threats?" She arched a brow, past caring whether anyone might be listening. She leaned closer, holding his gaze. "Throw me in your dungeon. See how far it gets you. As I recall, it worked so well last time."

"There are worse fates than prison," he murmured, attention dropping to her lips. "I could make your suffering so sweet. I'd have you begging in a matter of hours for relief."

Wren pressed up onto her tiptoes and brushed her lips lightly along his, a tingle running down her spine at the contact. "Promises, promises."

"Why do you have to always challenge me?" he growled.

"Because you're not God." Wren dropped back onto her

heels and twisted out of his grip. She walked away from him, head held high even as her heart raced.

"You never give your back to the enemy."

"Is that what you are to me, husband?" she called over her shoulder.

A slew of curses.

She smiled, satisfied with her victory.

CHAPTER 15

ARRIK

His wife was going to get herself killed.

And the very thought of it struck terror into the center of his black heart.

After their row, he had wanted to go after her. Maybe fight some more and kiss the stubbornness from her lips. But being king didn't mean a life of frivolity. He had duties that could not be ignored. Last evening and all day, he'd been ensconced in meetings.

He took a slow sip of his watered-down wine. Arrik didn't care for spirits. He hated how it dulled the senses. And in his line of work, that was deadly. Although he was half tempted to drink himself into a stupor to get out of this meeting and to forget his troublesome little dragon.

The advisory meeting had gone on for three hours now and had no signs of finishing any time soon. Arrik knew fine well what his advisors—most of them Soren's—were hoping for.

They wanted Arrik broken and impatient—whittled down to a greenhorn who had to admit he knew nothing about ruling. But they didn't know just how strong his resolve was, nor how far his patience could extend.

A man with waxy skin, hooded eyes, and thinning flaxen hair, droned on and on about tax levies on the merchant classes, speaking as if Arrik were stupid. He stared down the man, making him stutter. They could play their games for now. Soon most of them would be gone, replaced with his own men when the time was right.

Arrik just as equally couldn't risk alienating some of the most powerful families in the kingdom. He had to be careful. Cautious when it counted, and bold when it didn't. Every move he made had to be perfect, otherwise Soren's men would tear him down.

Or Idril's.

He fingered through the reports already knowing what they said. He wouldn't be upping the taxes. The highborn class was already taking advantage of the smallfolk. The men in the room were some of the wealthiest in their kingdom. Arrik wasn't about to rob from the poor to line the pockets of the rich. A sentiment that Wren would have agreed with if she could see past her own prejudice and morality.

Arrik scowled at the documents, not reading a single line, and shifted uncomfortably. His back still hurt from the terrible sleep he'd gotten last night. His mind should have been focused on the meeting, but he kept thinking about how they'd parted. How he'd lost his temper.

After what had transpired in the dungeons with Ever, Wren had refused to let him sleep in their bed. *His* bed. Perhaps a year ago he would have staunchly ignored her and forced his way in, but her feelings *mattered* to him.

Despite himself, he wanted her trust.

Her love.

It was foolish, but he couldn't help himself.

Shane didn't even seem to understand it.

Arrik would have to keep an eye on his alliances. They'd been friends most of their life—Shane had followed him into the most dismal of battles with unflinching loyalty—but everyone had a breaking point, and Arrik could tell Shane was reaching his.

He shifted in his seat again as another spasm of pain ran through his back. In any case, Arrik had resentfully slept on the floor. The shadows under his eyes and an ache all the way down his spine were proof of it. It certainly wasn't making this meeting any more bearable.

Surprisingly, though, he didn't regret it; he didn't want to be a brute with Wren.

His mood darkened.

Even though a brute was exactly what he'd been in the dungeon.

He was still furious about everything Wren risked by her outspokenness in front of his men—furious at Kalles, too, for deliberately riling her up—yet now it was guilt that was plaguing him. He'd been rough. There was no excuse for that.

He had to make it up to her.

Long after Wren had fallen asleep the night before, Arrik

had stared at the ceiling, trying to figure out his wife. Her view of the world was very black and white. If Ever had been part of the bombing, would Wren really protect her? He'd spoken with Josenu and all the spy had revealed was that Ever had treated Wren with respect and kindness during her time with the rebellion. Had his wife gone to the woman's aid out of misplaced loyalty?

He couldn't fault loyalty.

The horror on her face as she'd called for his men to unchain the older woman was burned into his mind. Guilt was new to him. But every time he recalled his wife's reaction, the uncomfortable feeling would rise up. How would he have reacted if Shane or Ronan had been the ones strung up and beaten, by Wren's command no less?

It would have torn him apart.

No wonder she had looked at Arrik as if he were a monster.

"...which brings me to the topic of your wife, Your Majesty...Your Majesty?" the flaxen-haired man inquired politely.

Arrik shook the fog from his head, inwardly cursing his inattention, before staring at the man in question until he expanded on his point. He coughed softly. "Her Highness has been observed and reported to be—*ahem*—altogether too *crass* and *foreign* for the palate of the Verlantian court to stomach. Might you be able to—*ahem*—enlighten her on how things are done here?"

"You presume to cast judgements of your queen?" The question was dangerous.

"Never, my lord. There has just been talk about her

barbaric origins, and though perhaps our queen would like some instruction in the way her new people do things."

And there it was. That word again: *barbaric*.

Wren wasn't barbaric, and neither were her people. His wife was fierce and loyal and terrifying to behold, but she wasn't barbaric.

He was.

He pursed his lips in thought. She did need to learn Verlantian ways. "I do think that could be best achieved by my wife spending more time in the company of the court. With our people."

A murmur of approval.

"Might I suggest she visit some of the most influential families in your court? Making connections and friends would be well received among your peers," suggested a younger man with a pointed chin and dark hair—Arrik was fairly certain Astrid herself had ensured his place as an advisor to the king.

Another murmur of approval.

Arrik hated the thought of Wren leaving him behind, but he also knew that it was the right call: one he would have suggested himself had his wife not been the one who had to be subjected to it.

He relented and said, "You have my permission to organize a tour of the usual families for Queen Wren to visit over the next two weeks."

"And...another thing," the same man said. He glanced at everyone else in the room before saying, "We have all agreed that it would be best for Her Highness to be the one that leads the execution of the caught rebellion members. We believe it would show the Verlantian people that her sympathies rest with the families who lost loved ones."

It was a smart move, but how would Wren react?

Ending the meeting, he strode through corridors back to his chambers, and to Wren. He hesitated at their door. Ronan arched a brow at him, and Arrik steeled himself for what was to come. It would be a battle to get her to accept the role of executioner, but it was important for him to see if she was truly on his side. Executing the captured rebellion members was an inevitability; Wren had to be aware of that.

At least, by her hands, their deaths would be swift and painless.

Thinking about the prisoners gave him an idea.

He entered their chambers and closed the door behind him.

The moment Arrik laid eyes on Wren sitting on the floor, overlooking the gardens with unseeing eyes, he knew he needed to make amends.

He walked to her side, dropped to his knees, and clasped his hands over hers. She didn't flinch away, but nor did she look at him either.

"I'm sorry," he said truthfully. "I think you know I'm sorry, but that doesn't mean I don't have to say it. I should never have treated you that way. You were hurting and I made it worse with my temper. You deserve better."

For a moment it seemed as if his little dragon was going to simply ignore him, but then her shoulders sagged, and she sighed heavily. When her red, swollen eyes found Arrik's, he realized with a new stab of guilt that she'd been crying.

"You cannot treat me like that, then apologize and hope

things will be better. How do I know it won't simply happen again?"

He squeezed her hands gently. "Change isn't easy for me but know that I *am* trying. Because of you. *For* you. I like who I can see myself becoming, but I can't become that man overnight. Be patient with me."

"I don't want you to change for me. I want you to change because you want to be better for yourself and your people. We don't have to become the people our parents hoped to shape us into. We get to choose, but we can't do it for someone else. That's not real change."

He shook his head. "That's not true."

"It is, you just don't know it yet. I will not be responsible for your actions."

Arrik dropped his head and kissed the back of her hands. "I am sorry."

She pulled her hands from his and his stomach dropped until she cupped his cheeks and gazed into his eyes. "I appreciate the words, but actions matter more. *Show* me you mean what you say."

In that moment, he knew she was his salvation from the darkness. That despite everything he'd done to gain Verlanti, it would mean nothing without her by his side. He was so tired of being alone.

"Will you forgive me?" he rasped. "I'll stay on my knees all night for my queen if that's what it takes."

That, finally, elicited a ghost of a smile from his beautiful wife. When she got to her feet he followed suit.

"I don't need you on your knees. I need you to stand beside me and see me as your equal."

"I do." When Wren gave him a dubious look, he added, "I swear it is so."

"Then show me that you want a partner, not a doormat."

He cupped her cheek. "I don't want any version of you but the real, authentic you beside me. The one who'll call me out on my poor behavior and not let me get away with it."

"...then why does it still feel like I'm being kept in the dark?" she asked, voice so soft Arrik barely heard her on the wind.

He took her hand and led her from their chambers. There was something else he needed to show her.

"Where are you taking me?"

"To meet someone."

Her steps slowed when they reached the stairs that led to the dungeon, trepidation on her face. "What are we doing here?"

"I'm bringing you here because I trust you," he murmured, "and because I'm hoping it will demonstrate that you can trust me."

Wren's face was impassive in the low torchlight. "Lead on."

Those two little words gave him hope.

And hope killed.

CHAPTER 16

WREN

She hated being in the dungeon again. It always reminded Wren that she was one wrong word away from being locked up again, even though she knew the dungeons couldn't keep her contained so long as Trove was around to save her. Still, it weighed on her mind like lead as Arrik directed her to a cell she had previously taken no notice of.

It was very dark, so Wren had to peer through the shadows to see who was being held within the iron bars. A brown-skinned man, with close-cropped hair and a similar facial structure to Rowen. That it *wasn't* Rowen filled Wren with such an overwhelming surge of relief that she almost gasped. He might not be her husband—might not be the man she loved so ardently in the past—but she still cared for him and did not wish the Verlanti dungeons on him.

Realizing that the prisoner was Vadonese sent a jolt of

recognition through Wren. She *had* seen him at the last rebellion meeting with Rowen. *An envoy?* Wren mused, taking in the bruised and bloodied appearance of the man with distaste.

She turned her attention to Arrik, and he grimaced.

"He hasn't spoken a word. Hence the beating."

"That's very gracious of you," she said stiffly.

"Wr—"

"Her," rasped a third voice. The Vadonese prisoner. He pointed a somewhat shaking finger at Wren. "I'll talk to the dragon princess. Alone. I shall not talk to anyone else."

She blinked slowly. What the devil was this now?

Wren expected Arrik to laugh the prisoner down. To reject his request.

Instead, he placed the keys in Wren's hands, briefly squeezing them between his own, then promptly left the dungeon.

Leaving Wren alone with the man from Vadon.

What sort of trap was this?

She clenched the keys in her hand. Was this Arrik's way of saying that he was sorry? That he trusted her, and she could trust him? After everything that had transpired thus far between them, to trust Arrik now would be foolish. But she'd use the opportunity he'd given her, and gladly.

Wren unlocked the cell's door, which creaked ominously on its hinges, then dropped to her knees to sit in front of the man, despite the wet muck that covered the ground. "Who are you?" she asked him, softly, gently, but with purpose.

The man tilted his proud chin to meet Wren's eyes. She saw the same unbroken look she'd seen in Ever's expression.

The rebellion members were all made of far stronger stuff than the Verlanti crown could ever break.

"An am-am"—he coughed to clear his raspy throat—"ambassador of sorts," he said.

"For Vadon?"

He nodded.

"What do you want with Verlanti?"

"Verlanti?" The man spat his disgust. "We want nothing to do with these snakes."

"Then why are you here?"

"We don't want them anywhere near the Dragon Isles."

"Why are you telling me this?" She studied the man. He wanted to speak to her for a reason. "Vadon wants something from me? From the isles?" Wren thought back to everything Rowen had told her about his true purpose in Lorne. It hurt less now to think of it. "That's why you wanted me to marry one of your men. So Vadon could control—"

"Not control," the man interjected. He ran a tired hand over his brow. Looking closely, Wren could see that he was beginning to sweat from fever. Not surprising considering the conditions down here. A stab of white-hot anger filled her at the fact Arrik deemed it completely acceptable to send people down here.

Just like his father. Just like Soren.

Was that the path Arrik was heading down? Was he doomed to become just like the cruel old high king?

When the man didn't continue, Wren said, "If not control, then what?"

"Lower taxes," he said simply. "Better trade agreements. Priority trade for black diamonds. *No slave routes*," he added on, when it became clear that was what Wren was going to ask next. "If you can guarantee those things for us, then Vadon is yours to use as you will against the vipers."

Wren regarded this critically. It was all perfectly fair and good and true—too good to be true. She cocked her head to the side. "I'm looking for the downside to this agreement," she freely admitted. After all, the man was a prisoner of the people he most hated. He was hardly going to tell them anything Wren said. "I'm used to people requiring more concrete proof of an alliance. Everything you want are things I can only agree to at this point verbally. And something tells me you don't have just reason to trust me at that level quite yet. Why me? Why now?"

He offered a wry smile, and in that moment Wren could see, through the muck and the blood, a shadow of the striking man the prisoner was before he'd been detained. "You are known among your people to be fair. You hold much sway over the king. We've been waiting for you for a long time."

"I don't know you."

"But you will."

"So sure?"

"Yes, in the future, we *will* trust each other."

"Then what else do you want from me?" Wren slid a little closer on her knees. "What do you *need*, so that Vadon might fight alongside me and the Dragon Isles?"

This time the man's smile grew feral. "I need you to kill your husband. I need you to kill High King Arrik."

CHAPTER 17

WREN

Split loyalties. Dark deals. Bloody endings.

Was this really what her life had become?

Despite the fact she'd been telling herself otherwise, Wren always knew everything would come down to killing Arrik. It had been an inevitability right from the start. He had been the one who ransacked Lorne. Arrik was responsible for the deaths of her parents. For making Britta an orphan.

For imprisoning Wren and wrenching her away from her little sister.

But he was so much more than that.

He freed slaves, deposed cruel kings, and punished those who deserved it.

A sob lodged in her throat, and she stumbled, catching herself on the damp dungeon wall. Wren fought to control her emotions as her mind swirled around the deal she'd struck with the Vadonese envoy. His assistance would give her everything she needed to take back the isles. All he asked was for her husband's life.

And she'd said yes.

She heaved, bile burning the back of her throat.

Rebellion was one thing. Murder was another.

Another dry sob escaped her throat, but Wren turned the wretched betrayal of her conflicted feelings into a shallow cough. She forced herself upright and wiped her face with the sleeve of her dress, trying to compose herself.

Swallowing down her shame, she trudged up the stairs and came up beside Arrik once more. Her stomach churned at the soft smile he gave her, and the affection she spotted in his eyes.

"You weren't in there for long," he said, very obviously trying to keep his tone light and conversational as he gave Wren his arm for her to loop hers through.

She didn't hesitate. Holding on to him grounded her wretched soul.

He did not manage to hide his surprise and victory when she did, in fact, take it. But if she didn't, she felt altogether like she'd collapse to the floor beneath the overwhelming weight of all the responsibility that had been thrust on her.

"I-I wasn't?" she said, knowing her voice sounded hollow. Strange to her own ears.

"Only five minutes," Arrik drawled. His brows furrowed and his gaze took on a gleam. "Something's wrong. What did he say to you?" The harsh tone his voice took—the way

Arrik's entire body tensed as if ready to fight on her behalf—shook Wren to the core.

Her king hadn't said the words, but he truly cared for her.

And she was going to kill him.

"It was nothing." Wren waved a hand as if that could shoo away everything in her head. "He wanted to play mind games. It got to me a little, but I know what he was doing. I'll be all right."

"Hmm."

"You don't sound convinced."

"Unsurprisingly, I'm not inclined to believe rebel prisoners from an enemy nation."

Wren barked out a laugh despite herself, feeling like she was ready to crawl out of her skin.

Just channel your inner Astrid.

She could do this. With every word, with every step, with every breath, she settled back into herself and shoved the conversation with the envoy far from her mind. She didn't need to complete the task today. No agreement had been signed.

Emboldened, Wren took Arrik by the hand and tugged him in the direction of their chambers. "Let's have dinner outside, by the baths," she said, offering him a small smile that felt like it didn't quite fit her face. "I could do with inhaling the steam to clear out the smell of...you know."

Arrik glanced back at the dungeon and nodded in understanding. "If that is what you wish, dearest."

Dearest.

Every time she heard that word fall from his lips, another

piece of her heart became his. It was the way he said it. Arrik truly meant that she was his dearest, his most cherished.

Arrik whispered to one of the servants as they arrived in their rooms. He led her to their private gardens and laid out a blanket for them before sitting and holding a hand out to her. Wren stared at his palm before taking a step backward.

His brows lowered. "What's wrong?"

She gestured to her soiled dress. "I'm a mess. Let me clean up and I'll be right back."

Hustling back into the room, she practically ran past the servants and sequestered herself in the lavatory. Wren locked the door and slid down the smooth wall. She leaned her head between her knees as she tried to calm her racing heart.

How did she get herself into this mess?

All she had wanted was the isles and her freedom.

This was supposed to be her game.

Sure, she'd planned on taking the throne from Arrik, and at one time she wanted to kill him…but that had changed sometime along the way. Now she couldn't imagine a life without him.

She'd given her heart to the devil.

And it bloody well terrified her.

Get yourself together. Nothing has changed. Just continue on as you have been.

She slowly gathered her composure and exited the lavatory. Woodenly, Wren entered the dressing room, kicked off her slippers, and changed into a simple wispy black gown with no back. She slowly made her way back into the gardens and paused as servants placed bowls of grilled duck, salted fish, soft cheeses, fresh bread, sliced fruits, and other delicacies onto the ground.

She padded closer. "What's all this?" It looked romantic.

Arrik gave her a smile that reached his eyes and set her heart racing. "I wasn't sure what you liked so I got a little bit of everything." He took the wine from the nearest servant and waved his hand. "We wish to eat alone."

Wren nodded to the servants as they dutifully exited through their rooms. She turned to face her husband as he let out a long, low sigh, then with expert fingers undid the braids that kept his hair away from his face. When the wind blew the now-free silvery strands, he sighed even louder.

"They were giving me a migraine," he explained, stretching out his long body along the ground.

"Are you sure it was the braids that were causing the migraine, or me?" Wren replied, pleased that her voice came off as teasing rather than stilted.

He let out a short laugh. "The very long, incredibly boring meetings I had to preside over today may have had something to do with it."

"Ah." Wren sauntered closer and sat to his left. She popped a slice of peach into her mouth, appreciating the way the juice coated her parched mouth more than she could ever put into words. "Pray tell and complain."

He blinked slowly. "You really want to hear about my day?"

"I do." And she meant it.

He relayed all the boring but necessarily topics he'd had to listen to, as well as the simpering advisers who looked like they wished bloody murder on Arrik the moment they thought he wasn't looking. As he spoke, they ate, and took off their shoes, and stretched out their limbs so the sun could envelop every inch of them in its heat.

It was downright domestic, in a way that wasn't practiced or an act.

It felt natural. Scarily so.

"And then," he said, when they were nearing the end of a bottle of strawberry wine that made Wren's cheeks flush pleasantly, "just when I thought it was over, they brought up you."

She shook her head and rolled toward him, propping her head on her hand. "And what has your barbarian queen done to offend them this time?"

Arrik laughed, long and throaty, his head tossed back, exposing the strong line of his throat and his pointed ears. One she wanted to taste and bite.

Wren flushed. That was enough wine for her.

"Darling, your mere existence is sufficient to cause them grief. But, as it turns out, they actually had a good idea."

"Which is?"

He glanced at her out of the corner of his eye. "They want you to get out more. Meet more people."

"I have met more people than I can remember," Wren muttered, huffing out her chest in genuine frustration. "I talk to locals and merchants and—"

"By *meet more people* they mean the *right* people. Highborn families. Families with influence and standing at court."

"*Ahhh.* I can see why that would be necessary." She sighed. "I don't like it."

"Of course you don't," he sniggered. "I can arrange to

have the families visit the palace, if you'd like. That way you don't have to—"

"No," Wren cut in, "no. I'll go to them. It will look better in their eyes if I'm the one making the effort." Wren knew she was lucky that this was true, because it made it a far more convincing lie than anything else.

Visiting highborn families at their homes would make it that much easier for Wren to meet with the rebellion.

Arrik gave her an appraising look then glanced away. "Thank you," he said sincerely. "Seriously. You're doing me a far bigger favor than I deserve by doing this."

She perused his serious profile. "What aren't you telling me?" she asked, reaching for Arrik's hand to just barely squeeze his fingers. "What else did your advisers say?"

It looked as if Arrik would rather have his teeth cut out one by one with a rusty knife than tell her. But then he squeezed her hand, closed his eyes for a moment, then said, "They want you to head up Ever's execution. Not *perform* it. But...lead it. Address the crowd. Inform her of her punishment. That sort of thing."

Her breath caught.

"And that's...when?" It was as if someone else was using Wren's body to speak. She couldn't process what she was hearing. She knew Ever would be sentenced but hearing it decided was another matter altogether. Having the older woman's fate in her own hands was unbearable.

"...before you begin touring the highborn families. The beginning of next week."

"And you have proof she committed these crimes?"

Arrik nodded. "You may not speak about your connection with the rebellion, but I know you know that Ever holds power among the rebellion, Wren. She had to know about the bombing. There were families there."

She squeezed her eyes closed as if that would shut out the truth.

Wren wanted to fight. She wanted to scream. She wanted to cry and throw things and lop off the heads of every single one of Arrik's advisers—even the ones he liked—for pushing this fate onto her. But she had to hold her head high and take on the task as gracefully as a queen would. She had to lie.

No matter how it tore at her soul.

Ate at her heart.

Slowly, so slowly, Wren nodded and it broke her.

"Wren."

She met the king's piercing gaze, vaguely aware that she was digging her nails into Arrik's hand so hard she had drawn blood, but he hadn't said a word.

"I'm sorry." Her voice broke.

She tried to withdraw her hand, but Arrik placed his other one on top of it.

"You're allowed to say this hurts you, Wren," he said gravely, as gently as if she were the most precious person in the world. "You don't have to keep your emotions bottled up."

"It hurts," she whispered, fighting back tears.

"I know, dearest. I'm so sorry."

She didn't want to head up the execution, but she knew —she could see it in Arrik's face—that doing so would be a huge boon for him against the people who believed him to be the wrong king, and her the wrong bride.

"I'll do it, if you'll be there standing beside me," she croaked, not having to fake the thickness of her voice.

"Of course I'll be there beside you."

Arrik wrapped an arm around her waist and pulled her against his chest, his legs tangling with her own. His callused fingers ran through her hair and she wept, breathing in his salty, woodsy scent as if her life depended on it.

"I've got you, love. I will never let you go."

His words made her cry even harder. He meant every word from his heart and yet here she was lying in his embrace while death and deceit rested in her own heart.

Her pain was real, but her words were false.

She'd never be part of Ever's execution. She would find a way to save her friend.

Arrik pressed a kiss to the top of her head. "You're safe with me. Let it all go. Trust me."

And she did, but he shouldn't trust her.

She would do what Arrik wanted. What he needed. He would trust her so completely that he'd never see the dagger at his throat until it was too late.

He wasn't safe with her at all.

CHAPTER 18

WREN

The warm sunshine and gentle breeze eased her into consciousness.

Wren yawned, her face feeling tight.

Her eyes snapped open as a very large masculine arm pulled her tighter against a muscled chest. She looked down at the way Arrik possessively held her in his sleep and tried to keep calm as panic threatened to claw up her throat. How did they end up in this position?

She scanned the garden. The last thing she remembered was her husband playing with her hair. Wren glanced down at his hand resting on her belly and winced. She was becoming far too comfortable in his presence. Especially after what she'd agreed to yesterday...

Feeling stifled, she gently tried to wriggle out of his grasp, only for him to moan into her hair. Wren froze as his hand wandered the curved planes of her stomach, his thumb resting right beneath her breast. A shiver worked through her as Arrik stirred, nuzzling the back of her neck. Her eyes closed briefly as she savored the sensation. It felt... good...to be held. He made her feel so tiny, so safe in his arms.

"...g'morning," the king muttered, his deep voice thick with sleep. "Why are you awake so early?"

"The sun." She could think of nothing else as his fingers roved.

A soft sensual chuckle ruffled her hair that made goose-bumps break out along her arms. "Close your eyes and go back to bed, darling." She wiggled again and he hissed. "Keeping moving like that, little dragon, and we both won't get any more sleep."

She blushed and eased herself out of his grasp. Wren rolled away and swung upright, catching Arrik's eye. He was tousled and it looked *good* on him. His silken hair begged to have her fingers run through it.

A lazy smile spread across his lips, a little bit of the devil gleaming in his gaze. "You've roused the beast, dearest. I suggest you come back into my arms or I might have to hunt you down."

She swallowed and shook her head. "I'd like to go for a ride, to clear my head."

His playful mood evaporated as quickly as smoke, turning into concern. "Are you alright?"

"I will be, but after what you asked me to do yesterday, I think I'm in desperate need of it."

He nodded, his brows furrowing. "By ride you mean...?"

"Trove. Yes."

Her husband didn't like it. Wren could see it in the set of his shoulders.

Arrik sat up and ran a hand through his hair and then over his face. "I'm sorry I had to ask you to head up the execution. Take all the time you need to clear your head."

She gave him a wobbly smile and stood. "I'm not sure when I'll be back."

"Will you take Shane and Josenu with you?" A question, not a demand.

Wren paused and stared down at the monster who'd stolen her heart. "Of course." Before she could overthink it, she leaned down and pressed her lips to his. He kissed her back with lazy abandon, like they did this every morning and had all the time in the world.

"What was that for?" he asked, his voice a bit rough.

"For speaking with your actions."

"With a reaction like that, I'll make sure to do it more often," he growled softly.

Her heart thumped painfully in her chest when she saw more than just desire in his gaze.

"Do be careful."

"I always am," she replied.

"That's debatable."

Wren rolled her eyes and walked away from Arrik, her smile faltering a little. "Don't get yourself killed while I'm gone, my king."

He chuckled. "You and I both know that my life is only yours." Arrik didn't know how true his words were. "I'll have dinner waiting for you."

"How very domestic," she called back from the dressing

room, quickly putting on her favorite pair of trousers and boots.

"Anything for my queen."

She snorted. "Dinner it is."

"I'll count down the hours," Arrik deadpanned.

As if anticipating her every move, Josenu and a surly Shane were waiting for her at the palace entrance. A moment later Leif materialized out of seemingly nowhere.

"Where have *you* been?" she asked, giving her friend a hug before setting off down the long and winding streets to the dock. Wren tugged at her hood to make sure her hair was concealed. No one needed to know that their queen was loose on the streets. "I haven't seen you for days."

He gave her a knowing look. One that said *Let's talk in private*, so Wren allowed a companionable silence to fall between them as they walked.

"I need to lose the bodyguards," Wren murmured a few moments later, catching Josenu's eye for a fraction of a second—too quick for Shane to notice but long enough for Josenu to work out what was going on.

Leif squeezed her hand and grinned. "But of course. Leave it to me." Then, loudly: "How about we check out the cloth fair down in the merchant quarter first? There's some imported silk from my homeland that I've been dying to check out since it first arrived by ship."

Wren *oohed* and *ahhed* as if the thought of shopping for cloth delighted her. "I would love that! Lead the way."

And so Leif did, turning this way and that way and altogether cutting as difficult a path through the increasingly manic, bustling crowd of the cloth fair. A minute or two later he said, in a low voice, "Go. Now."

She broke off from her friend and her entourage, sneaking behind a stall selling spicy, exotic fragrances alongside bolts of silk, before creeping onto the nearest roof with an efficiency Leif would be proud of. It was in this way that Wren made very quick work of reaching the docks, and Gunn's ship. Trove was nowhere to be seen, and nor was her brother. Perhaps sleeping off a drunken night?

She nodded at the first crewman she encountered. "Where's the captain's bedroom?"

The raven-haired woman—who towered over Wren—smirked as she said, "The captain is—ah—entertaining private company right now. He—"

"His bedroom, please." A command, pure and simple.

"Down those stairs and straight down the corridor," the woman relented, knowing a headstrong opponent when she saw one. "Don't think I didn't warn you."

After thanking her, Wren followed her directions, not bothering to knock when she reached the captain's quarters, and threw open the door. He deserved to be needled with as much trouble as he'd caused her in the past.

"*Mother of*—Wren?" Gunn yelled, dropping his blades onto the blanket. He waved down to the svelte figure of the woman sharing his bed. "Can't you see I'm otherwise occupied?"

Wren would have laughed if she wasn't here on a mission. She ignored the woman who watched her with dark eyes and pushed down her hood. "Where's Trove? I didn't see him outside."

Gunn let out a string of curses as he wiped sleep from his eyes. "Bloody beast has been terrorizing my men for fun. A couple of them lured him out with a fishing boat to get him to hunt and leave the main ship well alone. Hope you don't mind."

"If you think they lured him anywhere, then you're more stupid than you look. Trove will have gone out there simply to terrorize your poor sacrifices all the worse."

"Well, better them than me," he muttered. "But why are you here, really?" When Wren looked pointedly at the figure under his covers, Gunn shrugged. "She's deaf. Ask away. Or demand, as my precious sister is so prone to do."

Wren ignored the jibe. "Things have escalated at the palace. Where's Rowen? I need to speak to him. Ever has been sentenced."

A flash of understanding shone in Gunn's eyes. "Right. Of course. Do you remember the pub you first met me in? He's staying in a room above there. The southernmost-facing suite." A pause. "He's expecting you."

A knot formed in her stomach. "What do you mean?"

Her brother shrugged. "Just that he knew you'd come looking for him at some point."

Great.

"Thanks," Wren said, then without another word turned tail.

"You're welcome, *sis*," Gunn called, right before she slammed the door shut. "Marry your mistress, *brother*," she yelled back.

Muffled laughter followed as she stalked down the short hallway to the deck.

She ignored the looks passed her way and pulled up her hood over her hair as she left the ship to make her way to the tavern. There wasn't any time to waste. There was always someone wanting her attention or watching her. Wren's disappearing act could only last so long before someone would become suspicious.

It didn't take long to locate the pub, nor the southernmost room.

She hesitated outside Rowen's door. The last time they'd met it hadn't been on good terms.

Ever doesn't have time for you to dally.

Wren pulled in a deep breath and lifted her hand to knock when the door was opened from the inside. She blinked as a bronze-skinned woman with the most startling gold eyes Wren had ever seen walked out. The woman's hair was properly mussed, and a blush stained her cheeks. She didn't look surprised or annoyed to see Wren standing there, instead smiling politely before leaving down the corridor.

A twinge of hurt struck her.

Rowen moved on quickly, it seemed. He'd tried to kiss her the last time they'd spoke—said he still wanted her. She knew in her heart they hadn't been mere empty platitudes, but they clearly hadn't been "you and nobody else" confessions either.

Not that it mattered. She was married, and he was free to do as he liked.

Her gaze moved back to Rowen's room, and she forced herself to step over the threshold. Rowen stood half-naked washing his face in a basin in complete ignorance of her presence. Melancholy thrummed through her chest. It was quiet moments like these that she'd imagined in the past of them together. It was bittersweet.

The hurt Wren experienced felt old, like an echo, a ghost of a feeling. An old wound acting up in the rain.

They'd both changed.

They'd both made choices that led them here.

It was only fair they both could move on.

Wren wanted that—for both of them.

She coughed softly into her hand when Rowen made no attempt to turn around, clicking the door closed behind her for good measure. The noise made him jump.

He glanced over his shoulder and blanched. "Wren," he bit out, scrambling to grab a shirt and stand up straight. "That wasn't—she wasn't—"

"It's fine," she cut in. "You don't have to explain yourself. You're a free man."

"But I—"

"Look, there are no promises between us any longer. I am married."

He dropped his head, staring at the shirt crushed in his palms. "I don't know how to do this. It doesn't feel right."

"I don't know if it ever will."

He lifted his gaze, a sad smile on his face. "I miss you."

Her heart squeezed. "I miss my friend too." Despite everything, they'd grown up together and she still loved him, although differently than in the past.

"Why are you here?" Rowen asked.

"Because I need answers." She stared him down. "There is a Vadonese man in the dungeons. Who is he?"

All at once he became serious and professional—the man Wren knew and loved from his time in the Dragon Isles navy—the man who would tell her honestly what was going on, without softening the blows. But this time he wore a touch of wariness.

"You've seen him?"

"I have."

"Is he well?" Rowen urged.

"Well enough," she said slowly, scanning his face, noting the worry. "Why do I get the feeling the man in the dungeons is more important than he says?"

"And what has he said to you?"

Wren narrowed her eyes at Rowen's evasion. "I came to *you* for information, not the other way around. Stop tiptoeing around the matter and be straight with me. We don't have time to play games. Who is he?"

"He's one of the younger sons of the King of Vadon," Rowen stated harshly.

Wren blanched. "Please tell me you did not say what you just said."

Rowen chuckled hollowly. "If only..." He ran a hand through his hair. "You don't need me to tell you how important it is that he isn't harmed."

She forced back a retch, glad that she hadn't yet eaten that morning. Things just kept getting worse. "He's a bloody Vadonese prince?"

"Prince Kade. The fourth son of the Southern Isles."

"If he's executed, there'll be all-out war," she whispered,

wiping her brow with her hand. She was already holding Verlanti together by a thread. "How could you let this happen?"

"Like I just handed him over to the king," Rowen retorted as he began pacing the room. "We didn't expect to get raided. None of our safeguards went off."

"Not one?"

Rowen's lip curled. "Not one."

That was problematic. "You have a spy." The signs were clear as day.

"We're handling it."

"I hope so." A crown spy was dangerous for her health. If she met with the rebellion again, she'd have to be in disguise.

"We need to get Kade out." A pause. "We'll need your help."

"Done." She'd already wanted to get him out in the first place, but with the origins of his birth revealed, it was a necessity now. "What do you need me to do?"

Rowen glanced out of the window before saying, "Josenu told me that Arrik himself holds the key to the prince's cell. I need you to get it for me."

"Consider it done. And what of Ever?"

Rowen paused his pacing and slowly faced her, his expression a blank mask. A chill ran down Wren's spine as he took one step toward her.

"We can't save everyone."

"What are you saying?" She glared at him when he held up his hands placatingly.

"You know as well as I that there won't be enough time

to get both of them out. I heard she's in bad shape. She's a liability to covertly break out."

"You can't be *serious*, Rowen!" Wren growled, balling her hands into fists to stop herself from shaking some sense into him. "Whatever happened to *no man left behind*? The reason you all escaped the raid was because of her! You would leave her to rot in the dungeon? To be executed?"

Rowen gave her an unbelievably sad smile. His shoulders sagged. It was as if it pained every fiber of his body to force out the words: "Ever made her choices. She knew what came with the territory. Our priority has to be Kade. War hangs on his life, not Ever's."

"What happened to you?" Wren murmured.

"Life."

She shook her head and took a step toward the door. "The boy I grew up with would never sacrifice his friends."

"That boy grew up."

"Growing up doesn't mean you have to exchange your values, Rowen. I'll get you the keys and get Ever out myself." Wren spun on her heel and yanked the door open.

"Wren, I'm sorry."

"So am I." She slammed the door behind her and thundered down the steps.

If the rebellion wasn't going to help her, then she and Leif would work something out alone, just like how they'd broken out Idril's slaves.

Everything would be okay. She would make sure of it.

Her head was full of such thoughts—working through plans, rejecting some and accepting others—as she wound her way back to the cloth fair.

Stalls blurred past her as partly-thought-out plans ran through her mind.

There had to be a way to get Ever out.

A large hand wrapped with a cloth smelling thickly of chemicals clamped over her mouth. Wren screamed against his hand as the burly man yanked her against his chest. Her eyes watered and the world tilted as she ripped the dagger from her hip and blindly stabbed backward. A howl of pain echoed in her ears before darkness claimed her.

CHAPTER 19

WREN

WHAT THE DEVIL HAD HAPPENED?

It was like crawling through mud, trying to work out when and how and where and why she was.

Head throbbing, Wren cracked her eyes to try to get her bearings. She lay on a mound of filthy hay, in a nondescript stable. Piles of animal manure were lumped in one corner of the wooden building. Ropes were tied around her wrists, and dirty weapons lined the far wall.

It wasn't promising to be sure.

Who'd kidnapped her?

The rebellion?

Idril?

The crown?

No matter what, it didn't bode well.

Careful not to make too much noise, she tugged on the ropes binding her hands and feet. The coarse material itched against her skin, but they hadn't been tied tightly.

Clearly, whoever had kidnapped her had no idea how proficient she was with ropes, given her upbringing surrounded by a world-class navy. That ruled out the crown and the rebellion. Could it be Idril? Or perhaps a simple smash and grab?

Wren lifted her head slightly and scanned the empty stable as she made slow but steady progress out of the rope that bound her wrists. Then, once her hands were free, she quickly undid the cordagearound her ankles.

She rolled her neck and did a quick assessment of her body. She was bruised, but nothing was broken, and her clothing was still intact. Not a smash and grab. Her hidden knives had been confiscated, which was a problem, but they'd be stupid to leave her in a room with weapons and no guards.

Wren made to get up when the stable door opened.

Blast it all.

Too far from the weapons to do anything.

Time to play the fool.

She wrapped the rope loosely back around her ankles, then hid her untied hands behind her back, where they had first been bound. The element of surprise would be her only advantage. She needed to listen and be patient.

A deep rumbling voice became clearer as the door was opened quickly, though the sun shining behind them obscured their faces from view.

She blinked against the light and stared at their boots as her sight righted itself.

Four pairs of boots.

Four against one wasn't good odds.

The stable door closed, and Wren could see the men more clearly.

It was abundantly clear: soldiers or assassins they were not.

They were lowborn, working-class men, with not an ounce of fighting muscle between them. One of them was wielding a pitchfork like it might accidentally stab him. Another a hammer. One of them had both of Wren's daggers in his hands, though the way he held them told her all she needed to know about his inability to use them properly.

The fourth man was unarmed, and wore a smile that she didn't like one bit. He swaggered toward Wren, looming over her.

"Good," he sneered. "You're awake. Torture is hardly enjoyable when one is sleeping through it."

"Torture?" Little did they know she'd survived more than they could ever do to her.

He smirked, an earring in his pointed ear glinting in the low light. "Only the best for our bastard's queen."

So this was about Arrik, not her. "I supposed you wish to send a message to your king? I hardly see how this will do the trick. The monster lives to torture me."

All four men laughed.

"That's not what we have heard," the man with her daggers said. "We think our king likes his precious dragon whore a little too much. He's taken too much from us, and now it's our turn to take from him."

"Hurting me will not hurt him."

"But it will hurt his hold over the isles," spat the man with her daggers. "He will suffer the way we have suffered."

"How have you suffered?" Wren asked, biding her time.

"The bombing took my son. He took my son!"

"I'm so sorry for your loss," she said, meaning every word. Wren couldn't imagine losing a child. "That was not the king's work, but the rebellion's."

"And why do you think they attacked if not to protest the monarchy?" the man with the hammer said.

"Soren was ruling then."

They didn't care. They were out for vengeance.

The first man waved a dismissive hand. "Who cares who's responsible for it? All that matters is that the message we can send—the only one that will *matter*—is directly to the king. And since it seems like the only thing he values is *you*... I guess it's your unlucky day, *my queen*."

"I am the queen of nothing. I am your king's war prize," she replied softly. "This will not bring your loved ones back."

"It will make me feel better," the one with the hammer snarled.

The other men joined in, distracted for the moment.

The time had arrived.

They didn't see it coming.

The first man who'd spoken to her—the unarmed one—lurched forward to wrench Wren up by the ropes tied around her wrists, but as soon as he tried to touch her, Wren roared in his ears and trapped him in a headlock. A moment later he was sprawled on the ground, and Wren had "undone" her loosened ankle restraints.

Movement exploded in the small stable.

The man with her daggers cursed and swiped at her.

"Wrong move," she taunted, adrenaline coursing through her as she dodged two jerky, unpracticed swipes toward her. A knock to the back of the man's head with the edge of her hand was sufficient to cause him to drop to his knees.

Wren grabbed her daggers out of his loosened hands and edged out of his reach.

Two down. Two to go.

"Who's next?" she challenged, directing her attention at the man with the hammer. He had lost the confidence he'd previously possessed when he'd been sure of his ability to overpower her. "Afraid?" she murmured.

He backed away, eyes wide.

Strike.

Wren didn't let him escape. She came after him, only striking out to attack when his back hit the wall. Wren dodged his wild swing, then stabbed him in the leg. Not fatal —not immediately—but serious enough to cause agonizing pain. The man yowled. Wren just barely avoided the hammer, which clattered to the floor before its wielder did.

"I told you that you didn't want to hurt me," Wren growled, and spun around to face her final opponent. "That leaves the pitchfork." His arms trembled as he held the pitchfork in her direction. His gaze darted to the door behind her as if he wanted to flee. But she wasn't in the mood to let him off easy.

Nobody kidnapped her and got off easy.

"P-please," he stammered, hands shaking as much as his voice. "We didn't—"

"You meant to torture me. Kill me."

"But we didn't—"

"Didn't what?" Wren cut in. "Expect me to fight back?" She smiled and carelessly tossed a dagger in the air.

The man was so transfixed by the action that he didn't notice her throw the other one at his shoulder until it was too late. He screamed, crashing over the first man just as he tried to get back up. She took a running step and kicked him in the ribs for good measure, before yanking the blade out of the final man's shoulder.

"I am the dragon queen. No one touches me without bleeding."

He gurgled but fell silent.

"Was that it?" Wren called out, wiping sweat out of her eyes before pocketing her knives. She still felt woozy, the drugs in her system not quite flushed out. She needed water and rest and to get out of the bloody heat. Unbidden, her brain flitted to Arrik's chambers and the cool solace it promised.

It felt so much like *home* that Wren recoiled as if something had burned her.

The door to the stable came crashing down, and she was starkly brought back to the present.

"*Wren*!" Leif cried, storming in with a furious Josenu and Shane in tow. They staggered to a stop when they discovered Wren standing before them, covered in blood but looming over her fallen opponents.

"What the devil?" Shane muttered.

"Um..." she began, unsure what to say. She coughed awkwardly. "How did you find me here?"

Josenu took a moment to observe what had transpired,

then pointed a thumb at Leif. "He seemed to just *know* where you were."

"We'll discuss how he knew exactly of your whereabouts later," Shane said, glaring at Wren's friend with unbridled suspicion. "Are you alright, my queen?"

"None of the blood is mine," she murmured as Leif embraced her, a wave of relief overwriting the adrenaline. Exhaustion weighed down on her. "I'm truly fine. Thank you for coming to my rescue."

When she pulled away, Leif wore a fake-stern expression. "Seems like a waste of my dragon princess-homing abilities if you save *yourself*."

"Would you rather you found me de—?"

"*Ahem*," Shane cut in, disgruntled beyond measure. "We need to get you back to the palace. You've been missing for six hours. The king is...not pleased."

That was an understatement if ever Wren had heard it.

"I'll take her back," Leif said. "The two of you should round up her kidnappers to take them back."

Shane narrowed his eyes. "Do not presume to give me orders...but they do need to be dealt with."

"Have they not received punishment enough?" Wren asked. "They are mourning their lost children."

"An attack on you is an attack on the crown. This cannot stand."

Wren glanced to Josenu, who nodded in agreement with Shane. "He's right, my queen."

She took another look at the poor souls on the floor. They'd made their beds and now they'd have to lie in them.

Leif took her arm and directed her toward the door.

As they headed out, Josenu gave Wren's shoulder a gentle squeeze. "Don't worry me like that. You forget that you have more people than simply Leif who values your safety. And we're not all as...loose...with our interpretation of 'safe' as he is."

Both Wren and Leif choked out similar laughs, but then Wren gave Josenu a genuine smile. "I know. I appreciate it. I'll take better care of myself. I promise."

She, Leif, and Josenu all silently knew what this meant: next time Wren needed to go off to meet the rebellion, Josenu would not be left behind. In this regard, his role in Arrik's trusted sphere of bodyguards was incredibly useful.

Shane cut a look their way. "Don't dally, my lady. The king awaits you."

A warning.

She rolled her eyes at the guard just to rile him and turned her attention back to Josenu. "For my tour of the highborn," Wren said, "will you act as my primary guard?"

He nodded. "It would be my honor."

"Go back *now*," Shane interrupted, so close to yelling that even Wren, who reveled in antagonizing him, knew better than to hang around. With a final smile at Josenu, she and Leif made quick work of returning to the palace.

"You might want to clean up before seeing your darling husband," Leif murmured just as they reached the royal chambers. He opened the door for her. "I don't imagine he'll like seeing you so...beaten up."

Wren laughed hollowly as she stepped inside. "I hardly have a scratch. Just a few bruises." She was bloody tired. "He should see the other men."

"Oh *should I*?" The king's deep voice washed over Wren.

She went cold.

With a silent, furtive nod, Leif slipped out of the room and closed the door, leaving Wren to turn around and face the man to whom the wickedly, cold voice belonged.

Arrik was the perfect embodiment of his voice, a thunderous giant of ice making his way toward her. She'd never been one to back away from him, but the haunted, taut pull of his skin and the murderous fire in his eyes was enough for even her to take a half step back from her husband.

"How was I supposed to predict that I'd get kidnapped?" Wren reasoned, attempting to be bold but hating how small her voice sounded. She knew this was her fault, and so did Arrik. Running around without an escort was too dangerous. She was no longer just the adopted daughter of the Dragon Isles.

She was queen of two kingdoms.

"You have guards for a reason."

"I do, but I'm not a child or a soft lady of your court. I was raised in the navy." She took off her cloak and tossed it onto a nearby chair.

His jaw clenched. "And yet I find you bruised and covered in blood. Why did you abandon your escort?"

She knew he was upset, but Wren didn't appreciate his tone. "I didn't know I was forbidden to go out on my own." Adrenaline rushed through her system again like an old friend. Instead of backing away, she stormed forward to meet Arrik right in the middle of the room. "Am I not the queen? Do I not hold freedom within my grasp?"

"Freedom?" Arrik threw back his head and laughed, the

beads in his hair clashing together angrily. "You cannot have freedom without responsibility, *wife*. You almost *died* today for your blasted freedom—"

"They were desperate, lowborn farmers," Wren countered, squaring up to the king despite the fact he towered over her. "They were in pain—angry with you. The monarchy. They never stood a chance against me."

"You stubborn, troublesome female! This isn't about your skills."

"Then what the devil is it about?" she yelled back.

"*This*."

She gasped as Arrik roughly yanked her against his chest and promptly swallowed any more questions she had with his lips. They stumbled backward, the fingers of his right hand sinking into her unruly hair to cradle her head. Her back slammed against the wall, the king pinning her to the spot. He kissed her with an urgency she had never felt. It was as if he was trying to imprint her on his soul.

Heat spiraled in her belly; she was helpless beneath his urgent touch, her heart and body responding as they belonged to Arrik—he the master and she the puppet. Goosebumps ran across her skin when he bit her bottom lip. She sighed, the sound seeming to unleash something wild inside him.

Arrik's hand curled tighter in Wren's hair, a slight burn but she liked it, craved it even. She dug her nails into his chest as if she had claws, wanting to anchor herself to him—for him to *feel* her—feel all the frustration, pain, *love*, and fear she had churning inside her heart. Where her husband had always appeared to be cold like ice, now he was a blazing inferno intent on consuming her and leaving nothing but ash in his wake.

He pulled back suddenly. Wren's eyes popped open and she stared up into his glaring eyes. His chest heaved against her own, her lips swollen and sensitive from the ferocity of his kiss.

He'd unmade her.

With just one kiss.

"I know you're hurting about Ever," Arrik growled, voice more of a rumble. "I know you needed space to work through everything that has been set upon your shoulders. But I draw the line at you risking your life. If you refuse to take care of yourself, then I shall claim your life as mine."

"Isn't that what you've already done?" she snapped back.

He gritted his teeth, and tugged on her hair, although not unkindly. "We are both in a situation not of our making. How many times do I have to try to make it right so that you believe me?"

"You can never fix what you've done." She flinched at her harsh words.

Arrik cracked a sharp smile. "Now there's the truth. You think I don't know you. That I can't see through your lies? That I can't see your soul? That's where you're deceiving yourself. Your soul mirrors mine. We are two halves of the same. I will not go in circles with you. We cannot fix the past, but I am determined to build something new with *you*. You have a choice, my queen. We serve as one, or we are nothing."

Her heart raced. "Nothing? Does that mean you'll let me go?"

He leaned close and skimmed his lips over her cheek until they rested just beneath her ear. A shiver ran down her spine.

"Stop pretending to be a caged little wife. You're a dragon. You can leave any time and yet you stay. I think I've stolen part of your soul just as you've stolen mine."

His words were too close to the truth.

Arrik pulled back and lifted her chin, caressing her bottom lip with his thumb. "Stop running from me and start running to me."

"I don't know how to," she said unbiddenly, hating how vulnerable she was.

"We will learn together." He stroked Wren's face tenderly, tucking a lock of tangled hair out of her eyes, and her breath caught. "Trusting someone doesn't come easily to either of us. But when I was pacing this bloody room thinking you were dead somewhere, I couldn't breathe."

"I'm sorry," Wren said, and she meant it. The fingers that she'd so roughly dug into Arrik's skin now loosened, running across his chest, down his waist, and then around his back. Her pulse raced as she embraced the dark king who'd taken everything—including her heart. She placed her head against his heart, savoring its strong beat. "I truly am."

But the unspoken truth behind Wren's words was even tougher for her to swallow.

She'd fallen for Arrik.

Properly, with all her heart, fallen for the man who

looked like he was going to burn the world because someone touched her. The villain would have taken all but promised to give all.

The monster she loved.

And Wren was going to kill him.

CHAPTER 20

WREN

"You want me to attend *what*?"

"The council meeting," Arrik repeated, a small smile curling his lips as he took in Wren's expression. "Not everyone is happy about it, but since you've agreed to all of their requests, they didn't have enough cause to protest their queen sitting in on the next meeting."

She took this as the quiet victory that it was.

Upon entering the council room, it became very quickly apparent that *most* of the—largely— old men were unhappy with her presence at their meeting. Wren knew Arrik was trying to systematically remove all of the council members he disliked or distrusted, but clearly that process was slow-going. Civil unrest was altogether a large threat.

Some things took time, but still...regime change was the best time to effect real change, like abolishing slavery or improving relations with Vadon or the Dragon Isles. Her stomach twisted with a now-familiar guilt.

How can you think such things when you have his demise planned, you wicked girl?

A thread of pride wound around her chest as she watched Arrik easily taking charge of the meeting from a weaselly-looking man who was trying to insist on taxing the lower classes more. Her husband cut a striking figure.

"I don't know if you remember," Arrik said mildly, "but it was those very lower classes who kidnapped my wife and sought to murder her as an act against the crown. So I'd wager they wouldn't take well to increased taxes." The man looked thoroughly put in his place, but then the king continued: "Rather, I think it would be a good idea at this point to decrease tax on the lower classes and fractionally increase tax on the very upper echelons. I'm *not* negotiating on this," he added on, when the room erupted in protests.

"But our former king swore taxes wouldn't be increased!" argued one man.

"Why should the upper classes pay more when the lower classes pay *less*?" cried another.

"I am not our former king. Our coffers are lower than ever thanks to war," Arrik boomed out, quietening everyone in one fell swoop. "Verlanti simply doesn't know it yet. The poor are getting poorer while the rich are getting ever more reliant on trade overseas to maintain their lifestyle, because the lower classes cannot possibly put any money back into the economy. Have you not seen the state of the streets outside of your own little corner of the city? Soon you will be ruling slums, not provinces."

That seemed to sober the group.

Wren knew exactly what he meant. She thought of Lillia, the starving child she'd helped the year before, and her sick mother, for whom Lillia had been stealing to support. That such poverty existed side by side with the decadence of the upper classes was nauseating.

No kingdom was perfect, but there was room for improvement.

For everyone.

She tapped her fingers on the chair as the room grumbled in dissent and decided to speak up.

"Do you know how many homeless or impoverished people there are in Lorne?" Her voice rang out over the group. All attention moved in her direction. She took a deep breath and lifted her chin. "No? Then I'll tell you. There are none."

The weaselly man snickered in derision. "I find that hard to believe."

"Lorne is not perfect," she acknowledged. "But in this matter, we excel."

"We? Do you still count yourself an islander?"

That was a slip of the tongue.

She nodded graciously, even though she felt anything but. "I will always be of the isles just as you will always be an elf. But make no mistake, I am *your* queen."

That wiped the smile off the advisor's face. "So how did the isles manage it, *my queen*?"

She made a pointed look at Arrik, who nodded, before continuing. This was his court, and she wanted to make her moves carefully. "We tax the rich triple what you tax here, and tax the poor next to nothing. Funnily enough, such an attitude encourages people to look after their fellow neighbor and view riches not in terms of gold and diamonds but in the strength of their community." A small smile. "There's a reason you don't see many in the Dragon Isles adorned in our own black diamonds. They hold little worth to us."

"I don't believe it," spluttered one of the many faceless old men. "Verlantians would never stand for such a thing."

"Your people would never support caring for its own people over a small handful of individuals sitting on a pile of diamonds like a *dragon*?" Wren countered, delighted at the irony of her statement.

"What my wife is trying to say..." Arrik cut in, coughing to hide a laugh when the room once more burst into protests, "is that there is a time for plenty and there's a time to be conservative. My father stretched out that time of plenty for far too long for far too few people. It's time to change that before it financially ruins us forever."

And that was that. The men could say nothing against their king so they moved on to the next topic of conversation, then the next, and the next. Wren was content to listen and only occasionally interject. By and large she agreed with everything Arrik was saying, though she disliked how often he compromised just to appease the upper echelons of society.

Give them a choice to join or be against you, or burn those who choose the latter.

She inwardly winced at her own thoughts. When had she become so bloodthirsty? Her gaze wandered to the king.

Was it Arrik's doing, or was it part of her nature that had always been there? Deep down, Wren knew that she'd always had a dark streak and little patience for stupid, selfish people.

"Vadon has been poking at our borders again," a man with red hair said over an hour later. He was someone her husband had chosen and was at least three decades younger than the next youngest man. Going by his scars and burly shoulders he seemed to be a warrior, just like Arrik. "There was an attack on one of our ships."

An attack? She sat forward in her chair. Would Vadon really be so brash?

"Can we prove it was them?" the king asked, his icy gaze intense.

The man shook his head. "They were stealthy as always. We need to increase our force on the south of the isles."

She clenched the velvet arms of her seat. Would another war be brought to the gates of her people?

Arrik considered this, glancing at Wren for a second. She knew he was going to say no. All because Verlanti's naval forces were still being used to keep the Dragon Isles in check.

She schooled her expression. The guilt she'd been feeling for days now dulled just a little.

The room discussed naval forces for another half an hour, but eventually the conversation dwindled and all eyes turned to her.

"The rebel execution is still set for sundown two days from now, yes?" someone asked.

Arrik nodded. Wren just barely avoided a grimace. She

knew she had to get Ever out before then, even though right now it felt impossible.

But two days. It was so little time...

"And the tour of the kingdom will follow," the king said.

"And is former High Queen Astrid still set to accompany Queen Wren?" the weaselly man asked.

That was new information.

She blinked slowly and offered a careful, calculated smile to the group. "I wouldn't have it any other way, my lords." The words almost choked her.

She didn't like the notion of Astrid being so close. The woman was a snake, but in reality it would make it easier for Leif to keep tabs on her, since Wren still hadn't been able to decide if it was better keeping him back at the palace or traveling with her. Now that decision had been made for her.

Wren's life was a series of dangerous and strange events.

An execution of a friend. Travel with a depraved, power-hungry queen mother...

The assassination of the king.

She shied away from the last one, instead imagining herself at home with her little sister. Guilt once again plagued Wren. When was the last time she'd written to her sister? Was she truly losing herself?

Just keep holding on. You will see her soon enough. Do what you need to do to get back to her.

That's what scared her.

Wren would have to lie, steal, and murder to get back to her sister.

Would she really throw aside her values to regain the isles?

The short answer was yes.

If she had to act like a barbarian in order to get what she wanted, then that's what she would do.

After all, it's what Arrik had done.

Arrik retrieved Wren and the two of them exited the council room a united front. A bitter taste like bile rose up Wren's throat.

She was no better than her husband.

Perhaps worse.

Because she knew better.

CHAPTER 21

ARRIK

For the first time in a long, long time Arrik was nervous.

Not because of the execution that was due to happen the following day, though that on its own was just a cause to be nervous. He'd been to many over the years, but this one would be hard for his wife, and in turn hard on him. He wasn't even anxious for the tour of the kingdom which Wren was due to embark on in two days. Even now, he hated the idea of being apart from her.

He paced outside their rooms, feeling his guards' gazes on him. It was unbecoming for a king to pace like a caged animal, but Arrik couldn't help it.

He was sneaking his wife out for a romantic dinner, just the two of them.

It was the first time in their relationship that he felt like he could. Things had changed between them the other day for the better. In fact, it seemed like each day got better.

Arrik knew after her kidnapping and the last council meeting that he had to do *something* for his little dragon. Something to ease the tension in her shoulders and show her that married life and ruling would not always be heartbreak and stress and trouble. He wanted to show his fiery wife that he cared about her and her needs, make her feel listened to and seen.

He huffed out a breath and clasped his hands behind his back, his shoulder pulling slightly. To that end he'd spent a large part of the day conducting a very dangerous game of Lure the Giant Dragon to a Secret Cove. He had to hope, after all the fatalities he'd only just avoided, that Wren would accept his surprise evening plans.

The door opened to their chambers and he was rendered speechless. While she was dressed plainly by Verlantian court standards, Wren took his breath away with just a pair of thigh-high boots, trousers, and a simple linen shirt that showed her curvy figure that he longed to run his hands and lips along. In fact, he'd take much pleasure in removing each piece of clothing from her…

"And where, exactly, are you taking me?" Wren asked, cutting through his wicked thoughts. She closed the door behind her and gestured to her outfit. "This isn't typical attire for the evenings with your court, my king."

He liked it when she called him that. *My king.* Like she owned him.

"Just trust me. You'll like it," Arrik replied, once he figured out how to use his tongue once again.

"Trust *you*?" she said, a teasing glint in her eye.

"Yes, trust me," Arrik laughed, feeling the knot in his chest somehow both tighten in anticipation and relax in joy at being able to laugh like this with Wren. It was a rare thing where he felt free enough to be honest about his emotions.

"Very well," she murmured, trying to make him out. "What do you have planned?"

"A surprise." He held his hand out. "Come with me?"

She didn't hesitate. Wren slipped her hand into his and it felt like winning a war. She'd gentled to him. The trip through the city was a blur of nerves and witty banter as his wife tried to get the truth out of him. She almost had him a time or two, so it was a bloody relief when they reached the docks.

"Are you planning on drowning me?"

"Not today, dearest." He grinned outright when he helped her into a small rowboat and she shivered at his touch. She was as connected to him as he was to her. "It isn't far, and I swear it's worth it."

Wren still looked dubious, but she nevertheless allowed him to unmoor the boat, take the oars in his hands, and use long, sure strokes to pull them out of the bay.

"No guards?"

"Not this time."

"How shocking. I could kill the king and no one would know."

"You like me too much to kill me," he retorted. Arrik smirked at the blush that colored her cheeks. Wren might be sassy, but she was shy in other affairs. It charmed him.

By the time they reached their destination,a hidden cove

just past the edge of the bay, which few— if any— people knew of, Wren began growing more interested.

"Where are we?" she asked.

"Patience, my love." He secured the boat and sighed when she jumped off before Arrik had even tied it up, skipping into the cove as if all the weight that had been placed on her shoulders had been lifted.

He watched her like she was a dream that was about to disappear any moment.

Little had he known what a treasure he'd found in the Dragon Isles all those months ago.

Wren held her hands out. "So what now?"

"It's a surprise," he said, gently careening Wren in the right direction with a hand on the small of her back. Arrik's fingertips grazed her skin through the thin linen and she shuddered.

But not in disgust.

Her deep blue eyes caught his for a moment, an explosive look over her shoulder before the dim, flickering light of fire caught her attention. She turned her head in the direction of the flames, her mouth forming a soft *O* when she saw what he had prepared for them.

"This is...oh, wow," she murmured. "When did you— when did you prepare all of this?"

"Just this afternoon," Arrik admitted, feeling self-conscious as he watched Wren take in his idea of what he *hoped* was a romantic evening. He'd never wooed a woman before. "I thought you could do with getting away from everything, even if just for a night."

Torches in sconces lit up a small cave, which had been decked out in multiple plush carpets to soften the stony ground. Upon this was a mahogany table laden in all of Wren's favorite foods, and two bottles of her preferred peach wine.

"Do you like it?"

She beamed at him, and it felt like his entire body had been set aflame. "I love it."

His nerves melted away and they just...*were*.

No expectations.

No family.

No grudges.

The two of them gorged on food and wine, the evening air cool on their skin when the blistering heat of the day finally broke. They talked and laughed and made fun of each other. He watched his wife over the rim of his wine goblet, soaking up her happiness and all of the little trinkets of information she revealed.

How she hated tomatoes with all her might, though she had never tasted one before setting foot in Verlanti. Her favorite color was green. She loved to read.

But not only did she open up to him, she asked questions too.

And he held nothing back.

About how he was a lousy fisherman though he'd lived by the sea all his life. How his favorite color was in fact not black but blue. He loved to play cards.

They both favored the evening, when the sky was bleeding over the endless expanse of ocean and the sky and water felt like it was one cohesive painting—like the world simply kept going round and round and round, uninterrupted by the goings-on of mere mortals.

With confidence he didn't feel, Arrik set down his wine and took Wren's hand. He lifted it to his lips and kissed the back of her hand like they had all the time in the world. She said nothing, just watched him. Arrik stood and pulled her with him. Hand in hand, he led her to the mouth of the cave. The waves gently lapped at the stone. He sucked in a sharp breath when she leaned her cheek against his arm, content to be near him.

"Thank you for tonight."

"It's not over yet," he rasped.

"Oh really? What else do you have planned?"

"Well..." he began, running a hand through his hair before eyeing the water. "There should be a special guest appearance tonight, but I'm not sure where—"

Her eyes snapped to his face. "What did you do?"

"A little bit of bribery," he revealed, nodding to the water. "I may have lured a certain creature to this cave and then bribed it with a haunch of pork not to eat me."

Her eyes widened and she slapped a hand over her mouth as giggles erupted from her. He grinned down at his wife, her laughter the balm to his soul that he didn't know he needed.

Arrik rolled his shoulder. "Your beast was not very happy with me. I shall bear a few bruises for the next couple of days."

"You're lucky that's all you have," she muttered.

Wren closed her eyes and hummed a soft, haunting melody that made the hair along the nape of his neck rise.

The water by their feet began to bubble and the telltale midnight blue snout of the dragon surfaced.

Arrik held his ground as the beast eyed him. The dragon still wasn't his friend but they had common ground now.

They both would kill for their woman.

His wife released his hand and he watched with increasing fondness as Wren knelt in the water, trilling and humming and singing a song in a language Arrik could not understand. She held out her hand and the massive water dragon pressed its snout gently into her palm. It was miraculous, almost magical.

The beast sang back, its trill echoing around the cave. Arrik felt the meaning in his bones—melancholy, joy, loss. Woman and dragon sang about home. Their song eventually faded as the sun completely disappeared over the horizon.

"That was beautiful," he murmured, afraid of breaking the spell.

For a moment it seemed as if she had forgotten he was there, sniffling as if to keep back tears, but then she looked up at him with a mischievous glint in her eye and blinked any moisture away. She'd shut away that part of herself, and while he wanted it, Arrik wouldn't push.

"Come on," she said, sitting on the edge of the rocky cove. She began tugging off her boots. "Let's go swimming."

Arrik laughed and crossed his arms, but his laughter dried up when his wife boldly stripped down to just her linen shift that stopped at her upper thighs. She smiled at him in a way that made him want to capture her and bear her down to the ground. Although, the dragon would probably put a damper on things.

"Come on, my king. You're not afraid, are you?"

He scoffed and began unlacing his shirt. "Never."

"Then a little shy?"

Arrik held her gaze as he loosened his belt. "Of my body? Never. In fact, look your fill."

She was the first to look away, blushing once again. "You elves and your lack of modesty."

"So says the woman who stripped in public."

"This is hardly public," she tossed over her shoulder as he finished stripping off his own clothing.

Arrik padded closer and sat behind his wife. She shivered as he moved Wren's hair over her left shoulder and pressed a kiss to the exposed skin. "You are right. This is not public. I would not share your beauty with anyone. It is mine."

"So possessive," she snorted, glancing up at him.

He kissed the corner of her mouth. "You have no idea, dearest."

She shivered against him and jumped out of his arms and into the water. Arrik eyed Trove, who watched him with dark eyes.

"I'll be very put out if you eat me," he said, slipping into the water as Wren surfaced.

The beast grumbled but otherwise made no movements toward him. His wife swam to Trove's side and grabbed hold of his horns. The dragon's frills vibrated as if excited, and he darted forward.

Wren let out a whoop as they sped out of the cove, Arrik swimming leisurely behind them, not able to keep up. It was a beautiful night—the horizon the deep purple color before dissolving into the perfect blue of night. The stars had woken, shimmering off the dragon's scales. Wren slid behind Trove's frills and trilled. Trove leaped out of the water, diving back in. Woman and dragon rode air and water, gliding through both like silk.

Unbidden, a stab of guilt threatened to destroy Arrik's rare feeling of contentment. He'd taken this from her. Taken her dragon and culture away. It was cruel and he was ashamed. Someday they both would be able to go back to the isles and she'd be able to live that way again. At least part of the time.

He startled when Trove and Wren emerged from the ocean just an arm's length away, water splashing over his head. Arrik plastered a smile on his face and pushed his braids from his face.

She frowned, and all her happiness evaporated. "What's wrong?"

He caught Trove's unblinking eye, gulping down his trepidation and guilt. "I'm sorry."

Wren's brows knitted in confusion. "For what?"

"For what happened to your former dragon. I shouldn't... not even one of those beautiful creatures should have been harmed, least of all yours. They are pure majesty, and their deaths rest on me. I'll have to carry that for the rest of my life."

Wren watched him long and hard from her position on top of her dragon, looking every inch a dragon queen—not a princess—as she towered above him. "We are not responsible for our parents' choices," she said at last. "What is done is done."

"You are too gracious." He didn't deserve her. *Ever.*

Wren's expression softened and she reached down a hand for Arrik's. "I am not. Now come," she murmured, "join me."

"I—wait!" Arrik protested, but it was too late.

His wife clicked and the beast helped push Arrik onto his back with a kick of his leg, and before Arrik knew what was happening, his arms were wrapped tightly around his wife's waist.

She patted his arm. "Don't let go!"

Arrik opened his lips to speak only to get a mouthful of seawater as Trove took off through the water. He spat out the salty brine and glared at the beast. The dragon had surely done it on purpose.

"Hold your breath!"

He got one good breath before the dragon dove beneath the surface. The coral lit up in blues, greens, and purples around them, illuminating a fantastical world Arrik could have only dreamed of. His lungs burned and he saw spots a moment before they broke the surface.

Arrik spluttered salt water all over the back of Wren's head and wiped at his stinging eyes. The most beautiful sound reached his ears.

Wren was laughing. Louder and more joyously than he'd ever heard from her before.

This was her element. *This* was what it meant to be a dragon rider.

And you have her all to yourself. You have neatly clipped the wings of your dragon.

The thought made him want to rage. Could nothing be easy or simple? Did he always have to be the villain?

He shoved away his dark thoughts and took another deep

breath before they plunged into the sea. Time ceased to exist as they explored the secrets of the ocean.

Eventually, his ears threatened to pop, and Wren had started to shiver. They were forced to retire for the night. Arrik rowed the little boat back to the docks while Wren lay on Trove's back, singing softly to her dragon. Once she'd said goodnight, the dragon disappeared beneath the waves and ships like a ghost.

The quiet between them as they made their way back through the city and into the palace was easy. Her hand slipped into his and they simply strolled together to their chambers. He glared at the guards when they glanced in her direction. She hadn't gotten properly dressed, and to be honest he was quite serious about no other man seeing what was his.

It was a quiet affair getting ready for bed. Companionable. Easy. Sleepy.

He stood outside and watched the moon as she changed. Arrik wanted ten thousand nights like this, then ten thousand more for good measure, and another ten thousand after that just to be safe. It had been a long time since he'd felt so much peace.

"I'm decent," she called.

Arrik smiled and muttered, "If only you weren't."

"What was that?"

"Nothing," he answered, stepping inside.

Quickly he changed and crawled into bed. They were long past sleeping apart, although she still didn't like sharing blankets.

Her eyes drifted to his bare chest and it felt like a physical touch. He crawled onto the bed and beneath the covers. Wren squeaked as he pulled her into his arms and brushed the hair out of her face.

"This okay?" he whispered, studying her face in the low light. He'd never been a gentle man, nor had he a soft upbringing, but he wanted that, for her.

Wren nodded, snuggling into his arms. *Willingly.*

She smelled of salt and ocean; her hair and body were slightly damp, but he reveled in it.

Arrik yanked her closer as she turned in his arms and curled up. "It was my mother who taught me how to swim," he said, already halfway to sleep.

"I have to admit she can't have been a very good teacher," Wren said, the bite of a sly smile in her voice. "You are slow, my king."

Arrik tickled her before he could stop himself, delighting in the feeling of Wren squirming in protest against him. "Anyone would lack in skill next to you. You're like a fish. Or a—"

"...dragon," they both said in unison.

After a moment, Wren whispered, "Is it a good memory? Learning to swim with her?"

"Mhm."

"Then I hope you never forget it until the day you die."

There were no more words after that.

He pressed a kiss to her damp, tangled hair and closed his eyes. Exhausted for once because of a good day, and with a head empty of what the next day would bring, he fell asleep holding the second woman he'd ever loved.

CHAPTER 22

WREN

LEFT, RIGHT, PARRY, STRIKE.

That was the usual pattern to Josenu's sparring. Today, however, the man seemed determined to change it up—to spar with Wren at a punishing speed. But she was thankful for it.

It helped keep her mind off what was to come that very evening.

Don't let your mind drift. Fight.

They were waiting for Kalles. The troublesome piece of the royal puzzle.

He'd formed a plan to get Ever out. When Josenu had broached the subject with Wren, she could hardly believe her ears. It had to be a ploy of some sort, but the ax had never fallen.

When she'd asked why he wanted to help, his answer had

been, "It'll be fun to see what sort of mayhem breaks loose when the prisoners get out," he'd said.

Quite frankly, Wren still had no clue if she could trust him, but his motive *did* track with why he'd given Wren a dagger on her wedding night, and why he'd been helping her "fit in" with the Dark Court of Verlanti. Kalles seemed to thrill in chaos and causing problems for his brother. And as long as it didn't hurt anyone, Wren couldn't care less about what he got up to.

Besides, Leif had been shadowing him alongside Astrid, and had informed both Wren and Josenu that the youngest prince wasn't working with anyone else. He was a lone agent.

And now he was working with Wren.

At least for the time being.

"Enough!" Wren cried out, exhausted, when Josenu whacked her across the back of her calves with the flat side of his sword. She dropped to her knees to catch her breath. "I surrender."

"What's the score now? Three to me and two to you?" She heard the grin in Josenu's voice without looking at his face. *The rat.*

"Yes, and I just know you're going to rub it in my face until the day I die, so let me have some peace from your gloating for a single day, please."

Josenu snickered but otherwise complied, giving Wren a hand up to her feet. The two of them were thoroughly disheveled. Wren smoothed down her hair when she saw the mess her opponent's was in.

The spy didn't bother following suit. He glanced over at the rest of the training grounds. "I can only fight so well against you because I've watched all your other fights like a hawk. You'll probably beat me...one day."

Wren peered at him. "You're better than Ronan."

"Yes."

"And Shane."

"Correct."

"I'd say you're on par with the king and yet you hide it." Something she'd noticed over the last month.

"Your point being?"

"What are you doing being a simple palace guard?" Wren bit out. "Why aren't you the captain of the guard or...or something? You don't make sense."

Josenu offered her a wan smile. "I think I'm doing my best work exactly where I am." They both knew what he meant: acting as a double agent for the rebellion.

Grimly Wren nodded. "I see your point. Speaking of doing your best work, where the devil is Kalles? That no-good, drunken—"

"Speak of the devil and he shall appear," Kalles said, voice full of mischief as both Wren and Josenu wheeled around to face him. He placed his hands on his hips and smiled. "You have something for me, I believe?"

Careful that nobody was watching, Wren slipped Kalles the keys she'd pilfered from Arrik before he'd woken that morning. It had filled her with guilt, especially after the night they'd shared, but all it took was one thought of Ever and that guilt was washed away. "Is everything in place?" she whispered.

"I'm offended you think that I would fail." He tucked away the keys. "I drugged the guard already. Now, I just have to dress Ever in their clothes and smuggle her out. It's simple enough."

"Good."

"But I do need two things from you."

Josenu cursed beneath his breath and she stiffened, trying to keep her expression as smooth as possible. Wren didn't want to give anyone anything to gossip about. "What?" she managed.

"Don't look so worried."

Wren smiled, but it wasn't friendly. "What do you want?"

The youngest prince, a pale shadow of his oldest brother, merely laughed. "It's nothing you cannot give me, Wren. Just a kiss and a secret, and I'll do all that you bid me to do."

"How dare—?" Josenu began, outraged, but Wren gently waved him off. She strode right up to Kalles, placing the barest of kisses on cheek.

When she pulled away he smiled like he'd won the kingdom.

It sent a chill of unease up her spine. There had been nothing sexual about the kiss—not even from Kalles—but he seemed happy nonetheless that Wren had kissed him. Wren cocked her head and scanned her brother-in-law from head to toe.

Was he simply lonely? So starved for real affection that he sought to trick it out of people?

Without any real thought, she hugged him for good measure. Everyone needed a hug.

For a moment Kalles stiffened beneath her, but then he relaxed into the embrace and hugged her back. She held on tight, even when he sighed in relief. It was imperceptible to everyone but her.

"You are a stealer of secrets, dear sister," he softly accused.

"I don't know what you're talking about," she murmured back.

"You have a way of discerning what someone needs and giving it to them. That's dangerous."

"Enough riddles, Kalles. What secret would you like to know?"

"I know your secret already," he mumbled against her ear. "It's not your body my brother is obsessed with, but your soul. And you're finally beginning to notice."

Wren flinched and pulled back, but Kalles didn't let her go. "What do you—?"

"But be careful," he warned. "Don't let my brother taint your heart more than he already has. He has a way of destroying everything good in his life."

"Kalles..." Wren slowly let the younger prince go, though she only moved an inch or two away from him. "What do you know?"

"Too much."

"Why give me the blade on my wedding day?" she pressed. "It was Vadonese. What games are you playing?"

But Kalles didn't respond. He winked and simply walked away.

"What did he say about the king?"

Wren startled at the sound of Josenu's voice. "What do you mean?"

He grimaced. "I could see it in the way you flinched. You

have a certain look about you when Arrik is mentioned." A pause. "You have to be careful. So much hinges on—"

"I know," Wren sighed, shoulders slumping. "I know. I think I might get some rest before...before tonight."

The spy bowed. "Until tonight, my queen."

She retreated to her chambers, staring blankly around the room. Her gaze landed on the rumpled bed. She had woken in Arrik's arms warm and comfortable. For a split second, she was happy.

Wren's stomach dropped. The days of false happiness were numbered, but only she knew it.

CHAPTER 23

WREN

"THE QUEEN MOTHER," ONE OF THE SERVANTS ANNOUNCED.

Why was she not surprised that Astrid had come to visit?

The queen mother floated into the chamber looking as perfect and put together as if she were going to a party, not an execution.

"Why are you wearing black?" the woman complained, waltzing inside like she owned the place. "It's so dreary."

Wren narrowed her eyes at her own reflection in the mirror. "It's an execution. It's a serious event." *Never mind that there won't actually* be *an execution if everyone plays their part right.*

Astrid laughed hollowly, then opened a bag she'd been carrying to reveal a rainbow chiffon gown for Wren to wear. "The execution is for scum who murdered the people of

Verlanti. Their execution is a celebration. A *happy* event. The people expect you to be happy alongside them. Don't you want justice for them, Wren?"

There was nothing Wren could say to that. "I also wear black and silver because these are my king's colors. I seek to honor him with what I wear." She scanned the colorful dress. "I don't think he would approve."

Astrid wiggled her eyes. "I think he would once he saw it on your body."

"I can see why. There's hardly any fabric to cover my chest," she grumbled.

"I wouldn't worry. You're not as voluptuous as I am in that area, so it should suit your tender sensibilities quite well."

Wren wasn't entirely sure what was going on. Astrid had never been so obviously snippy with her before. "Is it really your custom to wear such bright colors?"

The queen mother pouted. "Do you not believe me? I can call for my ladies-in-waiting as well as other women from court."

That was the last thing Wren wanted. Plus, she didn't want to alienate Astrid.

She held her hand out. "I believe you, my lady. It's just not my custom."

Astrid cooed. "What a good girl you are to adopt the customs of your people. Now let me help you get dressed."

Wren's skin crawled at the idea of Astrid touching any part of her body, but she curbed the reaction and slipped out of her black dress. The queen mother helped her into the peacock gown. She grimaced. Alongside her scarlet hair, it felt altogether far too much. Did Astrid seek to humiliate her?

She looked to the elven woman, but only spotted approval.

Odd.

"Shall I do your hair?" Astrid asked.

"No, I can do it myself. Thank you, my lady."

Wren braided back her hair from her face and it clashed with the dress. It was severe compared to the bright number Astrid had forced upon her, but it suited her mood.

"Wren?" Arrik's voice called.

She spun around as he entered their rooms, his gaze moving between his stepmother and Wren.

"Ready?" he asked, giving Wren a once-over with the same approval as Astrid. Even he was dressed more brightly than usual, in a pearl-and-opal waistcoat and gray trousers that were almost lilac. The pale colors were striking against his sharp features and silver-blond hair.

"Color," she muttered.

He frowned. "Not my preference but tradition."

"I told you, darling," Astrid said in a singsong voice. "And you almost wore black."

She nodded once. "Thank you again." Wren turned her attention back to the king, feeling like her legs might give out any moment. "Ready," she managed, allowing Arrik to take her hand and lead her from their rooms, Astrid trailing behind them, content for a swarthy guard to accompany her.

"Are you alright?" Arrik murmured.

"I have no answer to that," Wren whispered back. If all went well, Ever would be free, but there would be a hunt for the traitor. If all went wrong, both she and Ever would die today.

The long marble corridors gave way to four large, ornate doors that led to the execution courtyard.

Arrik paused just before the door and squeezed her fingers. "Prepare yourself."

She nodded and braced herself as the guard flung open the doors.

A wall of jubilant, violent noise bombarded Wren as they stepped into the courtyard. A bonfire was lit, and torches full of powders that changed colors blazed from tall wooden sconces that danced. There were jesters and musicians and a crowd almost a thousand deep, all in the same gaudy colors that Wren now wore.

She understood why: justice and revenge were sweet. But celebrating the deaths of human beings left a horrible taste in her mouth.

Life was precious. It was to be mourned when it was lost.

Bury your feelings and get through this night.

She pasted a pleasant look on her face and leaned into Arrik. "Where were you all afternoon?" Wren asked lowly, as they ascended the dais from which Wren would pass her judgment.

"Duty called," he said through a vicious grin, waving at the crowd. Shane, Ronan, Ares, and Kalles were already on the dais, also waving to the crowd. She lifted her own hand and locked eyes with Kalles.

He smiled carelessly but his eyes were desolate. The prince shook his head once.

Something had gone terribly wrong.

The rumble of drums filled the air, getting louder with every moment, and Wren's stomach dropped to the floor when Ever was marched out and tied to a post directly below the high dais.

No.

Her ears rang and a bout of dizziness crashed over her as a soldier began calling out the woman's crimes. It was all Wren could do not to sway on the spot. Arrik's gaze slid to her arm, not missing the way she held on to him.

"You can do this," he reassured her in hushed tones—words for her only. "You can. I know it's hard, but you can."

She could never tell her husband that she was never supposed to *have* to.

"And so, for the crimes aforementioned," the soldier finished, "the rebel Ever has been sentenced to death by stoning." The roar of the crowd grew, and someone threw a rotten apple at the woman.

Ever didn't even react.

"Wren," Arrik urged, a few moments later. He squeezed her hand. "You must go forward and sanction it. Remember?"

Wren didn't trust her voice, so she nodded, fighting not to stumble down the flight of stairs, her ridiculously bright dress wrapping around her legs. All her people cheered and swore and screamed in delight.

She made her way to the middle of the courtyard to face Ever directly.

"*I'm sor—*" she mouthed at the older woman, but Ever shook her head.

A warning.

"It was always going to end this way," Ever croaked, her voice hoarse and ragged from dehydration. "In this life…I've lost so much. Suffered, and continued suffering, to ease the suffering of others. I will find peace in death. So do what you must and know that you have my thanks."

Wren wanted to cry. She wanted to flee. Heat pressed at the back of her eyes.

The crowd hushed.

Instead, she stood up straight and asked, loudly enough for her voice to be carried, "Do you deny your crimes?"

"I do not," Ever said, clear and straightforward.

Heart pounding, Wren turned from her friend to face the closest soldier. There was no way out of this, but she couldn't watch Ever be stoned. The older woman deserved a clean, quick death.

Wren indicated toward his bow and quiver. "May I have these?"

The soldier, stunned, handed them over without a word.

The crowd cheered and yelled Wren's name.

Dragon queen. Dragon queen. Dragon queen.

Their queen.

A lone tear tracked down her cheek.

Wren nocked an arrow to the bow, spun around to face Ever, and shot her straight through the heart.

The courtyard went silent. Wren could hear the blood rushing past her ears.

Her shot had flown true. Ever was dead.

No pain. No suffering.

"May she burn in hell," Wren spat out, and the crowd went wild.

CHAPTER 24

ARRIK

HE'D BROKEN HIS WIFE.

Arrik had always known today would be hard on her. He'd known it, yet still he was shocked that Wren actually did the *executing* at the execution.

In that moment, she was the Verlanti queen. Sharp, ruthless, and coldly beautiful.

Yet he hated it.

He still didn't know why she'd shot Ever. It didn't make sense.

When he'd descended into the revelry to retrieve his queen, she'd said nothing, nor looked at him. Arrik had escorted her back into the palace, their steps echoing down the dark, haunting hallways of stone.

Wren was silent as they made their way back into their chambers. He couldn't blame her; he didn't know what to say either. He had no idea what words his wife would find comforting, or which would make her feel worse. He glanced at Shane, who watched Wren with new respect and a touch of compassion.

Good. His second needed to make peace with his wife.

The silence seemed to grow as they entered their chambers.

"Do you need anything?" his friend asked after Arrik led Wren over to the bench on the edge of their room which overlooked the bathing garden. It was her favorite place to sit in the entire palace.

Arrik shook his head, then reconsidered his answer. "Food," he said quietly, so Wren couldn't hear. "Nothing heavy. Wine."

"Understood." Shane left and shut the door behind him.

Arrik inhaled deeply and turned to his wife.

It was the first time they'd been alone since she'd woken in his arms that morning. It felt like a million years ago. Arrik closed the distance between them, hesitating for only a moment before attempting to embrace her from behind. To comfort her. To support her.

His wife shrank away as if his touch were poison. "How could you let this happen?" she whispered, head hanging low as she stared at her shaking hands.

"I don't understand what you mean," Arrik replied.

Wren stood up and turned to face him.

He took one look at the empty, anguished look on her face and held his hands out. "I'm so sorry." Her eyes locked on his, and that anguish turned to fiery rage. So she didn't want comfort. She wanted to fight. He'd been ready for this.

She stabbed a finger into his chest. "You used the rebellion. *You*, not the other way around. You used them to gain the throne and now you're executing them for crimes *you* put them up to, all so you could gain further favor with your people! You're despicable, and I hate you."

Perhaps in other circumstances Arrik might have believed Wren, but not after the last few weeks. Arrik recognized the fury in her face. The frustration. The despair. It was all directed inward, because Wren herself had been unable to change the hands of fate. She needed someone to lash out at. Someone to scream at and punch all her emotions away.

Arrik could be that for her. "Do you want to hurt me?"

"I want you to admit what you've done."

He'd give her what she wanted—what she needed. "So I used them," Arrik said coldly. "What else did you expect me to do? They were rebelling against my father, not me. It was within my rights to use them against him. They knew what they were getting into. They are not the innocents you paint them to be."

Part truth. Part lie.

Wren glared at him. "How could you *say* that?" She slammed her palms against his chest, weakly at first but then stronger and stronger still, until he took a step back so she didn't hurt herself. "You act as if you're trying to be a better person but you're not! All you do is *use* people!"

She slapped him. *Hard.*

His cheek stung, and she reared back to slap him again, but he caught her wrist and held it in his steel grasp.

"Did that make you feel better, my queen? To cause pain?"

"You're the one who hurts everyone!"

"I use who I have to, but it's for the greater good," he growled back.

"The greater good? It's only good if it works for you. People aren't pawns, Arrik!" she yelled back.

With surprising grace and strength, Wren pulled out of his grasp, spinning around to try to land a kick against his gut. But Arrik, once more, caught her, his arm wrapping around her calf and twisting until Wren lost her balance and the only thing keeping her up was Arrik himself. He yanked her against him, her leg curled around his waist.

Wren bit out a cry of frustration, scratching his arms. "Let me—rot it, let me hit you!"

"Only if you can!" he shouted right back, catching her wrists in his hands. "But you don't *want* to hit me. You want me to fight you. That's a different thing."

She screamed and leaned forward to bite his shoulder.

It bloody hurt.

Arrik gritted his teeth but refused to let go of his queen. "Let it all out, dearest. I can take your violence and rage. I will bear it to keep you from breaking. Give it all to me."

Wren sobbed and bit him harder.

He groaned and leaned his cheek on her head, sweat beading his brow at the pain. "I don't want to fight you, my love. I *won't* fight you."

His wife froze in his arms and then she began to tremble.

All at once, the tension that had been holding her

upright dissolved in a fit of tears. She collapsed into Arrik's embrace, soul wrenching sobs wracking her body.

Instinct told him to take Wren to the sea, but he didn't want her grief to be public.

Gently, he lifted her into his arms and carried her to their bathing pool and walked right into it, fully clothed, and sat down with Wren cradled against his chest. She clung to him, rainbow dress floating around them like watercolor spreading across a page.

"Shh, it's all right," he soothed, stroking her hair as she let out a fresh wave of sobs. "I've got you. I won't ever let you go."

He rocked back and forth with his wife broken in his arms.

She was grieving for everything she had lost. Everything that had been taken from her, physically, mentally, and emotionally. A tear slipped down his own face as he tried to hold her together.

Arrik had a massive share of the blame when it came to everything that had happened to her, but he was too selfish to let her go. *He* wanted to be the one to help her heal, to give her everything she needed, and more.

She tossed her head back and began to sing, but it was more of a cry.

Goosebumps rose along his arms as she mourned and clung to him.

A shadow from the sky cut through the twilight air, darkening the bath in ever-increasing circles, the lap of wings rustling the plants surrounding them.

Trove.

His tail whipped back and forth, destroying part of the garden, scattering leaves and flowers in every direction. The massive creature crept forward, his eyes locked on Wren. He rested his head on the edge of the bath, his snout bumping against her until with one hand she finally released Arrik and stroked Trove's nose.

The dragon crooned and cuddled closer, as gentle as a cat. His feline eyes trained on Arrik and the king swore they narrowed as if Wren's current state was all his fault.

Arrik supposed it was.

The three of them lay there in and around the water, man, woman and dragon, until eventually Wren's sobs began to ebb, and Trove hummed her into sleep.

The air developed a chill and Wren shivered in his arms.

He eyed the dragon and then his wife. Trove watched him through slitted eyes.

"I am not stealing away your mistress," he said sternly to the beast. "She needs to be warmed."

With that, Arrik slowly climbed out of the bathing pool, cradling Wren to his chest, and backed away from the dragon. Trove followed crawling on his belly, watching each movement. He even went so far as to wedge himself into their chambers, snout resting at the side of the bed.

Arrik stripped Wren before changing her into dry bedclothes and laying her on the mattress as if she were blown glass. Trove rumbled and Arrik made sure to tuck her in on the dragon's side. His wife would find comfort in that.

He stood at the foot of the bed, watching his wife sleep and her dragon eye him, before changing into his own dry clothing and slipping into bed.

She murmured and reached for him in her sleep.

Arrik's throat tightened as Wren settled in against his chest and her breathing came out low and slow. He stared at the ceiling, and it struck him in that moment how important his wife was to him.

I would burn the world for her.

The thought scared him.

He'd been fighting for the Verlanti throne for so long, the idea of anything surpassing that seemed unreal. But what terrified him more was the *certainty* of it. In his bones, he knew he'd commit the vilest acts of violence to protect the treasure he held in his arms. Was that love? The all-encompassing desire to protect and cherish another person? She occupied his thoughts too often. When Wren smiled at him, he felt peace. Was love a poison or a tonic? No one had shown Arrik a scrap of kindness but for his mother. Even now he could hardly remember what she looked like. So how was he supposed to rule the kingdom he'd dedicated his life to and also love the little dragon his soul cried out for?

Trove huffed and wiggled out of their room, the dragon's scale scraping along the marble floor. He winced, hoping it wouldn't wake his wife.

"Arrik."

Wren's voice was like a bell in the night. Clear. Pure. Beautiful.

He glanced down at her as she turned in his arms to face him. "I'm sorry. Trove was a bit loud in his departure," he rasped. His heart was beating so wildly that it hurt. When Wren placed a hand over his erratic heartbeat, and pulled his own hand over hers, it hurt even harder.

Wren didn't answer with words. Her lips found Arrik's, and she closed her eyes, and when Arrik slipped a hand around the nape of her neck to force her lips closer to his as if he could press his love into her skin, she opened her mouth, inviting him to slip his tongue inside.

She was velvet and spice.

His wife moaned, her fingers tightening around his.

The sound awoke something feral in Arrik. Something violent.

He rolled Wren beneath him, his entire body crushing her into the mattress as he kissed with pent-up frustration, longing, and desire. He knew he should be gentle after what she'd been through today, but he couldn't find it within himself to pull away. Part of him was worried she'd disappear if he stopped.

Wren's legs wrapped around Arrik's waist; she arched her body into his own in a way that had him see stars and biting out curses. "More," she murmured between kisses. He growled into her mouth, stroking her face before running his fingers through her hair to expose the column of her throat. He needed to taste her there too. It wasn't enough.

He was starved for his queen. A shudder ran down his spine as she raked her nails down his back, and then somehow pulled him even tighter against her.

She wanted this, but a little bell was going off in the back of his head.

He didn't want this to be a mistake. Arrik wanted this moment to be everything. She had to *crave* this just as much as Arrik did. He had to hear her say that. Over the years, he'd done many bad things, but stealing from the woman he loved would not be one of them.

"Tell me what you want," Arrik breathed against her lips, even as she dug her heels into the back of his thighs, urging him closer. Sweat beaded on his forehead as he held himself still.

Wren's eyes fluttered open, dark and heavy-lidded with desire. "You."

He kissed the corner of her mouth, not able to help himself. "It's been a long day, darling. I don't want you to regret this," he said gruffly.

Arrik didn't want her surrender. He wanted her to choose him.

She glared up at him and wrapped his braids around her fists before giving them a good yank. He winced as pain shot through his scalp, but it only made him burn hotter for her.

"Listen to me, my king," she snapped. "I want you, Arrik. I've wanted you for...far longer than I could ever admit to. Things will never be rainbows and butterflies between us. We're violence, passion, and grit. Today, made me realize who I really am. I know what I want for the future and I'm tired of fighting it. Now...stop fighting your queen."

It was enough to unspool him entirely. Arrik didn't know who began throwing off each other's clothes first—him or Wren—but it didn't matter. All that mattered was skin-on-skin, bodies pressed against every available inch of each other like they were both starved.

"You must know how much I've longed for you, Wren," he said, his entire body thrumming with tension. He reached down and hitched her right leg higher until their bodies pressed together in a way that made him want to lose himself in his queen. He felt more than saw the blush that spread across her cheeks.

He smiled devilishly down at Wren. "Your wish is my command, wife."

One thrust was all it took for his queen to yield to him with a hiss of pleasure and pain. In that moment, he wondered just who commanded whom, because he would give everything just to stay like this forever.

CHAPTER 25

WREN

It would have been easy for Wren to wake up and be overcome with guilt and regret over what had transpired last night, but the feelings would not come.

The fact was, she felt contented and unashamedly happy.

That was her dilemma.

She stared at Arrik's face, so sharply cut and handsome, and pursed her lips. Just because they slept together didn't mean anything had changed. It couldn't. He had made mistakes, done bad things, and needed to pay for them.

But do you really need to be the judge, jury, and executioner? Haven't you hurt enough people?

The thought struck her painfully in the chest at the reminder of Ever. There wasn't a choice. Wren's feelings for her husband couldn't have an effect on her choices. There were so many people depending on her.

"...g'morning," Arrik mumbled sleepily, pulling her in close and kissing her as if it was the most natural thing in the world. She melted against his chest, not shy about all the naked skin pressed together. After what they'd spent the entire night doing, she supposed it was. It startled her how easy it was to kiss him back like nothing was wrong—to mold her body to Arrik's and let him envelop her in his scent, his presence, his everything.

She gulped as she spotted more than affection in his ice-blue eyes as he pressed a kiss to the top of her shoulder.

"How are you feeling?" he whispered, drawing patterns on her hip.

She shivered, all too aware of his touch and the desire swirling in her belly. "I'm fine."

He paused his kisses and scanned her face. "I wasn't too rough?"

So, the big bad monster was concerned. It made her smile. "I'm fine. In fact..." She slipped her leg over his hip and brushed her finger over the tip of his pointed ear. "I'm feeling quite hungry."

A slow smile curled his sensuous lips as his kisses drifted farther down her chest. "What a coincidence. So am I."

Several hours later, they'd lost themselves in each other, bathed, and eaten together.

Wren was stepping onto the carriage which would take her on the first leg of her tour of the highborn families of Verlanti. A small part of her didn't want to leave Arrik behind, but she shoved that thought away. He'd taken her body but she couldn't allow him to take any more of her.

She frowned when he stepped on after her, wearing a grin.

"Why are you getting on?" she asked with an arched brow. "I thought I was traveling with Astrid." Wren had been dreading it all morning. One had to stay on their toes when entertaining the queen mother.

Arrik huffed out a laugh. "You think I could force that upon you immediately after yesterday? No, I changed my schedule a little so I could tour the first couple of cities with you. Astrid will meet us at our first destination."

Relief swept over Wren, so overwhelming that she sagged into her seat. Arrik wrapped an arm around her, ordered the driver to go, and then they were off.

She watched the countryside go by and groaned. "What about Leif?" Wren asked, feeling guilty that she'd forgotten about him. He was supposed to be traveling with her too. "And Josenu?"

Arrik pointed out of the window to a carriage trailing behind them. "They're both in there. I thought you'd—ah—like a little bit of privacy today. They can join us if you wish." He glanced out the window and stared hard.

It was blatantly obvious that Arrik hoped Wren would not ask her friends to join them. She couldn't help but laugh, loudly and clearly, as if there was nothing wrong in her life at all.

His head snapped in her direction as she slapped a hand over her mouth. Arrik's eyes crinkled with affection, and he pulled her hand away. "Don't hide your laughter from me. It's a joy to hear your happiness." His expression turned serious. "I hope you always laugh like that around me, Wren."

She gulped and glanced down at her lap. "I can only endeavor to try," she said, hoping her acting skills were sufficient at hiding the dread she felt upon hearing his words.

They didn't have forever. Their time together was numbered.

The carriage was pulled along by resplendent black horses at a lazy pace, Arrik clearly in no rush to reach their first destination. He spent the journey sharing stories of his childhood with Wren—the happy ones, which were few, and the sad ones, which were many. Wren found herself getting lost in the tales, forgetting about her duty and her goals and her intention to betray him.

She wanted to know everything about her husband, and be there as he continued to grow into a new version of himself.

But their bubble of happiness was abruptly popped when they finally reached a city on the coast—Wren vaguely thought it was named Beleiras—and she spotted not just Astrid and some of Arrik's advisers standing in front of their host's home for the night, but Lord Idril too.

Her stomach curdled.

"Why is he here?" she asked Arrik in a hushed tone, as he exited the carriage before helping her out, too.

"It's just politics," Arrik said. He squeezed her hand reassuringly. "You've got this. Don't worry. He won't last long under my reign. But I need to know where he is and what he's planning at all times until he's gone for good."

That did not reassure Wren nearly as much as Arrik had

clearly hoped it would. She felt sick to her stomach at the prospect of having to sit down to dine with her disgusting, lecherous, evil sire.

It took more strength than Wren thought she possessed to give a polite hello to the bastard as they exited the carriage. Idril was sure to shoot her a smarmy look while kissing the back of her hand. She wiped it away in her skirt as she followed a servant to her room for the night, leaving Arrik behind with his nobles.

"See you tonight, my queen," Idril called.

She didn't look back but kept moving forward, no matter how much she wanted to stab him in the throat.

Wren passed the next hour with Leif, who'd snuck in to check in with her and give her an update on Astrid, getting ready for dinner and coming up with increasingly elaborate ways to murder Idril.

"Sorry," he said, between mouthfuls of butter biscuits he'd pilfered from the kitchen. He crossed and uncrossed his legs upon her bed, ever the fidget. "I wanted to let you know this morning that both Astrid and Idril were here—my contact in the kitchen here let me know very late last night. But you were indisposed, so..."

A blush heated her cheeks. "It was a rough night."

Leif paused his chewing and cocked his head. "I just bet it was." His tone was knowing.

Wren glared at him and then stole two of Leif's biscuits despite his protests. Time to change the subject. She sighed enormously and got to her feet. "Best get dinner over with. Do you have any information on *why* Astrid was here already?"

"Nothing that doesn't confirm what we already knew: that she's working with Idril."

"That doesn't make me feel any better. Do you think he's still working with Vienne and the rebellion, or do you think he's gone solo?"

Leif shrugged. "At this point it makes no difference. If you do what you need to do, then we both know Idril won't survive much longer." A low chuckle. "Or perhaps he'll be first, depending on his behavior tonight."

"Don't tempt me. Right"—Wren swooped down to plant a kiss on his cheek—"I best be off. Don't get crumbs all over my bed, you hear me?"

"I would *never*," Leif said, scandalized, though his lips twisted into a mischievous grin as he wiped down the covers nonetheless.

Wren would have rather remained in her room gossiping with her best friend all night, but she had a duty to uphold. She'd never wanted the crown; the navy and her dragon had been her love. This part of ruling was not something she enjoyed. So though she'd have preferred being flayed alive, she made her way to the dining hall, where Arrik was waiting for her by the door so they could enter together.

He pressed a quick kiss to her temple and squeezed her waist before they were directed to seats at the head of the table, as was befitting a king, with Wren on his right-hand side. Idril was on his left, Astrid on Wren's right, and the rest of the table was filled out by half a dozen of Arrik's advisers as well as the host for the evening, Lord Forster, his outrageously young wife, and his two eldest sons.

She knew not to judge others, but it was really hard not

to gape at Lord Forster's wife. She was clearly younger than even his youngest son and was pregnant. Wren suppressed a shudder. The lord in question had to be at least seventy years old.

"Dearest, you're staring," Arrik muttered underneath his breath, humor coating his words.

Wren forced her gaze away from the odd couple and examined the dinner group anew.

Of all the advisers present, she trusted none of them. A quick glance in Arrik's direction confirmed he felt the same way.

"I must thank you for being such a gracious host to so large a party," Idril said, once wine had been poured. "This is quite a delectable spread, Lord Forster. And I'm not just talking about your wife."

Wren gagged at the sleazy comment, but she hid it behind a napkin. That was rather gutsy of him unless they were allies of sorts. Out of the corner of her eye she saw that Forster's wife was made incredibly uncomfortable by the comment, but her husband and her sons were laughing uproariously.

Definitely not a love match. The poor woman. All the riches and circumstance, yet she had no power. Just another puppet.

"It is a pleasure to have you here again, Lord Idril," Forster said, confirming what Wren had already suspected: that the man was in Idril's pocket. "I must admit to selfishly wanting you here to get an update firsthand on what's going on with the Dragon Isles."

Wren sat up straighter, but a gentle hand placed over hers

—Arrik's—told her not to speak. So she did what she had learned from Leif, and listened.

Idril's awful gaze cast itself over Wren. He scratched absentmindedly at the scar she'd left on his face before saying, "I have a shipment harvested from the isles that's just about ready to dock. The captain on board says all seventy slaves are in good health and working order."

Some of the color drained from her face before her anger burst into an inferno.

She violently kicked Arrik beneath the table when he grabbed her hand to stop her from speaking.

Slaves. They are talking about slaves in front of Arrik, and he isn't condemning them for their actions. Slaves from my home.

"Shocked, my queen?" Idril cooed. He clapped his hands together and laughed. "I have a surprise for you, my lady. And especially for you, my king."

Her stomach lurched. Any gift from her sire was anything but.

Idril snapped his fingers as if Forster's servants were his own to command. "Bring it in."

"Calm down," Arrik whispered into Wren's ear as if he were telling her a secret. "He wants you to react. They *all* want you to react. You have to play the game. We both do."

Still Wren felt like she couldn't breathe as a silver platter was brought in and placed on the table directly in front of them. When the servant lifted the lid, she couldn't stop herself—she dry-heaved into her napkin.

Sitting upon the platter was Vienne's head, her eyes that were so much like her sister's, Wren's mother, glassy and lifeless as they stared up at Wren.

Arrik arched a haughty brow and waved a hand at the head. "There's a time and a place for such things, Lord Idril. I know you enjoy being dramatic, but over dinner is hardly the time for heads on a plate."

"On the contrary," Idril said, still laughing. "I rather think it's the perfect time. Had you not raided the rebellion when you did, Your Majesty, I'd never have been able to catch their leader unawares. I'd say the two of us make a rather perfect team at weeding out rats, don't you think?"

While Wren had never been fond of Vienne—had actively disliked her—she was still kin. Wren hadn't wanted to see her dead.

This is what she gets for playing with fire. For getting into bed with Idril. For compromising on her beliefs and letting him run the show. He's a monster who will slaughter anyone in his path.

But enough was enough.

Wren could be still and silent no longer whilst a table of vipers cackled at the disgusting sight before them. Only Lord Forster's wife was sympathetic, having caught the similarities in Vienne's face and Wren's, and made the conclusion most of the table were too bullheaded to realize.

"What relations you have, my lady," Idril said with a smirk.

"Indeed, sir," she retorted sharply. Her meaning clear—that he was just as bad.

She stood up abruptly and eyed the group with a cold smile. "I find myself not in the mood for tedious company." Wren didn't bother to mutter an apology before all but storming from the dining room in a flurry of silk.

It did not surprise her when she heard heavy footsteps following.

"Quite the spectacle," Arrik called.

She tossed a glare over her shoulder. "Me or Idril?"

He huffed. "I won't let anything happen to your people," Arrik reassured Wren as she picked up her pace and tore down the corridor toward her room. "And I won't break my promise. Idril was trying to get a rise out of you, trying to rile you up—you know how much of a snake he is. And you let him."

"That was Vienne. My aunt."

"I know. I'm sorry." His words were sincere but not enough.

She had heard over dinner the truth of Arrik's plan to maintain power, and abolishing slavery was nowhere near the top of his priorities.

She flung open the doors to her rooms, her husband hot on her heels.

"Get out!" Wren growled, spinning toward him.

He slammed the doors behind him, scowling right back. "These are my rooms too."

"You said nothing in there against him—*you had no intention of abolishing slavery, did you?*"

"Things like this take time," Arrik protested. He held out his hands in a placating gesture. "You know my stance on the matter. You know I don't mean for this to be forever. You cannot judge me for doing what needs to be done to bring peace. I will not cripple my kingdom."

"Your kingdom, my lord? Not ours?"

He scoffed. "You know what I meant."

"No, I don't. I wouldn't never let someone who committed murder dine at my table."

"Vienne was guilty."

"Even so, where was her trial? Where is your justice?"

"*I* am justice."

Wren laughed hollowly. "And there it is. You are the above the law." She looked away. "Get out."

"Please, Wren. Trust me on this. I need to know if I can trust you."

"Get *out*," Wren spat again. "I've proven my loyalty again and again, when you haven't done the same once in return. Leave me be."

Arrik cursed and spared one last glare her way before leaving the room, slamming the door behind him.

The tears finally came.

But she had a point, and he knew it.

CHAPTER 26

ARRIK

It had been a while since Arrik had visited the Beleiras docks, but he'd been studying who had been coming and going for several months now. As such, Arrik recognized most of the ships docked there, but recently a small handful had been seen coming and going that he was not so familiar with. It was easier to try to puzzle this out than agonize over how to comfort his wife when Idril had so badly messed with her head.

He would fix it. All he needed was Wren's trust, and time.

"Brother."

Arrik and Shane, who had accompanied him down to the docks, turned. Kalles was walking toward them with Josenu trailing behind him. Arrik nodded. "What do you have for me?"

"My Southern contacts reported movement on the

border," Kalles said, uncharacteristically serious. "They think an attack is imminent if the shipping levies aren't lifted soon."

When Kalles came to Arrik the day after the attack on the docks to inform him about how exactly he'd obtained the Vadonese blade he gave Wren to murder Arrik, he knew it was high time to take his brother at far more than face value. Through all his drinking and drugs and general debauched behavior, Kalles had been building an information network to keep track of the Southern Isles—something which Arrik and Soren before him had been unable to do.

Though Arrik still couldn't be certain of his younger brother's loyalties—Kalles hadn't minded the idea of Wren murdering him all in the name of fun, after all—the information he had been able to give him regarding the movements of Vadon had proven invaluable so far.

Arrik glanced at Josenu. "Does this have any bearing on why you're here?" He'd had Josenu tail Astrid the last few weeks after he discovered Wren had tasked her friend, Leif, with the same job. Wren had an impeccable sense of who to trust and who to watch. If she was watching Astrid around the clock, then that meant the viper wasn't done simply because her husband was dead.

"My men inside Idril's house believe that he'll be making a political move with Astrid, and that they'll take advantage of the unrest with Vadon to sneak up on you when you least expect it."

It wasn't a surprise and it was a smart move. Considering the current turmoil at court following Soren's death, and the fact most of his naval force was still tied up with the Dragon

Isles, Idril's plan was the last thing Arrik was equipped to deal with. But something had to be done and quickly.

"Speaking of Astrid..." Kalles murmured, sidling closer to Arrik, "I've heard rumors that she has some of *your* advisers in her pocket."

"Oh, Ronan, you're back," Shane called out as the burly man joined the group, cutting through Kalles and Arrik's whispered conversation. Ronan waved several slips of paper at them as he came over. "What did you find out from the sailors?"

"It's as we thought," he said. "Three of those 'merchant ships' were disguised Southern war vessels."

"That certainly tracks with what you just told me," Arrik said, nodding at Kalles. Then, to Ronan: "Have my men move into place. We can't risk any Vadonese slipping past the dock. Another attack on the capital would be dire."

Especially if Astrid and Idril have teamed up to take advantage of the unrest.

Ronan, Shane, and Josenu murmured among themselves as they coordinated which guards and soldiers would be on which shift. Arrik suppressed a sigh; he was so tired. He'd known ruling wouldn't be easy, but each day brought a new horror.

He wished he were with Wren.

As if reading his mind, Shane said, "I was just about to tell you before your brother arrived: Wren left the house."

He straightened, immediately on edge. "Why didn't you lead with that? Where is she?"

"I don't have a report on that." Shane pressed his lips. "I seriously believe that she's playing you, Arrik."

“Now that simply isn’t true.” It was Josenu who spoke, his voice loud and clear and unfaltering. He glared at Shane, then turned his attention to Arrik. “She hasn’t left all day. She’s still in her room. You know I have men watching her on your behalf.”

Shane’s face turned an ugly shade of puce. “Are you calling me a liar?”

“No,” Josenu replied calmly. “I’m calling you out on a mistake and for blackening *our* queen’s name.”

“I know she left the bloody house!”

“Did you see it with your own eyes?”

“Did *you* see her stay?” Shane countered. He took a step toward Josenu in an attempt to intimidate him, but the blond man stood his ground, unperturbed. “I trust my men. She left.”

“I have men on her door *and* her window. She hasn’t left.”

Shane pushed Josenu, incensed by the man’s cool, collected demeanor. But even Josenu had a limit, and he shoved him back.

Arrik ran a hand down his face. Here were two of his best men fighting over whether Wren was where she was supposed to be, all the while Vadon was planning an attack on Verlanti and Idril and Astrid were plotting to overthrow him.

It felt like the world was imploding on him. Arrik was beginning to wonder if he had any idea who he could trust anymore.

“The two of you, break it up!” Arrik bellowed, at the end of his patience. He pointed at Josenu. “You, head back and confirm with your own eyes that my wife is where she’s supposed to be. Ronan, organize the guard for the dock. Shane, come with me to Delia's manor." It was where Arrik would be staying for the night. Delia was an old, very wealthy woman with ties in Vadon Arrik was in desperate need of.

Kalles put up a hand. "And what about me?"

"*Stay sober*."

His brother did a jaunty bow. "I wouldn't dream of drinking, my liege."

Arrik turned on his heel and stormed off, before anyone could see just how close to losing it he really was. Shane followed him, his silence almost as damning as if he shouted.

"What?" he barked when they were alone, his guard following behind them. "I can feel your discontent."

"Watch your back, Arrik," Shane warned. "I know Wren has done everything you've asked of her so far, even though it hurt her. But that's—"

"But that's *what*?" Arrik demanded, when Shane didn't immediately elaborate. He pinned his friend with a dangerous look. "Tell me truthfully what you're thinking or I'll cut your tongue out of your mouth."

They both knew he wouldn't, but Shane answered nonetheless. "She has all the signs of a perfect assassin. There is, quite literally, nobody else in a better position to get rid of you than her. Do you really trust her with your entire kingdom...and your life?"

"Of course I—" But something caused Arrik to stop what he was saying. What Shane suggested had a kernel of truth to it. Arrik would be a fool if he didn't admit to that. Just because the thought of Wren betraying him shattered his very soul into pieces didn't mean it wasn't a possibility. He dragged a hand over his jaw, wishing he could scream or kill something. "I will handle the queen if it comes to that," he finally told Shane, before stalking off.

Could you really? If you had to condemn her as a traitor?

His mind and heart said two different things.

He didn't know any other way to find out Wren's true intentions other than by asking her. Arrik had to prepare himself for the idea that the next time he saw his wife, the conversation they had might very well be their last.

CHAPTER 27

WREN

KALLES WOULD HAVE LAUGHED HIMSELF TO AN EARLY grave had he known Wren was currently standing inside a brothel. That was, if Kalles had spoken a word to her since Ever's execution. Something had clearly gone wrong that he either didn't want Wren to know about, was too ashamed to talk about, or couldn't *risk* talking about for fear of getting caught.

Either way, Ever was dead. Now Vienne was too.

And Wren had to face up to the rebellion in the back room of a lowbrow brothel and try to convince them that she was still able to assassinate Arrik despite all her previous failures.

Liar. Liar.

Heart heavy, Wren walked into the room, Leif in tow. All eyes turned to her. Mostly everyone was glowering and glaring, especially Bram. He looked like he wanted to kill her on the spot. The only exceptions were Rowen and Prince Kade, the freed fourth son of the King of Vadon. The prince offered her a smile that was actually genuine, but she didn't have the heart to feel happy about this.

He'd been freed and Ever had been killed.

She rubbed at her chest at the thought of her friend.

No time for weakness. Get it together.

"Where's Josenu?" Kade asked politely. "I want to thank him for his hand in getting me out. And the young prince."

Ah. Suddenly it dawned on Wren that Kalles may have had higher priorities to attend to: ensure Prince Kade's escape above all else—save Ever if he could. Wren couldn't blame him *or* Josenu if this were the case, but it still stung. Why was it that the people *she* wanted to save constantly had to give themselves up for the greater good? When did any of them get a happy ending?

Wren swallowed and held her chin up. "Josenu had to stay behind to guard my door, to keep up the appearance that I'm still there. Kalles is back in Verlanti."

"Why is it that both of our leaders are *dead* because of you?" Bram spat. He was livid, and rightfully so. The room clamored with agreement.

"You cannot put Vienne's death on me," Wren said, fighting an itch in the back of her throat when she said her aunt's name. "She knew the risks of working with Idril."

"And Ever? What of her?" He stabbed a finger at her. "You killed her with your own hands!"

"Would you have rather I let the crowd *stone her to death?*" Wren yelled, losing some control. Her emotions were too close to the surface. Even though the woman's death *was* her fault, both Wren and Ever knew she had done the right thing in the end. Even if it would haunt her the rest of her days. "I saved her an agonizing death. I did more for her than any of you could have done at that moment in time. You can hate me for that but not find fault in my mercy."

When nobody in the room spoke back to her, Wren turned her attention back to Prince Kade. "I helped set you free. I intend to uphold the rest of my end of our deal. Will you?"

He smiled. "Of course. You have proven yourself honorable. Our agreement stands."

She didn't smile back. Honor wasn't a word Wren would use to describe herself. She'd lost her honor months ago.

Wren pulled out a thick ream of paper from her pocket. "Then I want it in writing. I'm not dealing in verbal promises. Too many of them have been broken as of late." She thought of Arrik, and her disgust at his refusal to abolish slavery. She wasn't going to back down from this.

But to her surprise Kade's smile widened, and he, too, pulled out a long piece of paper. "You and I think alike, Dragon Queen. This is an agreement from the Vadonese king, my father. I think you'll find it contains everything we agreed upon back in the dungeon."

Her eyebrows rose. How had he procured such a document already? Had they anticipated her actions?

He handed it to Wren, who allowed Leif and, reluctantly, Bram, to read it over her shoulder. As discussed Vadon wanted lower taxes, exclusive first sale rights to the Dragon Isles' black diamonds, and better trade routes in return for their full military support against Verlanti, to ultimately bring peace for all three nations.

It took Wren a while to flit through the jargon, ensuring no nasty surprises were held in store once she signed it.

"Where are your men now?" Wren asked, eyeing Prince Kade suspiciously. "If we're going to attack, we need to attack imminently."

Kade and Rowen exchanged a look. "They're already in Beleiras' port."

"And if Arrik happens to find them?" Her husband had eyes everywhere. It couldn't be a coincidence that their first stop had been this city.

"Then we have more men who came through Verlantian port two days ago, who have now ridden into Beleiras," Rowen said, flashing her a familiar grin.

"Don't look so smug," she replied gravely. "The king is not a fool."

Bram snorted. "Where you are concerned he is."

Her stomach tightened with dread but she ignored it as Rowen spoke again.

"Don't worry, we're going to make the Verlantian Dark Court pay for what they did to our home. All will be well."

Wren stifled a sob when she heard Rowen say *our home*, because he meant it. Despite his deceptions through the years, and not meeting eye-to-eye over everything in the rebellion, at his core he was an islander. That reassured her more than anything.

She exhaled and stared down at the treaty clutched in her hands. Wren was past the point of no return. Arrik wasn't going to abolish slavery. He was going to keep working with

Idril so long as he stood to profit from it. He believed that he would get rid of the evil man, and soon, but Wren knew better. She had seen it before—how easily one's moral compass could be twisted just a little bit, then a little bit more, then a little bit more, all in the name of an end goal that apparently justified the means it took to get there.

Wren had to stop Arrik before he went too far.

Before she lost herself completely.

She took the pen Kade held out to her and signed the agreement, her name a bold black slash at the bottom.

It was done.

She'd betrayed her husband in a way she could never take back.

As she left the brothel, feeling a million pounds heavier than she had done when she'd entered it, Wren heard the sound of footsteps rushing to catch up to both her and Leif. She turned, not sure she was able to deal with a confrontation with anyone.

Bram.

She braced herself for the verbal attack that was to come.

"You let Ever die," he seethed, his face like thunder. "You could have saved her but you favored a deal with the Vadonese over saving your own friend. She was on *your side*, you snake. She trusted you!"

Wren doubted Bram would ever understand what had truly transpired, nor the acceptance Ever had had about her own demise—how it had brought her a strange sort of peace.

Nor would he ever understand the grief that would haunt Wren forever because she couldn't save her.

So she said nothing, instead staring Bram down with a stony expression that took all of her strength to maintain. Her silence only served to infuriate the man. He pulled out a dagger and squared up to her, growling under his breath like a wolf.

As if he frightened her. As if he could take anything from her that she hadn't sacrificed already.

"If you don't succeed with murdering your barbarian husband, *I will come for you*."

"I don't doubt you will," Wren said, unflinchingly. She chuckled humorously and held out her arms. "I will welcome it."

Bram searched Wren's face for a long time after that, seeking some sign of her insincerity but ultimately finding none.

"You're different." He cocked his head, lips turning downward. "You're broken."

"And?"

He pursed his lips. "Don't do anything stupid."

"As if you care."

He didn't refute her statement, but his expression softened and all fight left him. Without another word, he strode back the way he'd come.

She watched him go and startled as Leif slipped his hand into hers. He led them away from the brothel and back through the city in silence, neither of them quite knowing what to say to each other. It was only when they reached the edge of Lord Forster's estate that Wren finally spoke. "You can't be around when I do this."

Leif looked confused. "Arrik isn't here. He's—"

"I know, but I'm supposed to see him in the next couple of days before we leave the city." She swallowed hard. "I can't afford to have you anywhere near me, just in case—in case—"

"Something goes wrong," Leif finished for her, anguished understanding twisting his fine features.

"I can't lose another friend," she croaked.

He pulled Wren in for a fierce hug, not letting go even when she tried to pull away in order to keep up her stony defenses. He held on, and on, and on, singing a nonsense song Wren recognized from their time together in the Verlanti dungeons, and then she couldn't take it anymore.

Her walls crumbled.

Wren hugged Leif back with everything she had, letting loose the torrent of pain she carried around since Ever's execution. Leif's shoulders shivered, too, and when a few errant tears dropped onto Wren's skin she knew he was crying alongside her.

"I don't want to go back inside," she admitted between sobs. They wracked her chest so hard it hurt to breathe. Leif gripped her forearms, his hold slightly stronger than necessary, but it helped ground her. Slowly but surely, Wren got her breathing under control, and finally the tears abated.

"You've got this," he said, his dark eyes on her hers. "You know you do. Your sister depends on it...and so do I. You can do it. You're stronger than anyone I know."

"I love you," Wren whispered, pulling Leif back in for another hug as if it might be their last, because it could be.

"I love you too," he said, before pulling away and walking off to spare Wren the agony of doing so herself.

She shook off her grief and straightened her cloak.

There was nothing left to do but walk through Lord Forster's estate gates and straight into the lair of her enemies.

And into the arms of her corrupt love.

CHAPTER 28

WREN

WREN ONLY KNEW SHE'D FALLEN ASLEEP BECAUSE A DULL thump roused her from her fitful slumber when the world was dark and cool and otherwise silent around her.

Strange, what woke me up?

Her eyelids fluttered open, heavy with sleep. Wren brushed the hair out of her eyes and flinched as she spotted the shadow of two people looming over her. Wren grabbed a dagger from beneath her pillow and bolted out of bed, heart pounding. Her bare feet scrambled on the floor as she scanned the room, ears ringing. There were, in fact, three shadows in the room, but one of them was slumped over by the door.

Josenu.

Unconscious.

Rot it.

Whoever had broken into Wren's room was clever enough to take her friend and bodyguard by surprise.

Please don't be dead.

She turned her attention back to the figures standing at the edge of her bed. Regardless of his state, Josenu would have to wait until later.

"What do you want from me?" Wren demanded, voice booming with a confidence she did not feel as her eyes adjusted to the darkness. The figures seemed familiar—one tall and commanding, the other smaller, daintier, slipping through the air as if made of silk.

Lord Idril and Astrid.

Not good. There was only one reason why they were here.

A flash of metal was brought out of Idril's pocket, a thin, wicked-looking blade with more reach than Wren's own dagger. She had no clue how adept he was at fighting, or whether she could best him with her own skills. Wren was a seasoned warrior, but so was Josenu, and he was currently crumpled on the floor.

But they took him by surprise. But you're wide awake. Don't go down without a fight.

Astrid slid onto Wren's bed to recline over the covers, stretching luxuriously with her arms over her head as if she were a cat.

"Oh, Wren," she crooned, black eyes like shining coals cutting through the glim light of the room. They were locked on her, serious and calculating despite the tone of her voice and her relaxed demeanor. "You really should have heeded my advice from the beginning. You were given so many chances. And yet still it's come to this!"

Wren gritted her teeth. "And what is *this*, pray tell?" She had to stall them while she worked out a means of escape. Just as she'd done with her kidnappers, so too could she best her current opponents. She just had to *think*.

As if sensing where her mind had gone, Idril stepped away from the footboard to stalk up to her, remaining just out of reach of her dagger. He held out his own blade, warning her to stay cornered in place. "I think you know what's going on, dear daughter. Did you really think I'd let you go after you so viciously attacked me?" Idril smoothed his fingers along the scar on his cheek, his face a facsimile of grief and agony before his lips contorted into a sneer. "Nobody touches me, not even you. You should have known your place. You should have *begged* to be part of my family. To serve me."

"And you think *she* would have let me work with you?" Wren countered, putting on as haughty a tone as possible as she nodded with her chin toward Astrid. She let out a bitter laugh. "The dear queen mother had it out for me from the start."

"On the contrary, my little dragon..." Astrid said, sliding onto her front to rest her face on top of her hands, "of all the people in my life lately, you alone were the one I was honest with. I admire your fierceness—your will. You look out for yourself, and anyone who stands in your way is merely fuel for your fire. How could I *not* want you as a lady in my court?"

"How flattering." Wren lifted her chin. "So what changed your mind?"

Astrid swung up to a sitting position, and for a moment Wren saw genuine displeasure on her face, as if Wren had truly disappointed her. *Crazy wench.*

"Because you started viewing Arrik as a husband, not a pawn. That was where you went wrong. Once Idril and I marry and take the throne, Ares and Kalles will step aside like good little boys. But Arrik? *Ha*... that bastard has to die. He always had to."

"I thought you wanted him."

Astrid laughed. "Only to torment his father and then take the throne."

"You're sick."

"Oh la, how your words wound me, my dear." She smiled. "I hate that it's come to this, but you will have to die with him. Lord knows I should have killed you before you could break my heart, just as I took care of Arrik's previous wives."

"All those innocent women," she murmured, horrified. "How could you?"

"They weren't innocent. They were power grabbing whores my husband had given his bastard son so he could keep his mistresses close." Astrid shook her head. "Know that I take no pleasure from this."

Again, it actually looked as if Astrid meant it. Wren stared at the monster who had comforted her on her wedding night. Who'd fed her words of advice and stroked her hair like a mother would. Astrid's affection *had* been real, in her own twisted way. But then Wren thought of everything Astrid had done. To Arrik. To Josenu. *She killed Arrik's wives. Their entire kingdom all thought he'd murdered them, but it had always been her*. All of Astrid's backstabbing and scheming and honeyed words of poison had blackened her soul beyond recognition.

She had to go. Her time was up, and so was Idril's.

But Wren wasn't confident she could beat them both.

"So why creep into my room in the middle of the night, attack my guard, and hover over my bed with a blade in hand?" she asked, trying to use her peripheral vision to find an escape route.

"Well, it would have been easier to poison your food at dinner last night," Idril explained, "but you ran off without so much as a sip of wine." His eyes shone with a lust for blood. "But this is better. I can kill you with my own hands, severing your mother's bloodline in the process."

Wren had nothing to say to that. Her mother fled to the Dragon Isles to be free of him. He was the reason Vienne was dead. But, whether he killed her or not, this would *not* be the end of Anneke's bloodline. There was Britta. Charming, laughing Britta, safe and sound back on Lorne. If Wren died, then the secret of her sister's parentage would remain safe with Leif.

Wren liked to imagine he would travel to the isles to regale Britta with tales of her brave big sister. Edited, of course, to remove the torture and the abject misery, and focusing on how Wren never gave up even in the face of absolute failure, all for her sister and her people.

"You'd kill your own blood?" she said, grasping at anything to keep him talking.

"Stop looking for a way out," Idril sneered, shadowing

Wren left then right when she tried to dart away from him. "You are nothing to me if you're not useful."

"Well said, sire," she retorted. "I didn't know you could be honest."

In her corner, boxed in by Astrid sitting on the bed, Wren was trapped. Idril didn't so much as dare to blink as he watched her every move. Wren knew, instinctively, that the dark elf wouldn't make a mistake in their current circumstance.

She needed a distraction. She needed—

"*Who goes there?!*" came a loud, shrill, panicked voice, along with the sound of the door banging open. Wren didn't bother looking at who had spoken. She used the miracle of a distraction to bowl right into Idril, knocking the blade out of his hands and sliding her dagger through his stomach and up to his ribs.

Heat spilled onto her hands and his mouth popped open and she yanked her hand back and stabbed him again, this time right into his black heart.

Her whole body trembled as the light faded from his eyes. Wren gagged and shuddered as his tall body slumped toward her own. Wren jerked away and he crumpled to the ground like a marionette with its strings cut.

You slayed one the monster. One to go.

Breathing hard, Wren spun around to deal with Astrid.

But the queen mother was gone.

"Blast it," Wren cursed, before searching the room for any more threats as her pulse thundered in her ears. She gasped and her heart seemed to freeze in her chest as she spotted the person who'd distracted Idril.

Leif.

She choked on a silent scream as her friend lay on the floor, panting and clutching his stomach. Wren rushed to his side and dropped to her knees. She touched his cheek, leaving a scarlet smear.

"Where did she hurt you?" she rushed out, dropping her dagger on the floor and wiping her bloody hands on her shirt. "Are you bleeding?"

"Caught me in the gut with a kick," Leif gasped. "Nothing else."

Heat pressed at the back of Wren's eyes as she grabbed him in a fierce hug. "I thought... I thought..."

"I'm okay," he wheezed.

Her hands shook as she pulled back. "Why are you...how are you here?" Wren stumbled out.

"I couldn't just leave you alone," Leif said, his voice cracking as tears rushed down his face. Wren had only seen the boy truly cry once before; now his tears fell like a dam that had just been broken. His shoulders shook against Wren, who by contrast found the strength to remain still and steady for them both. "I thought—I thought—what kind of friend am I if I leave you in danger just to save my own skin? And you asked me to follow Astrid. How could I do that if I was hiding away like a *coward*?"

"You're no coward, Leif," Wren murmured into his hair, stroking it like she would her sister's. "You saved my life. Thank you. Thank you. Thank you."

"No thanks are needed between us." Then Leif pulled away, wiped his tears, and shuddered some strength back into his spine. "I'll find Astrid, and then we'll make her pay. You can be sure of that." His gaze darted behind her. "Is he dead?"

"Yes," Wren replied, bottom lip wobbling. Idril deserved punishment but not by her hands in the dark of the night.

"It will be okay." He chucked his chin at Josenu. "You checked him yet?"

Wren blanched and scooted over to the spy's side and checked his pulse. It was strong. She gently probed his head and found a small bloody spot on the side. Carefully, she turned his head so his wound wouldn't touch the floor.

Leif hauled himself to his feet. She started to get up when he held his hands out. "Stay here and lock the door."

She half laughed and cried. "As if that did me any good before."

"I'm going to hunt Astrid down."

"Be careful."

"Always am." He ran off a moment later, sprinting out of the doorway as if carried by the wind itself.

Wren hauled herself up to her feet and strode to the door and closed it. Her lip curled. The lock was completely broken. Turning away, she scooped up her abandoned dagger and sank to the floor beside Josenu, her back to the chilly wall. From the corner of her eye, she could see Idril's left boot.

Don't look.

The night dragged on and her shaking subsided as she stared at the opposite wall, trying to erase the previous hours from her mind.

Josenu groaned, startling Wren from her thoughts. He clutched at his stomach as he eased into a sitting position.

"Careful," Wren croaked. "You've been hit in the head."

"And sucker-punched in the ribs too," he wheezed, gradually regaining focus. He scanned the darkened room, attention stopping on Idril's still form. "He's dead?"

"He is, but Astrid got away." More stupid tears filled her eyes.

Josenu glanced at her sharply. "Don't you dare feel guilty for protecting yourself. You saved my life."

"...he was my father by blood," Wren found herself saying, even though she hadn't told anyone but Leif and Gunn about that yet. "I murdered my sire. My soul is as stained as his."

"*Never* say that. You are nothing like him. He hurt people because it brought him pleasure. He was a selfish, evil man."

"People justify crime all the time in the name of justice."

"The fact you are saying that means you're not one of them." Josenu's smile was grim. "I had a feeling it was personal, the way you hated him. It's quite funny though."

"I don't see what could possibly be funny."

"We both had sires who were monsters."

Wren blinked, not quite understanding his words. "What do you mean?"

"Soren was my father," Josenu explained, grimacing as if the words themselves were bitter in his mouth. "Arrik wasn't the only bastard prince in Verlanti."

Suddenly Wren could see it. It was so obvious. Hadn't she always thought Josenu looked familiar to Arrik? They possessed the same elegance, the same pale hair, the same eyes.

You're a blind fool.

It also meant Wren had another card in her hands that nobody else had.

You're starting to think like a cold queen now.

"Why tell me now?" she whispered.

"Because I trust you."

"You shouldn't."

He reached for her hand and squeezed her fingers. "And that's exactly why I do."

Wren gave him a watery smile and returned the squeeze before releasing his hand. She slowly rose to her feet, mind and heart swirling with too many emotions. "We need to push our plan *now*. Leif has gone after Astrid, but we can't guarantee that will give us much time. We both know that *viper* will try to manipulate Arrik to save her own skin and rat us out."

"Arrik hasn't left the city yet," Josenu said, allowing Wren to help him sit upright. "He's staying at an old widows' manor in the north quarter. If you want, I can take you there now. But I'll have to let him know you're coming, just in case..."

Josenu left it unspoken, but Wren knew what he meant. *Just in case I fail, and Josenu has to keep up the double act for another day.*

Wren nodded, not trusting her voice. Her throat had gone as dry as the Southern Isles, each breath scratchy and sore when she inhaled. If she didn't go now she'd lose all the adrenaline in her system, and the ability to go through with what needed to be done in the process.

Before she left she armored every part of her in weapons —her two daggers, her bow, sharp pins in her hair, Idril's long and narrow blade. Her fingers drifted over the poison ring Bram had given to her months ago. She slipped the band of silver onto the index finger of her left hand. One never knew when a bit of poison might be useful. She stared blankly around the room.

"Are you ready to go, my queen?" Josenu asked softly.

She nodded and took in another painful breath and followed Josenu out into the night.

It was now or never.

CHAPTER 29

ARRIK

Arrik held Josenu's missive in his hands and read it for the tenth time.

Astrid and Idril had tried to kill Wren.

His wife.

His queen.

His *beloved.*

In the back of his mind, he knew he should do something, anything. But all he could do was stare at the bloody letter.

His dragon queen had begged him not to engage Idril. She'd even sent Arrik away and yet... he'd not changed his mind. Instead, he'd worked with the monster because it benefited him.

And it was *easier*.

His stomach lurched. Wren had almost died, all because he had sought the easy path to being king.

You really don't deserve her.

He crumpled the paper, his vision starting to go red.

"I should have been there," he thundered, throwing the missive to the floor.

His hands began to shake.

How dare they attack his queen.

He snatched a vase of flowers from the side table and threw it across the room. It shattered into a hundred pieces and scattered across the stone floor.

Get ahold of yourself. This is not the way.

Logically, he knew that, but he couldn't get ahold of his temper.

Arrik clenched his teeth together as shudders ran through his body. He'd only ever experienced this once before in his life... when his mother had died.

A harsh sob escaped him.

His mother had been the only woman who he'd truly loved.

Until Wren.

And it was breaking him apart.

He bellowed again and pressed his palms to his eyes. He'd known that he cared for her, even loved her as much as a degenerate like himself could, but nothing prepared him for the wealth of feelings that threated to choke him.

Arrik wiped his wet eyes and glared at his boots. He couldn't love like this again. It was too painful.

And dangerous.

For Wren. And for himself.

He began counting in his head and slowed his breathing until the room came into focus again. Arrik glanced at the round mirror hanging on the wall across from him. His appearance was much the same but there was something in his eyes that was different. Wren had changed him.

Cursing, he turned his back on the mirror.

He couldn't afford to be changed. The kingdom needed a strong ruler to keep it together in this time of transition. Wren was compromising that. She had too much control. His wife had reduced him to a weak man.

"Watch your back," Shane's words whispered in the back of his mind. *"She would make the perfect assassin."*

He'd brushed the words away earlier, but now Arrik couldn't keep them out of his head.

It was true that he was beyond relieved that his wife was unhurt but the cold, sharp side of his mind, the one Soren appreciated, saw how perfect Wren was suited for the job.

Guilty suspicion took root in his heart at the thought. How often had she lied to him? How many times did she say she hated him? How many times had she tried to escape? Was it really so farfetched?

Her sweet morning smile flashed through his head. He knew her. She held her emotions close to the surface. Those things weren't a lie.

He squeezed his eyes shut. "I'll drive myself mad."

A timid knock broke through his thoughts.

"Yes?" he called, turning to the door.

"Your Majesty," a servant murmured through the grain of the wood. "Your wife is here. Should I let her in?"

Fear wrapped around his heart. What if he sent her away? The feelings he was having were too much.

He quickly squashed the fear. Time to be the bloody king of Verlanti.

"Send her in," he managed.

The door creaked open.

The first thing Arrik noticed by the light of the torches and the dying fire in the hearth was that her face was wet with tears. Her eyes were red and sore as if she had been quite literally crying from the moment Astrid and Idril attacked her right until she stood before Arrik.

And it hurt him.

He wanted to rush to his wife, to take her in his arms and let her cry it all out. He wanted to spend all night concocting increasingly ridiculous, violent plans of revenge against anyone who sought to harm him or Wren.

Let the world burn, and we'll watch.

But he couldn't make his feet move.

He was rooted to the spot.

Doubts swirled in his mind. Could this all be an act?

Wren could well be his enemy, and Arrik's eyes were now fully open to that possibility.

Her rumpled robe fluttered around her feet as she stepped closer.

Something wasn't right.

"My king?" she said, a question in her tone.

"Are you alright?"

"I am," she said slowly, scanning his face as if she could ferret out his secrets.

Arrik turned from her and sat on the bed. He leaned

back against the headboard and watched his wife. "You sent me away and now you want me?"

Wren blinked. "I thought you would want me to come to you."

He did, but there was something wrong. He could feel it in the air. Time for a test.

Arrik held his hand out to his queen. "Come to me, darling. Let me hold you so I can know you are safe."

Relief surged over her expression and she rushed forward, taking his hand. Hers trembled as she stood at the side of the bed, watching him.

"Well, are you coming in?" he asked, closing his eyes and giving her hand a little tug. His breathing sped up and adrenaline thrummed through his body. He'd made himself as vulnerable as he could be. Now, time would only tell what his vicious little wife would do

His other hand crept beneath his pillows to the dagger he always kept there as she climbed onto the bed and then swung her leg over his, until she straddled his lap.

"Will you look at me?" she whispered, her voice uneven and full of tears.

Arrik opened his eyes.

His beautiful wife was above him, her scarlet hair pinned back apart from a few errant strands which tickled his face. Her heartbreaking eyes were full of such a conflicting sea of emotions that Arrik didn't know which one to focus on.

"I'm sorry," she said.

"For what?"

"For sending you away."

He released her hand and brushed a strand of hair from

her face. "You were angry. I understand. Are you sure you're alright?"

She nodded, and leaned closer. "Yes, now that I'm with you."

His queen captured his lips and kissed him hard. His fingers clenched around the dagger and the back of her neck. Why was it always like this? She made him burn.

"Wren," he growled, releasing her neck and the dagger. He needed her closer. Hell, if she attacked him right now, he'd die a happy man.

Arrik seized her by the waist to pull her closer, and frowned when he discovered her lovely curves were confined by a corset.

"What the—" he demanded, just as he felt the kiss of steel at his neck.

The world seemed to still as his eyes popped open and he stared up at Wren. His wife had her favorite dagger—the one with black diamonds in the hilt, the most outwardly expensive possession she had—pressed against the artery in his neck. He could feel the cool metal pulsing with his heart. Becoming one with him. Being part of him.

His gaze moved up her body, noting how the robe gaped open, revealing the armor beneath it. His little dragon hadn't come to bed for comfort but for battle. Arrik peered up into her face, into the hard expression she wore. She looked like the warrior goddess he had first spied from his ship, back when he'd plundered her land and taken her for himself.

He was so stupid.

Arrik chuckled, dropping his hands to his sides. "So this is how it's to be?"

"It's how it has to be."

"Are you going to kill me?" he asked. He could stop her. He could fight. Arrik knew it, Wren knew it, they both knew it. But he didn't move. Something compelled him to stay.

Wren trembled above him, keeping in perfect time with his heart. But she didn't move. Was she waiting for Arrik to say something?

His hand inched toward his dagger but he stopped when she pressed her blade harder into his throat.

"I don't think so, my lord."

He smiled sharply. "You know me so well."

Her jaw clenched and she swallowed hard. "You made it very easy."

Arrik searched her face for any signs of regret or weakness. "Was any of it real?"

"How could it be when you've kept me caged?"

That made him angry. More than the threat she posed to his life. He leaned into the knife, glaring up at his wife. "Don't you dare lie to me."

"Don't speak to me about lying," she snapped. "When you don't keep any of your promises."

"How long have you planned this?" he asked, eyes never leaving Wren's even when her blade pressed against his skin and drew blood. "Was it before or after you gave your body to me? Was that part of your plan?"

Wren let out a guttural roar. He'd gotten to his little dragon.

Her thighs pressed against him. "Do you think that's all that matters, Arrik? Me and you? And our feelings?"

Our feelings.

Now they were getting somewhere.

He wanted to say yes. With every fiber of his being he believed it. But he knew there was more to life for Wren than that. It was that core part of her that Arrik had been trying so hard to be better for, knowing he would ultimately fail.

"You could put the blade away," he said softly. "Put it away, and we can pretend this never happened. I've done terrible things, worse than this. Every couple has their challenges. This could be a story we laugh about in the future."

And he would. Arrik would put it behind them. After everything Wren had been through, it was the least he could do to give her a chance. To forgive her. To move on.

But he'd push her away. Never again could he allow her that close. She'd already damaged him.

Wren didn't reply. A single tear rolled down her cheek, eyes shining with grief.

"I can't." Two words that held complete resolve.

Something shattered inside him. "You won't."

He and Wren weren't going to be together. They weren't going to have their own twisted version of happily ever after.

Soren had been right.

No one would ever love him enough.

The last bit of hope died inside him. Ice crept through his veins and he relished the feeling. It was better than the soul shattering agony that would drown him if he let himself think about what was to happen.

If he couldn't have Wren, then he'd settle for the kingdom he'd acquired.

God save the queen.

CHAPTER 30

WREN

PRECISELY HALF A SECOND PASSED BEFORE WREN KNEW with dreadful certainty that Arrik was going to fight back and she could do nothing about it—his corded muscles and sheer size were more than enough to overwhelm her in such close combat.

Kill him. Just push the blade down and—

In one fluid motion Arrik tossed Wren, dagger and all, to the floor.

It was enough to shake Wren out of the frozen stupor that had paralyzed her into inaction. She rolled to her knees, and then popped to her feet, just as Arrik languidly climbed out of the bed as if he had all the time in the world.

Wren tore the robe from her body, tossed it to the floor, and backed up, putting space between them. One less thing to trip her up.

He touched the nick at his neck and then rubbed the blood between his fingers. "Always so violent."

"You're one to talk."

"This is your last chance, wife. Put the weapon down."

"Nev—"

Before she could finish, he barreled straight toward her.

Wren was reminded, then, of their first fight back on Lorne. The first time they'd locked eyes on each other. Wren, exhausted and injured and blinded by grief, had attempted to sneak up on the barbarian elf prince and murder him. But she'd been no match for Arrik back then—not in the state she'd been in.

Now she was fighting fit. She had learned from the masters of the Dragon Isles, she had learned from Leif and Bram and Ever in the rebellion, she had learned from fighting Josenu and Shane and Ronan...

She'd even learned from Arrik himself.

No one would ever take advantage of her again.

Wren ducked and rolled away from Arrik when he was mere inches from her.

"You want to play cat and mouse?" he taunted.

"As long are you're the mouse."

His lips thinned as they circled each other. "So this is the way it has to end, is it?" Arrik said, voice so tense it could cut through the darkness like the knife in his hand. A knife, even though he had a sword on his hip. A knife to match Wren's dagger.

He is being honorable. Fair.

The thought disturbed her. She shook her head.

"It always had to end like this," Wren replied tersely, hating how moisture escape her eyes. Arrik lunged and she lurched out of the way once more when he made to tackle her to the floor. She danced this way and that, too fast for him. Too light for him.

Thank the stars for Leif.

Wren cursed as she realized he was backing her up toward the widow, cutting off any escape. She growled and scrambled up the curtain as Arrik swiped at the fabric, tearing it from the wall. She stifled a scream and managed to land on Arrik's back. A year ago she'd never have been able to perform such a nimble feat.

"Really?" Arrik bellowed when Wren encircled her arms around his neck and her legs around his waist, cutting off his air.

He dropped his blade and pried at her arms but she held on as he dropped to his knees. Arrik sank his nails into her forearms. She clenched her teeth and held on despite the pain. Why wasn't he using his dagger?

"Fight," she hissed, as more tears filled her eyes, the room going blurry for a second or two.

"You really"—Arrik huffed in exertion against Wren's hold on his air supply—"mean to kill me this way?"

Wren swallowed down her sob and didn't reply.

The world lurched and she yelled in surprise when Arrik finally managed to slam backward onto the floor, crushing her beneath him. Stars blasted across her vision. This was it; there was no way she could shake off the monstrous man lying on top of her.

She wheezed and turned her head to the side just as the room lit up with light and heat. Arrik bolted upward and turned partly to cover her as another explosion went off near the manor, shaking the whole room.

She slammed her hand into his nose and wiggled away, managing to get to her knees, coughing and sputtering as Arrik pinched his bleeding, broken nose.

Why had he protected her?

She wiped the dirt from her face and placed her dagger against the artery in Arrik's thigh. The moment the metal pressed so intimately against his leg, he stilled and dropped his hands, blood streaming down his mouth and chin. Shouts could be heard from the corridor, then screams, accompanied by the cloying smell of smoke and the metallic tang of blood.

But to Wren and Arrik, the world might as well have been white and silent and pure. There were only the two of them, locked in a violent dance with each other.

"Do it," Arrik said an eternity later, his icy eyes never leaving her own. "Do it, and put me out of my misery, darling." He held his hands out to his sides. "I dare you to do it."

But Wren, once more...faltered. Her hands were shaking beyond control, her eyes too full of tears to even pretend she could see.

Oh stars, what had she gotten herself into?

Do it.

But her body wouldn't obey her mind. It was like it knew who she belonged to.

Arrik seized the moment, swept her to the floor, and

pinned her beneath him. She didn't fight it. She was done fighting. She'd had more than her fair share of chances and she'd failed. Despite everything, she couldn't take his life.

She was the most messed up, selfish human in existence.

Wren closed her eyes and waited for the blow.

"Oh no you don't. Open your bloody eyes."

She opened them, helpless but to obey. His eyes were blazing ice on hers, tight with emotion that had nothing to do with rage. He held his knife above Wren, hovering it against her throat.

Do it. This will only end if you kill me.

He inhaled sharply as if he could read her thoughts.

But Arrik didn't kill her. He didn't even try. With a curse he flung his knife away, running his hands through his hair as he almost blindly stared down at Wren.

"What am I supposed to do with you?!" he yelled, losing control entirely. He shook her shoulders as if he could force the answer out of her. "I can't do this. I cannot be the end of you, Wren. I don't want to live in a world where you no longer exist. I'm selfish and flawed and broken. But so are you. If I hurt you, it would be like hurting myself. We are part of each other and you know it."

Wren didn't bother trying to ebb the flow of tears as they rolled down her cheeks. She sobbed, ugly and unbridled, as she held her dagger out to Arrik for him to take it away.

He was hers, and she was his. There was no other way around the curse that had brought them together.

Arrik took the blade from Wren with a shaking hand, which only grew steady once he sent the weapon skittering across the floor. He pulled Wren up, embracing her like he was lost at sea and she was the anchor keeping him in place.

He sank his fingers into her hair and tugged her head back, claiming her lips with a ferocious kiss.

This pattern couldn't go on. It would kill them both.

She hiccupped when his lips dragged down the column of her throat. It felt like perfection. But it couldn't last.

It was only in that moment, when Wren heaved in a breath and oxygen returned to her brain, that she remembered just how much she had to lose if she surrendered to her feelings for Arrik and let him continue ruling.

They couldn't do this. *She* couldn't allow it. Love wasn't everything. Sometimes honor and duty meant more.

Wrapping her arms around her husband's neck, she clicked open the spike on her poison ring and sank it into Arrik's throat.

It seemed he didn't feel the sting; they were too engrossed in each other. With every passing second the drug worked through his system, and a few seconds later Arrik went straight as a board and pulled away from her.

"You..." he gasped, eyes wild and wide as understanding finally dawned on him. Wren couldn't find it in herself to say anything back. As gently as she could, she hugged Arrik, ensuring his convulsions would happen safely against her body.

A moment later, Arrik went feral in her arms, twisting and turning in so grotesque a manner Wren felt certain he was breaking his bones. He began to froth at the mouth, and for one horrible moment Wren thought she'd given him a fatal dose of the poison rather than enough to knock him out. He gurgled, his muscles relaxed, and he closed his eyes.

Wren screamed and began to shake. She'd betrayed her beloved.

And the door to the room burst open.

CHAPTER 31

WREN

Wren didn't have much time to dwell on Arrik's unconscious, drugged form; a battle was blazing hot and heavy around her and had now been brought directly to her.

Her pulse sped up when two members of the rebellion came in through the door, saw her kneeling over Arrik's apparently lifeless body, and shot back down the corridor with victorious grins. Letting out a sigh of relief, Wren spared a few seconds to check Arrik's pulse. Soft, but present and steady. He would wake up in a few hours with a headache but otherwise unharmed.

Except for his heart, which Wren had duly broken.

"I'm sorry," she whispered, pushing the braids from his face.

Everything was so messed up.

She quickly collected both of their blades and his sword, then stayed by his side.

Wren should leave him and enter the fray but she couldn't pry herself from his side. If she wasn't around, then there was no telling who would find him: friend or foe. A friend of the rebellion might stick a knife in Arrik's heart simply because they could, while a foe might sneak Arrik's body away to incite a *new* rebellion. Then all of Wren's sacrifices would have been for naught. And it was a good thing too. The next few people who entered the room were guards of the manor who didn't take kindly to her hovering over the king's bloody body.

She dispatched them, managing to knock them out instead of killing them. They were only doing their jobs. They didn't deserve death because of that.

She paced the room and paused by Arrik's side as she heard a pair of footsteps thundering her way. Wren braced herself next to Arrik and waited.

Covered in soot, sweat, blood, and wearing his near-permanent snarl stood Shane, though the snarl disappeared the moment he saw Arrik. His scarred face visibly paled, before blooming scarlet with rage.

"You *whore* of the rebellion," he spat, double-checking his environment before coming after Wren with his sword, swinging all the while.

"Shane, wait!" Wren cried, desperate for him to understand before he did something that couldn't be undone. "He isn't—"

"You're worse than Soren and Astrid and the rest of the rotted Dark Court!"

Wren parried Shane's attack, but it jarred up her arm, her shoulder, her neck. He was already a strong, imposing man, but now Shane was fueled by rage and adrenaline. In her current state, Wren wasn't entirely certain she could beat him.

But she didn't have to beat him. She needed him to understand.

"Think what you like," she said, when the two of them crashed together, their swords clanging against one another. Shane's eyes blazed like coals on Wren's. "But he isn't dead. I put him to sleep!"

A flash of uncertainty dulled the fire in his eyes, but then Shane let out a brutal laugh. "You think I'd believe that? You think—"

"Check his pulse," Wren growled, darting her eyes to the open door, "but be quick about it. Nobody can see me helping you." As a show of extreme faith, Wren lowered her weapons, though she knew Shane was more likely to kill her than to believe her.

Except this was Arrik she was talking about, Shane's best friend—brother by choice rather than blood, just like Leif with her.

Shane abandoned Wren and checked Arrik's pulse. His body visibly shook with relief when he realized Wren was telling him the truth.

"What do you want?" he muttered, glaring at her. "So that I can get him out of here alive."

"Nothing," Wren replied woodenly. There wasn't any hope for Arrik.

"Then why save his life at all?!"

Wren pulled at her hair in frustration, kneeling beside Shane over Arrik's unconscious body. "Because I don't want him to die. To see the life drain out of him—to have him leave me forever—I can't—"

"Rot it, you actually love him, don't you?" Shane's scarred face twisted with disgust, and he tossed his sword to the floor. "The two of you are fools. Worse than fools, you'll be the death of us all."

For some reason Wren found comfort in Shane's words. It was clear he hated her—would likely hate her until the end of time—but he equally could see that she and Arrik weren't lying about their feelings for each other.

"I need your help," she said, as an idea began to form.

"That's rich coming from you," Shane retorted.

"We don't have time for this. If you want him to live, I need you to follow my instructions."

"What do you need me to do?" Shane asked heavily, as if giving in put the weight of the world on his shoulders.

Her gaze flashed to the door again. They didn't have much time. "The rebellion has taken hold of Verlanti. You can be sure of that. As queen, I'll have to send you both to the dungeon, to await...to await your execution."

Shane clenched his fists around Arrik's shirt, the tendons in his hands looking close to tearing. But all he said was, "Go on."

"So I need you to let that happen," Wren said. "Go to the dungeon. Await your fate. But help me—trust me—and you can be sure your fate will not be your death."

Shane mulled this over, and for a moment it looked as if he was going to say no.

"I won't kill you," Wren added on, panicking over how little time they had left. "I can't do that to him. I'm not strong enough." Shane snorted but she continued on. "But I can't say the same for the rest of the rebellion. They will want to see both you and Arrik dead, *now*. The only way I can save you is through my power as queen, by getting you to the dungeon to await a public execution. Say you'll help me."

"Fine, *my queen*," Shane grunted, and all the fire drained out of him. He lifted his eyes and met her gaze. "Just know that I will come for you if you're lying. Nothing will stop me."

"Spoken like a true friend."

He glared. "I hate you for what you've done to him."

"If it makes you feel any better, I hate him for what he's done to me."

IT WAS SURPRISINGLY EASY TO TAKE THE CITY AFTER THAT.

It was smaller than Verlanti, which Wren knew the larger part of the Vadonese forces were currently taking down. Before the sun was up, the port city of Beleiras was Wren's, and victory over Verlanti as a whole was secured.

And that was it. Wren had killed Idril, taken Arrik down, and conquered their land the way their people had taken the Dragon Isles.

She would never bow before anyone again.

She should have been celebrating her victory and freedom. Wren should have felt happy.

Then why did she feel so hollow?

CHAPTER 32

WREN

There was a certain irony to the fact Wren had now conquered the nation that had previously conquered her own. They'd tried to bend and break and shape her into something resembling a Verlantian, but at the end of the day a dragon was a dragon.

And dragons didn't break.

They became queens.

"All rise for the queen of Verlanti," the official announcer boomed out, and everyone rose to bow as Wren ascended the dais to her throne.

She would never get used to this: the Verlantian court simpering and kneeling for her out of pure fear that she would call for their deaths. There was some respect lingering among them—Wren had danced with a pit of snakes and still come out the victor, after all—but there were a troubling number highborn who, she knew, would jump at the chance to see her gone.

She wasn't one of them. She would always be an outsider.

But right now that didn't matter. She *was* their queen, and she wasn't going to effect change the way Arrik had meant to go about it.

She was done with slow and gradual.

She wanted deliberate and *now*.

"My first order of business is to remove each and every member of the king's circle of advisers," she said, suppressing a smile at the wave of horror that rippled throughout the crowd. A few people dared to whisper that she couldn't do that, that she needed majority approval to remove even *one* official.

She coughed softly into her hand. "I think anyone familiar with the charter of these lands will see that the law only relates to a *king's* circle of advisers," she continued, still beyond pleased with the loopholes. Wren gave the court a cold smile. "Verlanti has never had a ruling queen before. As such, the law does not apply. And in any case..." This time Wren's smile widened—a challenge to those who would oppose her, to know that she wasn't scared. "If anyone feels strongly enough to do something about my ruling, they're welcome to try and change my mind."

A hush fell over the crowd. They knew what that meant.

Wren was *inviting* them to challenge her. To attack her. Because, ultimately, she would take them down, each and every one of them. It was confidence she did not necessarily feel in her bones but it was one of the most important lessons Astrid had ever deigned to teach her.

Never let them see you sweat. And don't crack. Stay icy.

Thinking of that viper, Wren turned her attention to the woman, who despite being held in chains between four heavily armed guards looked surprisingly graceful and elegant. Astrid matched Wren's stare with bold, unwavering eyes.

Wren wanted to have her executed. For Josenu, for Arrik, for herself. But in this case Astrid served a far greater purpose alive but *away* from the kingdom she sought to rule. Wren wouldn't make a martyr out of the queen mother. She had too many supporters at court. "To the former queen of Verlanti, Astrid, I exile you to the mines in the Dragon Isles. You will be stripped of all your worldly possessions before you leave."

Several members of the court let out audible gasps. At Wren's side, Josenu twitched with the effort not to smile in satisfaction. Wren had discussed long and hard with him how best to punish Astrid. The woman in question was furious, but under the weight of her chains she could do nothing but accept her fate.

"I'll kill you for this!" Astrid hissed.

"I'd like to see you claw your way out of those mines," Wren said, tone bored.

Let's see how well you fare in a land you sought to subjugate, with no money, no jewels, and no power behind you.

Next, Wren turned her gaze to Ares and Kalles, who were both dressed uncharacteristically demurely. They reminded Wren of Arrik, in his preferred black, and she fought back a stinging sensation in her eyes. She couldn't afford such emotions. She had the fate of two kingdoms in her hands.

"I am not without compassion," Wren said, "and I do not see the need to shed blood from those who have never sought mine. To that end, I offer Prince Ares and Prince Kalles their freedom, along with their personal wealth and possessions, if they renounce the monarchy and give up all of the lands the former High King Soren afforded them."

"I accept your conditions, Your Majesty," Ares said, inclining his head politely.

"I accept your conditions, Your Majesty," Kalles echoed, bowing, for once, entirely sincerely.

Wren had expected their answers. She had discussed her intentions beforehand. Though it had been clear by the time Arrik was imprisoned and the rebellion took over that Kalles had indeed been working with Vadon to remove his father from the throne and—of course—protect his own life in the process, Wren had not been sure if his older brother would accept losing his title and the inordinate amount of land he owned. But Ares had been happy to renounce it all in favor of living a happy, quiet life with his wealth firmly intact.

All that remained now was the hardest part of the entire day. The moment she'd been dreading for three weeks.

"Now we come to the sentencing of Shane, the former captain of the guard and King Arrik's second-in-command, and the sentencing of former King Arrik. Bring them in," Wren called out, though it pained her to do so.

Stay calm. Don't show fear. Be ruthless.

Shane was brought in first, looking harried and sleep-deprived and tormented beyond belief. Being in the dungeon for three weeks had clearly not been kind to him. A pang of remorse hit Wren's heart like a drum, but she didn't let it show.

"For aiding the former king instead of laying down your arms when it was commanded of you, I sentence you to death by public execution," Wren announced, keeping her voice as dispassionate as possible. "Do you understand this sentencing?"

Wordlessly, Shane nodded. With a tug on the chain around his wrists, he was pulled to the side, allowing Wren an unfettered look at the former king of Verlanti—her husband.

Arrik.

His glorious pale hair was a tangled, dirty mess of blood and soot and dirt, knotting around his face where once it had been painstakingly braided. His clothes were similarly a mess, black-on-black-on-black in layers of grime. He slowly lifted his eyes of ice and trained them on her.

She clenched her jaw. A challenge. Even in chains he would not make it easyon her.

"For crimes against the Verlantian people—for consorting with the rebellion and aiding their plan to remove the former king, and working with Lord Idril, a known conspirer against the throne, I sentence the former King Arrik to death by public execution. Do you understand this sentencing?"

The words rushed out, hollow; it hurt to even *say* them. To doom her husband with her voice to his death.

The room was so silent Wren could have heard a pin drop.

Arrik lifted his chin, a proud monarch even in rags and

dirt. The moment stretched between them. There was no love left in his eyes, only glassy indifference.

"I do," he said, his voice rough like sand against Wren's skin.

She didn't know just how much she'd longed to hear that voice. How much it hurt to have *not* heard it the last three weeks. She'd been so tempted to visit him but knew it would be dangerous.

Now she had potentially heard it for the final time in her life.

"Then we're done here," Wren said, to a cacophonic mix of cheers, roars, sighs, and sobs.

Just like that, the sentencing was complete. The short-lived former king of Verlanti and his right-hand man had been sentenced to death.

She stood and Kalles came to her side to take her hand as she descended the dais.

Wren held her head high as he led her through the throne room. She counted it a win to leave the poisonous court without showing a single trace of emotion on her face. It was easier to keep up a blank mask than to fake relief, or happiness, or grace. Wren wondered whether that blank slate would become her new normal. It was unnervingly easy to find solace in being numb—of feeling nothing.

But she knew that allowing herself to feel nothing would be the death of her soul: the very thing Wren betrayed Arrik for all in order to save it for him.

"Do you need anything?"

Wren stared blankly up at Kalles, trying to understand

his question. She needed many things but none of them were within his powers. "No."

Kalles studied her and squeezed her hand. "You can bear this."

"I know." *I can't.* "I can walk myself to my rooms."

He nodded and stepped away. "If you need me, just send Trove with a letter."

"I won't but thank you."

Wren watched him walk away and it was on the tip of her tongue to call him back. To ask him for something to help her sleep, to forget, but she swallowed down the desire. Losing herself to drink or smoke wouldn't help.

Kicking off her slippers, she left them behind and wandered the corridors. By the time Wren reached her room, it felt as if the day had lasted weeks.

"Would you like anything to eat?"

Wren turned at the sound of Josenu's voice, Leif trailing right behind him. When had they shown up?

"How long have you been there?"

Leif gave her a weak smile and held up her slippers. "The whole time."

Someone could have killed her. She couldn't allow herself to be lax like that.

She opened the door to her chambers and they followed her in.

"When is the last time you ate?" Josenu asked. "I can call for a simple dinner."

Both of them had taken to sleeping in her room at night, not daring to leave her side for even a moment. She understood why they were doing that—and why it was necessary—

but it also meant she'd not had a single minute to be alone with her thoughts. She didn't dare cry or shout or otherwise show emotion, even though they were her friends and she trusted them.

She needed to remain strong, even just as a front, for herself. *She* needed to believe that she could do this, that she wasn't always a strong gust of wind away from breaking down entirely.

Wren feared that if she let go, she might not be able to put the pieces back together.

She forced a wobbly smile to her face as she shook her head. "I'm too tired to eat. I'm just going to lie down for the night, if that's all right with the two of you. Sorry I won't be much company."

Leif looked like he was going to say something—to protest, no doubt, because he knew fine well when Wren was lying—but a gentle nudge from Josenu kept him quiet.

"Of course, Your Majesty," Josenu said, pulling Leif along with him into the corner of Wren's room, overlooking the bathing gardens, to quietly play some cards.

Wren lay down on her bed and closed her eyes, dully wondering if she would ever be able to convince Josenu to stop calling her "Your Majesty" when they were in the privacy of their own company. But soon her mind turned to darker thoughts of betrayal and assassinations and the look in Arrik's eyes when he realized Wren truly meant to turn against him...

As with the previous twenty-one days, Wren knew she would find no solace in sleep. She was exhausted beyond compare and she simply *couldn't* sleep. Her brain, her conscience, her soul, would not allow it.

She knew what she had to do.

It was dangerous. It was risky. But it had to be done.

Wren crept out of bed the moment she was sure Leif and Josenu were dozing and headed to the dungeons. To Arrik.

CHAPTER 33

ARRIK

IT WAS AN ODD FEELING, BEING ON THE OTHER SIDE OF THE dungeon's iron bars. Arrik had spent the last three weeks either dangling from chains on the ceiling or clinging to the bars, praying to God or the devil or anyone who would listen, to spare his life from the carnivorous fish that would love nothing more than to tear him apart.

Shane was faring worse than Arrik. He wasn't chained above the water, so had to cling to the bars of his cell for dear life whenever the tide came in. He'd always feared the fish more than most. He'd take a thousand cuts from a sword before becoming a live meal for the fish.

Guilt twisted Arrik's stomach. It was his fault Shane imprisoned with him. He was going to die because of him.

And because of Wren.

A fire lit up Arrik's heart at the mere thought of his traitorous wife. He *had* to be angry, otherwise he'd be heartbroken. But even anger was difficult to cling to in the dark, dank, dungeon.

You put Wren in here for days when you first took her prisoner, and even that didn't dull her spirit.

In some ways Arrik was fiercely proud of her, even now. She truly was a dragon. Someone to be worshiped. Someone to fear.

As if sensing his thoughts, the door to the dungeon heaved open, letting in both a ray of light and his tormentor. His wife didn't say anything as she stalked down the dungeon, her gaze glancing over Shane for the briefest of moments before she stopped right in front of Arrik's cell.

They stared at each other, impassive and silent. Wren looked like she hadn't slept in days—as if she, too, had been chained to the ceiling of the dungeon at the mercy of the tide and the fish. Dark smudges marred the skin beneath her eyes and she looked as if she'd lost weight.

"Have you come to gloat?" he muttered, staring her down.

"*That's* what you have to say?" Wren countered, a judgmental eyebrow raised. "After three weeks in here, that's all you can think to say?"

"Well, what would you prefer? Me begging for my life after you betrayed me?"

"*Betrayed* you?" Wren barked out a laugh. "After everything you and your people have put me through—murdering my parents, taking my land, holding me captive, forcing me into marriage—you talk about me *betraying* you? Wake up,

Arrik! With the path you were walking, I was always going to stand up against you. I learned from you."

He stiffened. "And what does that mean, exactly?"

"Oh, I don't know, working with Idril? Refusing to abolish slavery? Or we can go further back than that: you promised I could go back to the Dragon Isles and rule there whilst you ruled Verlanti, but that was a lie. You promised me everything and gave me nothing in return but lies!"

"Is that really what you think?" Arrik growled, shaking from his chains. "You think I'm the one who fed you lies rather than the other way around? What I did was necessary for the safety of Verlanti. You're the one who sold your body for a throne."

If there hadn't been several inches of iron bars between them, Arrik imagined Wren would have slapped him. Her eyes were blazing, teeth bared. "You can think that if you like," she seethed, "but at least I didn't sell my *soul* for it instead. And the fact I still have mine is what will save you now."

Wren unlocked the cell and stood by the edge of the gently lapping water without looking at him. Her eyes fluttered closed, and she began to sing. Arrik recognized the melody.

"Are you going to have your dragon do the dirty work for you?" he hissed.

Her song cut off abruptly and she stormed up to him, her chest almost touching his own. He inhaled sharply, her tantalizing scent begging him to learn closer. Stars, he was a weak fool.

She pulled necklace from the bodice of her dress,, revealing a set of keys.

"That's the difference between me and you, Arrik," Wren said calmly, unlocking his chains, before throwing the keys to their cells over to Shane, who'd been quietly watching their entire interaction. The water began bubbling, the telltale snout of Trove slowly rising to the surface. "You assume the worst in people, even those you love, whereas I always try assume the best."

There was the clink of a key in a lock, then Shane was in the cell with them. Wren fired him a warning glare when he stepped too close to her. He handed the keys back to her and she finally undid his final chain. With a splash, he fell into the shallow water, then promptly leaped onto dry land.

"This is your one chance to escape," she whispered.

Arrik couldn't believe what he was hearing. "You think I'll run away from all of this? Have you *ever* seen me flee from trouble?" It was insulting.

"If you don't leave, you'll die."

"Then I'll die with my dignity intact."

Wren stood up on her tiptoes and his traitorous heart leapt. He almost thought she was going to kiss him. Worse was that he would have let her. But Wren splayed out her hands across his chest instead, and with a heave she shoved him back into the water.

"Dignity is wasted on the dead!" she called out to him, though he could barely hear her over the rush of water in his ears. The moment he surfaced, Trove grabbed hold of him, locking him in an embrace so tight he could not have wrestled out of it. "Shane, if you don't want to die, I suggest joining him!" Wren cried, her eyes sorrowful as she watched Arrik and Shane, take hold of her dragon.

She was really freeing him.

This wasn't right.

They were supposed to fight.

To stay together.

Desperation hit him so hard it robbed Arrik of his breath.

This couldn't be the end.

"Come with us," he said, spitting out a mouthful of salt water. "Leave this place. This isn't your home. We both know that."

But Wren shook her head. "I still have work to do. I'm sorry." And she meant it. Arrik could see it. Could *feel* it.

She fished through a bag at her side and pulled out a hunk of meat, tossing it into the water to attract the carnivorous fish. The saddest smile he had ever seen played across her lips as she looked at him one final time.

"Take a good gulp of air. I mean it. The largest gulp you've ever taken."

Behind Arrik, he felt Shane holding on for dear life, muttering curses under his breath as he did so. The man was terrified. If only for his friend, to whom he owed a great deal, he pulled himself together, cursed Wren, and took a deep breath.

Then they plunged into the dark water.

She tossed the keys into the murky water.

It was done.

Why didn't she feel better?

CHAPTER 34

WREN

Wren didn't stop screaming even when the guards appeared.

"What happened?" one of them exclaimed in worry, bending low to check on their queen. She was hunched over, bent double, pretending to be in pain.

It wasn't too far from the truth. Not physical pain but emotional.

"He hurt me," she bit out. "That bastard—he *hurt me* and took the keys right off me!"

The guard motioned to his companion to head out and investigate the palace, and all exits out of the dungeon's water. "Don't worry," he reassured Wren, "we'll find him. And if we don't find him, that means the fish have got him."

Wren smiled grimly. "That would be a far more fitting fate for him."

After making a show of getting to her feet, Wren swayed out of the dungeon toward the throne room. A shadowy figure joined her in the corridor, Kalles' face uncharacteristically serious as he fell into step with her.

"Is it done?"

She nodded. "They'll look for his body but they won't find it." *If Trove gets them out...if Arrik and Shane can hold their breath for long enough...*

Kalles let out a bitter laugh. "Who'd have ever thought I'd help coordinate the *fake* death of my brother rather than a real one? Irony is a real wench."

Wren eyed him, feeling like an exposed raw nerve. "You aren't nearly as heartless as you pretend to be, Kalles. I know you care about him. I know you just wanted his attention, like when you were younger."

"Insinuate I have a heart again and I might just plan *your* death, Dragon Queen."

Wren wanted to smile but found that she couldn't. She was unbelievably exhausted; she needed to sleep for a month. She knew she'd be lucky if she got an hour later that night.

"Who are you kidding? I'm already dead inside."

Kalles stopped and stared at her in concern.

She waved him away. "Don't look at me like that. Come on," she told Kalles as they reached the throne room. "We have a kingdom to rule."

CHAPTER 35

WREN

THREE MONTHS LATER

"GUNN'S RETURNED!" A SERVANT INFORMED WREN ONE morning. She had only just sat down to breakfast—alone, because Leif wasn't due back until that afternoon—but as soon as she heard the news she leaped to her feet and snuck out to the docks.

She'd been waiting for Gunn's arrival for weeks now.

The pirate had smuggled Arrik and Shane out of Verlanti once Trove had surfaced in the bay. His ship had been responsible for traversing the sea and hiding the two of them in a place nobody would look for them: Neamh, a small island to the west of Lorne.

Since then, Gunn had been bringing them regular

supplies, along with letters Wren had written for Arrik and sShane. She had no idea if her husband had read them, for he had yet to respond to a single one.

When Wren reached Gunn's ship, breathless, it became quickly apparent that he wasn't there.

"Oh, he's in the tavern over there," one of the deckhands explained, when Wren expressed her confusion over where the captain was. The tavern in question was the one in which Wren had first met her half-brother, so with a nod of thanks to the deckhand, Wren wove her way over to the bar, careful to keep her telltale scarlet hair hidden beneath a hood.

It didn't take long to single out Gunn flirting with the barmaid. The rake.

"Leave her to her work," Wren whispered into her brother's ear, causing him to slam his knees beneath the bar in surprise.

He let out a filthy string of curses. "You think it clever to sneak up on a sleep-deprived pirate?"

"Pirate?" Wren countered, a sly smile on her face as she ordered herself and then Gunn a tankard of cold, frothy ale. She'd grown to like it over the last three months of secret meetings with her half-brother, as well as drinking with Leif, Josenu, and—to Wren's surprise—Bram. "I thought you were a merchant?"

Gunn laughed, then gulped down almost half the tankard in a matter of seconds. He sighed in satisfaction. "Stars, that hits the spot. We ran out of booze on the ship over a week ago."

"How terrible for you. How did you fare on the journey?"

"Better than I expected, if I'm honest," Gunn replied,

signaling for the barmaid to take his order of grilled sea bass and fried potatoes. "You're paying for this, right?" he asked Wren, before tacking on a sticky date pudding to his order.

She narrowed her eyes. "If you tell me straight-up about everything that's been going on, then yes, I'll buy you a bloody five course dinner if need be."

Gunn knew when he was getting a good deal. So he took another gulp of ale, settled onto his stool, and said, "The capture of High Lord Dravos in East Verlanti was a success. All of his slaves have now been liberated and are being helped off my ship as we speak. The rebellion will take over from there—helping them get jobs, rationing out food and shelter—you know the drill."

"Fantastic," Wren said, genuinely impressed. "It sounds like everything went off without a hitch."

"It helps when your opponent is as stupid as he is vain."

Wren snorted out a laugh. "And your men? Did you lose anyone in the process?"

"Simon lost a leg but he's happy about it."

"Why the devil is he happy about it?"

"Because the nurse who helped with his recovery is now sharing a bed with him every night." Gunn's eyes glinted with mischief. "I suggested he pass her my way when he was through but he didn't seem very—"

"*Behave yourself*," Wren warned. "You're a degenerate. I feel like I need to pray for your soul."

"My soul is cursed, dear sister."

She didn't believe that for a second. Gunn and his crew were doing an exemplary job at helping her clear out the worst of the slave-owners in Verlanti.

"I think you're too hard on yourself."

He shrugged. "Maybe, maybe not. Either way, it doesn't matter."

She let the subject rest. He had his demons and so did she. "We have more work to do."

"That we do," he agreed, taking another sip of his ale.

"When do you leave again?" Wren asked, suppressing a yawn merely *thinking* about organizing the next round of attacks against Verlanti's evil elite.

Gunn grimaced. "In two days."

"Two *days*? That's ambitious."

"We have to catch the wind while it's fair," Gunn said. He squeezed Wren's shoulder. "And if I want to get out to our place at the end of the trip, then I can't dally."

Code for Neamh.

"How is he?" Wren asked underneath her breath. She had been desperate from the moment she saw Gunn to ask about Arrik, but at the same time she was afraid. Afraid to know if Arrik wished her ill. Afraid to know if he was suffering because of her.

Afraid that he wanted nothing to do with her.

The barmaid arrived with Gunn's food, and after shoveling two heaping forkfuls of fish and potatoes into his mouth—and throwing a potato into Wren's mouth to make her laugh—he told her everything she was dying to know.

"He's angry, of course. He might always be, given the circumstances. But it's finally settling in that he won't be leaving the island. That's good for him, I think—accepting his situation is the first step toward a better life. His friend is faring much better. It seems like he's thriving out there."

That made sense. Shane always seemed like he'd rather not deal with people.

Gunn was very careful not to use any names as he gave Wren an update, something which they had both agreed upon at the very beginning. Names were dangerous after all, and Wren could not afford to give her enemies any leverage against her.

She handed her brother a parcel which contained letters for Arrik, Rowen's grandparents, Britta, and even one for Shane. For even though the man had decided to continue disliking Wren, and she him, there was something comforting in sending each other barbed comments with reckless abandon rather than keeping everything inside. It was cathartic. Therapeutic.

Stars, Wren wished Arrik would reply to her letters.

She hated that about herself. He made her so weak.

"Tell Rowen's grandparents it's time," Wren said softly. "If he's settling down—if he's no longer breaking things and a danger to others—then I think he'll benefit from meeting some people."

Gunn nodded, then cocked his head to the side. "At any point during all this time worrying over other people, have you worried about yourself?" He reached out a finger and stroked Wren's cheek. "You look tired, sister. Tired like the dead. You need to sleep."

"I'll sleep *when* I'm dead," Wren said, laughing humorlessly. Of course she was tired: abolishing slavery had not been met with joy, especially with the Vadonese who were bitter that hiring workers in their own lands was the price they paid for the very beneficial contract their king had signed.

Most people Wren met seemed to hate her for it, but by now she was used to people hating her. That didn't make it any less exhausting. The mere thought of more meetings or assassination attempts made Wren yawn. She was too bloody tired to be afraid.

Gunn chuckled softly. "Go back and get some rest, sister. I'll see you again in a few weeks."

Wren wanted to argue—to stay and enjoy the company of someone who *didn't* hate her for a while—but in truth the idea of lying down and doing nothing for a while was too appealing to resist. So after a tight hug and a goodbye, Wren skulked back to the palace.

She was relieved to discover Leif waiting for her in her chambers, though her best friend looked uncharacteristically glum when Wren sat down beside him on her bed. "Why the long face?" she asked, waving down a servant to ask them to bring red berry wine, some cheese, and flatbreads for them to share.

Her best friend huffed out a breath. "Having servants wait on us hand-and-foot whilst we gossip is fun and all, but we both know it isn't what we want to do."

Wren arched a brow. "And what, pray tell, is that?"

"Sneaking off on adventures!" he cried, waving his arms around to emphasize his point. "Fleeing from taverns full of pirates! Escaping dungeons on the back of a dragon!"

Wren could only sigh. "I miss all of that too," she said, mussing up Leif's hair when he rested his head on her shoulder. "I wish I had more freedom and time to spend with you. You know I do."

"I know, I know."

The two of them sat like that for a while, Leif lying against Wren as they ate and drank, until finally he turned to her and smiled mischievously. "You're very late, you know."

Wren frowned. "Late? For what?"

"You promised to meet with Bram down at the docks to discuss further reinforcements sent out to the highlands to push out the remaining slaves the lords up there are squirrelling away."

"Why did you wait until *now* to—wait, never mind," Wren said, leaping to her feet and rushing off to the docks. For of course she knew why Leif had held off on telling her: to spend time alone together. To *talk*. To have fun.

All things Wren could no longer afford to do.

Is this worth it? Wren wondered, huffing from exertion as she bolted through the palace. *Is it, really?*

With every passing day it felt like the answer was a resounding *no*.

CHAPTER 36

ARRIK

Many emotions had been at the forefront of Arrik's mind over the last three months, but even though they still resurfaced from time to time, all he was largely left with was boredom and bitterness.

The anger had burned itself out first. The rage, the frustration, Arrik let them loose in fiery bouts of energy, punching things, cutting things, running until no fuel remained for him to stay upright. Shane took the brunt of his friend's fury—Arrik insisted on sparring multiple times a day. For the first few weeks, more of Shane's skin was purple than it was pale, as was his own.

But the tiny island just off the coast of Lorne didn't hold much for Arrik to destroy in his anger. There were no other people, and no houses save the sparse, rundown cottage that he and Shane had to use for shelter. There weren't enough trees for Arrik to cut down and use their wood as a skiff—he could *see* Lorne, rot it, but the water was too wild and dangerous for him to risk trying to swim across. So he was stuck here, in an isolated, lonely prison, with nothing but rocks, moor, and rain to absorb his rage.

He'd hardly had a rational thought in the first few weeks, but now he had time to plot and plan, to find something to do. He wasn't getting off this island on his own, or even with Shane's help, so all that left was to eke out a life, however pitiful, upon it. If all he did was *survive*, then he might as well be dead.

He needed a goal.

He'd never spent this much time idle in his whole life. It was driving him insane.

Fixing up the cottage was an attainable goal. The rafters leaked, and the shutters that kept out the harsh northern winds were broken. What few trees grew on the island were tough, silvery birch trees. Arrik discovered, after he'd calmed down, that chopping them all down simply to make a raft would be a waste of the wood. The trees were old. You could cut down stray branches for firewood and maintain a house all without killing the thing.

He set about using his long-forgotten skills as a woodworker to fix the cottage. It was something his mother's father had made an entire life out of. Arrik had never met the man, but his mum had made sure Arrik learned at least the most basic aspects of the trade in order to honor him. As a child, Arrik hadn't cared for it; now he realized carpentry was infinitely more valuable a skill than all the prowess in the world with the sword.

In a matter of weeks he transformed old branches into new shutters, and fixed the roof and the floorboards, and even began fixing mere aesthetic issues both inside and outside the cottage for the sake of it. Arrik was proud of his work. He found himself looking forward to the weather warming up so he could begin working on a fence to section off the neglected garden, and then set himself to work fixing the garden itself.

While he was doing all of this, Shane fished. And fished. And fished. Arrik's best friend was an excellent fisherman—better than Arrik could ever aspire to be. It was like magic, the way Shane brought in food for the two of them, then even more so when he built a fire and transformed the fish into crisp, roasted delicacies. Arrik had never tasted so beautiful a tuna or a crab or an eel before.

In all honesty, Arrik had never seen his friend so happy, or so peaceful. How long had they been fighting for causes they didn't believe in simply because their king ordered them to? How many scars had Shane collected because of it? Retirement suited him. Arrik could see it plain as day with his own eyes.

But it wasn't enough for him. Arrik needed a clearer purpose than to simply fish and build and farm. He wanted more.

He just didn't know *what*.

Arrik gulped down another mouthful of spirits from the green bottle in his hand. It was poorly brewed, overly strong alcohol made for pirates, but since it was all Arrik had access to, it might as well have been the nectar of the heavens.

And he was nearly out.

When will Gunn return and resupply it? Arrik wondered tipsily, swirling the contents of the bottle with dismay. There was only half left, then one more bottle in the cottage. Not nearly enough to get him through to the next week.

Gunn had appeared three times so far, bringing scant supplies and letters from Wren. Letters from his *wife*. He hadn't read a single one, but he hadn't burned them either. Though he'd been sorely tempted. They lay abandoned but not forgotten under his bed.

He didn't know why he didn't simply get rid of them.

He liked the pirate who had rescued him and Shane from the back of Wren's dragon and taken them across the sea to the Dragon Isles. Arrik had tried to bargain with Gunn to take him elsewhere—to let him work as part of his crew, even—but Gunn was firmly in Wren's pocket.

Arrik wondered why. Why, and when, and how, had his wife pulled so many people into her orbit? To fight for her? In the days after his imprisonment, it had become clear Josenu had been working with her. For how long, Arrik had no clue. Given his history with Josenu, Arrik had never expected the man to turn on him.

And all for her. Had his wife promised herself to all those men?

He snarled and took another swig of spirits, then frowned as he spied a figure on the horizon. It wasn't Shane, who was away fishing off the shore and wouldn't be back until sundown. It wasn't an animal, either—all that lived on the island were birds. So Arrik stood up and shielded his bleary eyes from the sun.

It was an old couple, with bent backs and dark skin. Vadonese. He blinked, believing them to be a hallucination, only to see a young, pale child zooming around behind them in wild, erratic circles.

As they approached the cottage, and Arrik sitting upon its porch, he began to grow more certain that they were real. But with that certainty came suspicion. Who were they? What did they want?

"You need a bath," the woman announced as soon as they all stood right in front of him. She sniffed imperiously. "Have you not bathed once since you arrived?"

Arrik blinked slowly at her.

"You've made fair work of the cottage though," the man said, nodding approvingly. "I'll grant you that. We've been getting too old to maintain it. You have my thanks."

What the devil?

"I'll get a bath going," the woman said, ignoring him, before pushing past Arrik into the cottage. He could only stare at the old man as he sat down, pulled off a pack from his back with a huff, and held out his hand to Arrik expectantly.

It took him a moment to realize the man wanted some of the booze Arrik was drinking. Bemused by his new situation, Arrik was helpless but to comply. He handed the bottle over, and the old man drank long and deep as if the contents of the bottle were honey wine, not barrel-made white spirit made out at sea.

"I'm Cal," he said, voice gruff. "My wife's name is Aileen. That little girl over there is Britta. She's our granddaughter." Arrik swung his attention to the child, to the obvious differences in their skin tone.

She's too pale to be half-Vadonese. Was she adopted?

Britta was studying a bug with intense curiosity, not moving an inch as she did so. Arrik knew fighting men who were unable to maintain such a still demeanor, even when aiming a crossbow. It was impressive to say the least.

"Why are you here?" Arrik asked. He wasn't surprised when his voice cracked. He had barely spoken a word in weeks, not even to Shane.

"Wren tasked us with being your caretakers," Cal explained, and Arrik's mood soured. Of course they were here because of her. This was *her* domain, after all.

"I don't need your help," Arrik bit out testily.

"Sure you don't. That's why you're doing so well on your own." When Arrik didn't respond, Cal added, "But let's make one thing certain: if you so much as look at my granddaughter the wrong way—if you lay a hand on her—I will kill you. Do I make myself clear?"

"I would never harm a child." This was true. Not even to punish Wren would Arrik ever indulge in the thought of hurting an innocent child. "I'm not sure what the dragon queen told you, but that is not—"

"She said nothing bad of your character."

That brought Arrik up short. She hated him. Why not blacken his name?

Seemingly satisfied with his answer, Cal opened up his pack and handed Arrik a letter. When he saw Wren's spidery handwriting upon it, Arrik immediately ripped it in half and tossed it to the wind.

Britta chased the flying paper like both pieces were birds. It took her a while to catch them both, but when she did the little girl mutely handed Arrik both parts of the letter. A sense of shame overcame him.

Now you are acting like a petulant child in front of a literal *child. How far have you sunk?*

But Arrik knew exactly how far he'd sunk; he simply had no desire to get out of the hole he'd buried himself in. He stared at the letter one final time, tucked it into his pocket, and took a swig from the bottle when Cal handed it back to him.

Then Arrik sat there and watched Britta play, wondering if he'd ever feel joy again the way she was experiencing it.

Maybe that part of him was broken forever.

CHAPTER 37

WREN

SIX MONTHS LATER

Wren was tired.

Well, she was always tired these days, but tonight in particular she felt her exhaustion right down to the marrow of her bones. It was as if she'd aged sixty years in the last six months, yet the end was nowhere in sight.

Is this hell? Wren wondered, in the small hours of the morning when she was on the edge of laughing like a maniac at her lack of sleep. *Am I doomed to live like this forever and ever, with no rest or joy?*

There was no solace to be found in being queen of Verlanti. No gratitude or fulfilment, though of course Wren wasn't doing what she doing just so somebody would thank her. But something was missing. Something huge. Something meaningful.

Wren was coming to the end of her tether, yet still it felt like she'd never be able to fall.

That sensation—of running out of rope but never reaching the end of a fall—pervaded Wren's consciousness as her body finally succumbed to the heavy weight of exhaustion and she slipped into sleep. It was a rotten sleep, full of nightmares and full-body paralysis. The opposite of what Wren needed.

But it was what she had been granted, so Wren had no choice but to take it.

Eventually, however, it felt like someone *did* fall inside Wren's nightmare. But it wasn't her; it was someone *beside* her.

Wren forced her eyes open and was faced with Josenu tackling a masked intruder to the ground, slitting their throat for good measure. It took her a few horrible moments to work out exactly what had happened: the intruder's blade had been dropped mere inches from Wren's heart...her open window that had previously been curtained against the night...the sheets that had been pulled off her body...

An assassination attempt.

One which Wren had been too exhausted to handle herself.

"Stay in bed," Josenu ordered, calm when Wren was growing steadily frantic. "Someone come in here and clean up!" he yelled through the open door, before lifting the mask off the assassin's face. A man, with pale skin and pointed ears. Northern Verlantian going by the look of him.

Wren failed to suppress a shudder. "Revenge for executing Ramos and Wiley?"

Josenu nodded. "Most likely. Don't get up," he reminded Wren, when she attempted to swing her legs up and out of bed. "There might be other methods to kill you set up in the room."

So Wren did as she was told, because she knew Josenu was correct. It startled Wren how much it didn't bother her that someone had tried to kill her. The assassination attempts had come fast and thick since her ascension to the throne, some massive failures and some scary near misses. But they had become part of the fabric of her life now.

Part of the reason she was so tired of it all.

THE NEXT MORNING, WREN BARELY MANAGED TO STOP herself from dozing off during a council meeting. She'd worked long and hard with representatives from each region of Verlanti, along with Josenu and Ronan—who'd come around to working for Wren when he saw exactly what she was trying to do—to appoint a new council.

Now the meeting room was a mix of dark elves from both highborn and lowborn families, humans from the rebellion, and a couple of Lorne navy men Wren had sobbed her eyes out upon being reunited with them.

Rounding out the council was Rowen, representing

Vadon. He and Wren both knew having nobody from Vadon on the council would have been foolish, but she hadn't expected her former betrothed and childhood sweetheart to volunteer himself for the position. Wren had been unsure about it at first—working together for the rebellion had been uneasy at best—but as the weeks stretched into months, Wren found herself thankful that Rowen was here to help her.

It was like having her old best friend back. They knew how to work together. They knew when to speak out against each other, and when to be a united front. It was easy for them to talk and, more importantly, to listen.

Now more than ever, Wren was thankful Rowen hadn't died back when Verlanti first invaded Lorne.

"I'm telling you, the palace needs more security!" Ronan cried, his face as red as his hair as he slammed a fist on the table. "What happened last night—it shouldn't have happened. They always plan these attacks when Leif isn't around to shadow you, Your Majesty. You can't rely solely on Josenu when he's gone."

Wren knew this. But she didn't want anyone else in her chambers. Even though she'd come to trust Ronan, she still didn't feel comfortable having him in her room.

Sensing her discomfort, Rowen said, "More men in the gardens would provide security for the queen without interfering with her privacy. Don't you agree?" Wren could have kissed him for respecting her wishes. But then he ruined it all by saying, "In any case, security would be tightened with the introduction of more Vadonese in the palace. Have you considered Prince Kade's proposal since I brought it up to you last week?"

Wren barely managed to hide her grimace. She liked Prince Kade, and appreciated all that he had done for the rebellion. For the slaves. For the Dragon Isles. But Wren's feelings for the man ended there.

She locked eyes with Rowen. It didn't seem to bother him to suggest Wren remarry. This, at least, brought her some comfort. He wasn't in love with her anymore. They could be friends and allies without the shadow of their past haunting them.

"What would happen if I continue ruling *without* marrying?" she asked, careful to conceal her ire at the notion of getting married.

Everyone in the room exchanged glances, and a low murmur filled the chamber. It was the master of ceremonies who addressed Wren directly. "Marriage is required to produce an heir, but if you name one instead, then that would be acceptable. But it's frowned upon."

"Frowned upon? Why?"

"Because the heir may not be of royal blood, nor will they have conquered the crown by force. Verlantians are very traditional in this matter."

Marriage and the matter of an heir were still plaguing Wren's mind when the meeting was adjourned. She didn't notice when everyone filed out of the room, only looking up from her hands when she was all alone.

Save for Rowen, who was staring at her in obvious concern.

"What?" Wren asked, too tired to be polite. "What's wrong? What have I done now?"

Rowen chuckled good-naturedly. With slow deliberation, he poured Wren a glass of water from a jug on the table and slid it over. "Drink," he said, so she did.

The cold liquid soothed her parched throat, and she realized in that moment just how dehydrated she was. She tilted the glass and downed the water in one go.

"I don't know how to describe it," Rowen said, casting his gaze over Wren's face with sincere affection when she was finished drinking. "You have this—I don't know—*faraway* look in your eyes whenever you aren't in the middle of doing something. As if, as soon as you aren't propelled by forward motion, you simply cease to exist. I hate to see it. That isn't living, Wren. We both know that. Your place isn't here, and we both know exactly where it is."

Wren was touched by the startling observation. It warmed her heart to understand that, despite everything, Rowen was still a person who knew her down to her very core. They might not have been meant for each other the way she so staunchly believed back when they were children, but he still cherished her in a way nobody else could.

And she felt the same.

"Thank you for your honesty," Wren said, squeezing Rowen's forearm in appreciation. "I really mean that. But this is why I need an *heir*, blast it, and not a marriage. If I get married, how will I ever leave this place?"

But then Wren was struck with an idea, one which, until now, hadn't seemed possible.

Announcing an heir that would be frowned upon would

likely incite an uprising, but what if the heir was of royal blood? Someone the Verlantian people loved and trusted, who had shown time and time again they were willing to put in the work for *all* people in the country?

Wren had just the person in mind.

For the first time in many days, she genuinely smiled.

CHAPTER 38

ARRIK

"LOOKS LIKE RAIN. AGAIN."

"Is that really what we're going to fall back onto? The weather?" Shane gave Arrik a look of abject bemusement before returning his attention to his net. "I suppose it's better than you giving me the silent treatment for weeks on end."

"Shut up."

Shane chuckled, then shouldered Arrik out of the way. "Let me. We'll have nothing to eat for dinner with the way you're shaking it. I can feel your restless energy from over here!"

Arrik let his friend take over even though it rankled him that he made such a poor fisherman. He felt useless. So he picked up a few stones and began skipping them across the ocean's surface. It was a pointless skill, but he'd become rather good at it. One of the stones skipped twelve times across the water when Arrik's pointed ears picked up on the sound of footsteps on rock.

"You're scaring all the bloody fish away," Shane growled. "You're no better than a babe."

Arrik rolled his eyes and then scanned the rocky shore, peering at nothing until, eventually, a little face appeared from behind a pointed boulder. Britta. *How long has she been watching us?* Arrik wondered, somewhat discomfited. The girl was silent as the night when she wanted to be, picking over the landscape of her homeland with practiced ease that Arrik could have never emulated.

When Arrik didn't warn her away, Britta bounded over to join them, her eyes scanning the net, then Shane, with approval. Arrik knew from the last few weeks that the girl was *very* adept at catching fish, even with her bare hands.

"You should be with your grandparents," Shane sighed. He was fast becoming a grumpy old man, fishing being his private solace that nobody was allowed to interfere with. Even though Britta made a far superior companion for fishing than Arrik could ever be.

The little girl ignored him of course. She always did. She moved to the water's edge, dipping her toes in despite how cold it was, before selecting seashells to play with, seemingly at random. Since meeting Britta, Arrik had gleaned certain aspects of her personality, though other parts of her remained shrouded in mystery.

She rarely, if ever, spoke, but her face and mannerisms were expressive enough that Britta didn't really *need* to speak. She understood and adored nature. She knew how to cook.

She even knew how to work with wood, though she was still much too little to use an axe. But Arrik could see her calculating eyes taking in every swing when he chopped firewood, and sometimes she adjusted his posture or the angle of the ax to the wood to create perfect, fireplace-sized pieces.

The little girl was smart as a whip.

But she had other quirks. Tics. She was extremely particular about what she ate, and always without fail went to bed and woke up at the exact same time every day. When it rained, she cried if she couldn't go outside, and it sometimes took Cal and Aileen hours to calm her down. Arrik couldn't bear to hear her cry, so more often than not he relented and went outside with Britta to protect her from the worst of the weather.

When he spied an iridescent purple shell, Arrik plucked it from the water as if by instinct, giving it a polish with his shirt before holding it out for Britta. Her eyes grew wide as dinner plates; she wasted no time in scampering over to sit right next to Arrik's feet, hands held above her head for Arrik to drop the shell onto them.

She played with the shell as if it were made of gold, or black diamonds. Like it was precious. Then Britta began to hum.

The melody jolted a memory from Arrik, unbidden and at first unwelcome. It was a song he had heard Wren sing to Trove and, sometimes, in the quiet of the night when the only two people awake were her and Arrik.

A dragon song.

The sound was soothing, and though Arrik held some initial discomfort about why it was familiar, soon he found all his tension easing away. Britta and her high, clear, childlike voice were like a balm on his skin.

"*Arrik*!" Shane barked out, breaking through Arrik's bubble of peace like a hammer. His friend pointed out over the water. "There!"

Arrik scanned the surface where Shane was pointing, instinctively knowing what he was looking for. Bubbles. A snout.

The glimmer of green scales as an *enormous* emerald dragon surfaced from the water.

The creature was almost double the size of Trove, who Arrik had thought was massive. He was overwhelmed by the sheer mass of the monster.

"We need to go," Arrik bit out, grabbing Britta's hand to haul her away from the water. Beside them, Shane dropped his net and clambered away like a man possessed. But the little girl screamed as loud as a storm, scratching and kicking and biting at Arrik's hands and legs in dismay.

The dragon hissed, steam billowing from its nostrils in warning.

Arrik dropped Britta's hand, and the girl rushed back to the edge of the sea just as the dragon swam closer to reach her. Britta rubbed her hands up and down her arms and began to sing again. Before Arrik's very eyes the dragon calmed down and joined in the song.

The sound was mesmerizing. Arrik found himself locked and swaying on the spot, a hook in his brain inexorably pulling him closer to the dragon. So when Britta turned slightly and held out her hand for him, Arrik found himself helpless to obey.

"Arrik, don't—" Shane began, but he shut up when he realized his warning was fruitless. Arrik took Britta's hand, knelt on the shore beside her, and extended his other hand to the dragon. He held his breath when the creature's snout pressed against his fingertips.

He had felt like this once before, when Wren introduced him to Trove. It had been like nothing he'd ever felt before: to meet such a majestic creature with no motive whatsoever to subjugate it. To conquer it. He stood there before the emerald dragon as an equal, not a foe.

As a friend.

When Arrik saw Britta was waiting for his reaction, he grinned, surprising even himself with how genuine it was. The little girl squealed in delight, warming Arrik's heart from the inside out.

For the first time in years, Arrik experienced true peace. He wanted more of it.

He never wanted it to end.

CHAPTER 39

WREN

NINE MONTHS LATER

"So we end the month with only two assassination attempts," Wren told Trove, laughing dryly as he flew them both in lazy swoops and circles over the docks. Below them, Wren could just barely discern the flag of Gunn's ship. After Trove had aided in Arrik and Shane's escape, he had made himself scarce for a few weeks, but after his return Wren had made a point of flying with him daily over the city.

To remind Verlanti just who exactly was their queen. To remind them of her power.

To remind them that she was not a snake, but a dragon.

And Trove's back was the only place where Wren felt truly safe. Like herself. Complete. Or as close to complete as

Wren could be in the hot, humid, strange land that was Verlanti. For the place was no less strange to Wren than it had been back when she'd first been taken prisoner. She knew their customs, yes, and understood how the Dark Court worked off the back of gossip and subterfuge—though she'd been working hard to change that—but it felt as if she was learning about the country from a book in order to pass a test.

Not to live here. Not to be happy here.

But she'd found beauty and pleasure in simple things.

Although, it still didn't feel like home. She doubted it ever would.

Wren looked over Trove's side down to the bay below. She could just barely see her brother's ship. It was due to leave in three days and wouldn't return for three months. That was her deadline: three months. That wasn't much time to organize all that Wren had to accomplish.

But if she wanted to leave this foreign land for good, then three months had to do. Time seemed to simultaneous drag and speed by. Wren could hardly believe it had over a year since the death of her family. The pain was still there but it was an ache instead of a sharp pain.

With a heaving sigh, she kicked her heels into Trove, whistled a tune, and closed her eyes against the *whoosh* of air as Trove descended with startling speed toward the forest behind the Verlantian palace.

She knew who to expect when she landed and kissed her dragon goodbye, though it still shocked and amused Wren in equal measure to see the odd group that had banded together over the last nine months.

Josenu, Bram, and Ronan were engaged in a three-way fight, with Josenu currently in the lead. But Wren knew better than to underestimate Bram, whose sneak tactics she had become familiar with during her time in the rebellion. To the side of the makeshift sparring ring, sitting on top of a fallen log, were Ares and Kalles. Ares was laughing raucously at the fight as if it were live entertainment organized just for him.

He was such a dolt.

Given how much he knew about how everyone fought, and the fact that he was selfish down to his core, Wren wasn't surprised by this. But despite his massive self-preservation streak, Ares had proven more useful than Wren could have imagined. He was helping to train new soldiers, whilst also learning the ways of the Dragon Isles' naval force to improve his abilities at sea. She was genuinely intrigued to see what he would do next, and the kind of man he'd eventually grow up to be.

Kalles was drinking from a vat of wine, as usual, but he had been frequenting brothels and drug dens far less often. Wren took this as a good sign that the young man was making a slow but deliberate journey toward recovery. He still had a long way to go but she was happy to see more light in his eyes these days.

She felt in her heart that, in order to make a *full* recovery, Kalles had to pry himself out of the jaws of the Verlantian nobility. He was still so easily swayed, and without a change of scenery was likely to continue to be that way. But in any case, creating genuine friendships with Bram, Josenu, and Leif had done wonders for Kalles.

Leif was sprawled across the forest floor, fletching birch wood arrows with silver hair. A pang of longing filled Wren at the sight of the color. It only solidified what she'd come here to discuss; the only problem was that it wasn't a discussion to be had as a group. She needed to speak to one person in particular. She'd dallied long enough.

She needed to speak to Josenu.

The fight took another fifteen minutes to end, with Bram ultimately reigning as the victor when he took advantage of Ronan heaving all his weight into a swing against Josenu to knock him off his feet, taking Josenu with him. A dirty victory, to be sure, but a victory nonetheless. When they stepped out of the ring to gulp down water—or, in Ronan's case, wine—Wren gave them all a small wave, then indicated for Josenu to join her on the outskirts of the clearing.

His fair face was flushed and shiny with sweat when he strode over to her. "I wasn't expecting to see you until this evening," he said, scanning her face. His smile waned. "Is something the matter?" Always the protector.

"Nothing's wrong," Wren said, which wasn't the same as saying nothing was the matter.

Josenu caught on to the distinction immediately. "Say what it is you want to say, Wren." *Wren,* not *Your Majesty*, because they were speaking as friends.

Friends who trusted each other, and understood each other, and could see the best in each other.

Wren knew she was making the right decision.

"I was never meant to be queen over the dark elves," Wren said with a resigned smile. "We both know that. I was simply a tool to bring about change so a *real* monarch could rule."

"You are a real monarch," he said resolutely.

"One who understands their people. One who will be just and fair. One who their people can love."

"Our people respect you."

She snorted. "They tolerate me at best."

"You have to give them time. They'll come around. This is just a transition period."

Wren huffed and placed her hands on her hips. "Why are you making this so difficult?"

"What?"

"I want to appoint you as my heir."

Josenu's eyes widened, and he blinked slowly. "Me?"

"You." She clasped her hands together and waited as the gravity of what she was asking settled in.

"Why?" he croaked.

"Because you're the right person for the crown and the kingdom."

He ran a hand over his face and then shook his head. "I'm just a spy."

"One that knows much of his people both high and lowborn. You've lived in both worlds. That's extremely valuable and would make you a fair ruler."

His eyes narrowed. "I'm bastard born."

"So was Arrik but according to the law, you only need royal blood to become the heir."

He tossed his hands in the air. "This is ridiculous. You'll have a family. I won't need to be your heir."

Her heart squeezed. "That maybe so but I want them in Lorne, not Verlanti. The people need you."

"So you've made your decision."

Wren exhaled heavily. "I'm not commanding you to do this. I'm *asking* you to accept my offer."

"I never aspired to rule."

"And that will make you a great king."

He shook his head and released a disbelieving chuckle. "How long have you been planning this?"

"Since they brought up the subject of marriage."

Josenu met her eyes. "Is this truly what you want?"

"It is but I also believe it to be the best chance for your kingdom to settle and prosper. I'm not just thinking about what I want. Verlanti and Lorne are my priorities. But it's not only my decision. I will respect your choice no matter what."

He smiled. "What a queen you are. If only Arrik could see you now," he whispered.

She winced. Wren hadn't heard from her husband in nearly a year. She doubted he wanted anything to do with her. "I try my best," she rasped.

A sly grin spread across Jonsenu's face.

"I'll tell you what..." he said, moving back toward the sparring ring as Bram, Leif, Ronan, Kalles and Ares began to pay attention to what was going on.

"I don't like the look on your face," Wren said, though Josenu's smile was infectious as she jumped into the sparring ring after him.

Josenu nodded. "You know our customs, my lady."

And she did.

Wren rolled her shoulders and called out, "With these men as our witnesses, I challenge you, Josenu, to a fight. If you win, then things will remain as they are, but if *I* win, you become my heir."

All around them their friends rushed to the edges of the ring, eyes bright and fervent with the promise of a fight.

Josenu took out his dagger and flipped it in the air. "Let's see how badly you want this."

CHAPTER 40

ARRIK

So long as Arrik kept chopping wood he could keep his head clear of thoughts for thirty blessed minutes. He could hear Shane and Aileen chatting inside the cottage, no doubt debating the best way to glaze a fish. The two of them had formed such a ridiculously close friendship that Arrik often found himself laughing at them.

Considering Astrid had been responsible for the death of Shane's pregnant wife, he couldn't blame the man for finding solace in a maternal, gentle woman who wanted nothing but the best for him. His friend deserved to be part of a family.

It was clear Cal was happy for his wife to have the company too, and in fact the Vadonese man himself genuinely seemed to enjoy spending time with Arrik. Not for the first time Arrik wondered for how long it had just been Cal and Aileen and Britta, alone.

When was the last time they spoke to anyone else in the Dragon Isles? Why are they so isolated?

But the older couple hadn't given him any information about their past.

He glanced over his shoulder toward the cove.

Cal had taken Britta out to sea to go fishing. Personally, Arrik didn't feel like this was especially safe, but the massive emerald dragon had essentially become the little girl's shadow. If the beast was watching her every move, then Arrik had to concede that the elderly man and his granddaughter were likely as safe as they could possibly be.

It had been surprisingly easy to fall in the love with the little girl. She was sweet, smart, and didn't natter on all the time. He'd never connected with another human being so easily. In truth, Arrik had never had the opportunity to form such a bond.

Arrik rolled his shoulders and finished chopping wood. There would be enough to last for awhile. Cal was certain it would rain during the night and over the next several days.

Arrik set aside the ax and took a break to sit at the edge of the garden. It was neat and organized where once it had been neglected and unruly. He was proud of it. Not once had he ever tried his hand at growing anything. There was something immensely satisfying about seeing one's work come to fruition.

Movement passed the gate caught his attention.

Britta ran through the moor, barefooted as usual, signaling that she and Cal had returned from their fishing trip early. Her curly brown hair bounced around her round face wildly.

He found himself grinning at the little girl's free spirit.

A pang of melancholy followed.

When Arrik allowed himself less painful thoughts of Wren, he could see the ghost of his wife's fighting soul in Britta. The fearless way she'd fought against Arrik's forces when they'd invaded Lorne. Were all Dragon Isles lasses brought up this way? Arrik's sample size was a grand total of two, but both of them were fiercely independent, freedom-loving people.

It was something he had always admired. Always loved.

Seeing Britta live her life guiltlessly to the fullest made Arrik's heart thaw in a way he never thought it would again.

"Uncle Arrik!" Britta cried, beaming as she ran through the garden gate, hoping over vegetables, and bowled into him. He wrapped his arms around her. "The pirate came today," she said breathlessly, without even a stutter.

She'd barely spoken when they first arrived. It took some time for her to warm up to him but she stuttered here and there. Now, she hardly stuttered in his presence which made him feel like he was ten feet tall.

He gave her a squeeze, and she giggled. "Is that so? What did he bring?"

"This." Britta handed him a letter, Wren's telltale handwriting scrawled across it.

Arrik took it from her and slipped it into his belt, hating that Britta's face fell.

"How long are you going to ignore your wife?" Cal called out, stepping into the garden with a pack brimming with supplies.

Arrik put Britta down to relieve the man of his weighty burden, but he didn't respond to his question.

He didn't know how. He had too many mixed feelings. None of them he could make sense of.

He'd become king of more than half the world and she'd reduced him to a lowly farming recluse.

But Wren had also shown him love and grace in a place of death and lies.

Aileen peeked around the corner of the house. "Time for dinner."

LATER, AFTER AILEEN AND SHANE HAD SERVED THEM ALL A dinner of perfectly glazed pollock complete with a shrimp broth and double-fried potatoes, Britta tugged on Arrik's hand and pulled him into her bedroom.

"Tell me a story," she said, when Arrik sat upon her bed and Britta climbed into his lap. He wrapped his burly arms around her and placed his chin on her head, causing the girl to snuggle in.

"A story?" he mused, huffing an errant strand of pale hair out of his face as he did so. Arrik had always kept his hair long, but even *he* had to admit it needed a cut. "Let me see. Have I told you the one about the brave dragon princess whose scarlet hair flashed in the wind like a blazing fire?"

Britta shook her head as she played with one of his braids. "You haven't! Tell me that one!"

And though it pained him at first, Arrik told Britta about the woman who had changed his life forever. Or at least, a romantic, fictional version of events with a suitably happy ending. The child didn't need to have nightmares.

As he uttered the words, "The end," Britta released a small snore, and was completely limp in his arms. She must have tired herself out while fishing.

Arrik slowly stood, careful not to jostle her as he tucked the wee one into bed. She sighed and he brushed the springy curls from her tiny face.

"Sleep sweet," he whispered, making sure the covers were pulled up to her chin.

Silently, he crept out of the room and left the door cracked open. Aileen and Cal both sat by the fire, watching him with soft smiles.

"Thank you," Aileen murmured.

"No need to thank me. It was my pleasure." He headed outside, glancing over his shoulder at the older couple. Cal held Aileen's hand while he read. The moment was so peaceful and romantic that it made Arrik's heart ache.

Closing the door behind him, Arrik sat out on the porch, the spring breeze pleasant on his face.

He took a deep breath and pulled Wren's letters from his shirt pocket.

Then proceeded to stare at them in his hands as if that was sufficient to glean their contents.

Opening them somehow felt like defeat, but it also hurt. He wanted to hear news of home of... his wife.

The door opened, light spilling onto the porch as Shane came outside.

"Here," Arrik said gruffly, holding the letters out to his friend. "Read them."

He expected Shane to refuse, but instead his friend grabbed the letters and took his time reading each and every one. When he reached the end, he let out a resigned sigh that got on Arrik's nerves. What the devil did he have to sigh about?

"When are *you* going to read them?" Shane asked, handing the letters back to Arrik. "Because this is getting exhausting."

"What's that supposed to mean?"

Shane snorted. "Exactly what I said. Why are you hiding? You've never been a coward."

He had no answer for his friend. Part of him felt weak for keeping the letters. Why couldn't he just burn them along with his feelings? Yet he knew that was impossible. For Arrik knew in his heart that he was keeping the letters to be close to his wife, because he longed for her.

Because love wasn't easy.

It wasn't black and white.

And it hurt and healed.

He was terrified of what the letters contained. How had Wren changed, in Verlanti, without him? Had she met someone new? Someone who could love her without asking her to compromise on her values? Someone who could respect her, and cherish her, and worship her, the way Arrik wished he'd done from the very moment he met her?

The letters crinkled in his hands as he fought not to crush them.

A good man would wish her happiness in her life.

He was a good man.

He hoped that no such man existed. And if such a man *did* exist, then Arrik wished him dead.

If Wren had never truly loved him, Arrik still knew his own scorching, all-encompassing, terrifying feelings were true. He'd always love the fiery dragon princess who'd stolen his heart, body, and soul.

Even if she'd never feel the same way.

CHAPTER 41

WREN

ONE YEAR LATER

ONCE UPON A TIME WREN HAD NOBODY IN VERLANTI.

Nobody to miss and nobody who would miss her. Nobody to cherish and be cherished by.

But that had changed. For now, as Wren prepared to bid good-bye to Verlanti for good, she found herself surrounded by a multitude of friends.

Leif. Gunn. Josenu. Kalles. Even Ares and Ronan and Bram—though part of Wren wondered if Bram was happy to see her off simply to see the back of her. He remained behind to act as the new king of Verlanti's master of spies, while Ronan had taken over Josenu's position of master of the guard.

Ares, in a move nobody had seen coming, was joining Gunn's crew.

"All that talent, Ares, and you become a *pirate*?" Wren teased, when the man began hauling a crate onto the deck of the ship along with every other sailor on board.

Ares repositioned the crate in his hands with a huff, then said, "What better way to meet women that I'll never have to see again?"

Gunn barked out a laugh, then slapped him on the back. "Just no disrespecting them or breaking their hearts, all right? I don't want to be banned from any of my contacts because of your wandering eyes and hands."

Wren supposed it was the best move for Ares. He held no true love of his homeland, and now was heir to nothing. But he had all the money he could hope to have, and no familial expectations. That gave him freedom. That gave him all the choices in the world.

It was something Wren could appreciate.

"Are you ready?" Leif asked, interlacing his fingers with Wren's to pull her onto the ship when she grinned at him. He was coming with her much to Wren's relief and happiness. To be perfectly honest, the notion that Leif *wouldn't* follow Wren back to the Dragon Isles had been laughable to them both. It warmed her soul that her best friend, her brother by choice, was going to return home with her and make it *his* home too.

What Wren hadn't expected was Kalles coming along.

"If I'm staying here," he said, when Wren asked him for the fourteenth time if he'd lost his mind entirely. "Especially if you and Leif are leaving. There's nothing for me here, but there might be everything for me in Lorne. And if there isn't...well, I'll find somewhere else."

"That's good enough for me," Wren said, and meant it. She'd wanted him to escape the vipers of his homeland, after all. She'd simply never expected him to make that decision on his own so quickly. There was a doctor in Lorne Castle who had experience with addiction that she was eager to introduce to Kalles. Hopefully, with their help, he would get better. Live a happy life.

Josenu followed Wren onto the ship, helping Gunn and his crew load up the rest of their cargo. He handed her letters. "For Arrik, and for Shane," he said, eyes too tight when Wren took them from his grasp. "And for you," he added on, producing a final letter. "Don't read it in front of me. It's far too sentimental."

Wren let out a laugh, though it was wet with tears. "Heaven forbid the people of Verlanti witness their king cry *in public*. Are you ready?"

"No, but I will do what I must. Because I have to."

"I knew you were the right choice, Josenu."

"I was the *only* choice."

"You were still the best one."

"Enough of this," Gunn cut in, clucking his tongue impatiently. "We need to be off before the wind turns. It isn't like this is goodbye forever."

He was right. Wren was returning home and would rule the Dragon Isles in her sister's stead until she came of age and made the decision over whether she even *wanted* to rule. And if Britta took up the crown, Wren would be there right by her side, helping her.

So no, this wasn't goodbye. Wren and Josenu would rule their nations together and co-exist the way the countries should have from the beginning. Along with Vadon, a new era of peace would take over their little section of the world.

Wren grasped Josenu's shoulder but he pulled her into a hug instead. "If there happens to be a spare dragon you wouldn't mind sending my way, just let me know."

She chuckled. "I'll be sure to check out the Lorne Street Market and ship one out."

After that, Josenu retreated from the ship, and Wren watched as Gunn set sail and Verlanti grew smaller and smaller with every passing minute. Trove surfaced every so often so she knew her dragon was along for the trip.

The entire journey took ten days. The water was turbulent in the middle of their travels and Kalles was violently ill for most of it, but it was otherwise an uneventful trip. Josenu had been right. His letter had been full of sentimental words that made her cry like a baby. Despite all the trials of the last year, she'd gained more family and brothers than she knew what to do with.

Wren herself had never been seasick, but her ever-increasing nerves as they approached the Dragon Isles, and Lorne, twisted in her gut enough to feel like she was.

This was it. She was coming home. She was finally going to be reunited with her sister after all this time.

Over a year had passed. What would Britta look like? Children changed so much in just a matter of months.

Gunn docked in a tiny, private bay, which only the royal family of Lorne had permission to use. The moment it was safe to do so, Wren sang and Trove burst out of the water to land heavily on deck.

"Don't get yourself killed!" Gunn called over the rush of waves and spray of water that hit him in the face when Trove landed, clinging to the side of the ship for dear life as the deck leaned dangerously.

Wren laughed as she climbed onto the dragon, caught a parcel from Gunn, and launched into the air. "I'll try not to!"

It didn't take long before she spied an achingly familiar cottage. The rafters had been updated, as had the shutters across the windows, in a fine, silvery wood that looked likely to be standing strong until the end of time. Wren didn't need to ask to know who had cut down the wood, shaped and built with it.

Despite the nerves twisting her stomach, flying through the salt and the clouds and the scent of the Dragon Isles was setting Wren free. Every knot in her muscles, every pain she'd ever felt, every worry she was holding inside her, melted away to nothing.

She was here. She was home.

Then a tall, imposing figure with loose silver hair exited the cottage to stand in the herb garden, looking for all the world like a lonely deity. Wren's heart flipped in her chest.

"Faster, Trove," she urged, so impatient she was tempted to dive off the back of her dragon into the sea. But she resisted, and held on tight, and a few seconds later they landed on solid ground.

Arrik had spotted them by then, openly staring as she slid off Trove on adrenaline-unsteady legs.

Now that she was here, Wren wanted to run.

Take one step after another.

Wren forced herself to walk toward the man she'd betrayed.

The monster she loved.

He didn't move.

His hands clenched on the hoe he was using, and she warily watched him. Would he swing it at her? They'd always burned hot.

Wren stopped a few feet away from him, helpless to do nothing but watch as the surly elf summarily dismissed her and headed back inside.

That wasn't what she expected.

Some yelling.

A death threat or two, but not the silence.

A small figure bolted out the door at a blisteringly fast pace, and Wren's uneasiness evaporated.

"*Britta*!" she cried, all but dropping the parcel in her hands to scoop up her crying little sister into her arms.

Wren fell to her knees, sobbing and laughing so hard she couldn't breathe, her sister's wild hair in Wren's face.

"Britta," she said, pulling back to cup her sister's sweet face. "My love, I'm home."

CHAPTER 42

ARRIK

The moment Wren appeared before Arrik, it was as if his life had gone from black and white to full color. Had he even witnessed something *red* since her absence? Her hair was like fire, bringing him to life once more.

Yet when Wren descended off Trove and locked eyes with him, even though he was itching to close the gap between them, he'd made no move toward her. It was what he'd do when he reached her that troubled him. Did he want to kiss Wren or strangle her?

He honestly wasn't sure.

So he'd stormed back into the cottage instead.

What he hadn't planned on was the disapproving looks from Cal and Aileen like he was a naughty child.

He stormed past them and out the side door to the gardens to work with Shane, slamming the door behind him.

What reasons did they have to judge him? Arrik hadn't laid a finger on the queen. He hadn't even said a bloody word.

Shane arched a brow at him.

"Not a word," Arrik growled and began aggressively pulling weeds.

The two lapsed into silence and he couldn't help but clench his jaw when he heard the excited welcomes from Cal and Aileen through the open window.

His beautiful sanctuary that he'd worked so hard on didn't feel so peaceful anymore. She'd invaded his space and taken his makeshift family by just arriving.

He ripped a spiny weed out of the ground and kicked it away.

All afternoon he listened as Cal and Aileen crooned over Wren, regaling each other with stories that Arrik could not interpret as the excited tones died down. He and Shane worked away until dark, or as close to dark as the Dragon Isles ever got during midsummer. Arrik could feel blisters beginning to form on top of the calluses of his palms. But he worked through the pain because that was preferable to going inside the cottage.

Eventually, however, his stomach and his friend talked some sense into him. Arrik was almost bent double in hunger, and Shane could take no more.

"So you're going to starve yourself over facing up to her, is that it?" he drawled, slamming his hoe into the ground to rest his elbow on top. "That's awfully mature of you."

"Shut up," Arrik grumbled. He knew he wasn't being rational but he couldn't find it within himself to care. He was on edge and his wife was a problem he didn't know how to solve.

But Shane was having none of it. "I'm going inside now. If you want to come back in with me, then great. Otherwise, have fun sitting in the dark, hungry and cold and alone." The bastard had the audacity to smirk. "I on the other hand will be having dinner with the ravishing queen. Maybe she's looking for a new lover."

That was a low blow.

Arrik snarled but forced himself to leave the garden with Shane.

After washing himself off in the cold-water barrel outside the cottage, the two of them walked into the kitchen. Arrik's feet felt like lead with every step.

"Fancy seeing you here, my queen," Shane said to Wren. The lout went as far as to hug her.

Blast him. Arrik's jealousy came roaring to the forefront like the giant brute he was.

Get it together.

Arrik couldn't even look at her. He helped Aileen set the table, then collapsed onto a chair while the older woman and her husband began serving dinner to everyone.

"I'm very sorry to impose on your hospitality," his wife replied, a chuckle in her voice that Shane traitorously shared.

He didn't answer, but looked between Wren and Shane.

When had the two of them gone from hating each other to laughing with each other? Arrik knew that Shane had received a letter here or there from Wren, but he had imagined they were perfunctory.

Shane ripped into a hunk of bread and sighed with relief. "I've missed bread. Thanks for bringing some over. Speaking of—is it just you? I thought your little spy friend would come with you for sure."

Arrik glanced up through his eyelashes and caught Wren looking at him while awkwardly scratching her nose.

"Leif is with me, but Gunn's taken him straight over to Lorne. And, um, Kalles, too."

Arrik stiffened. "My *brother* is here?" he demanded despite himself. "What could he possibly do here?"

A flash of irritation crossed Wren's face, but she covered it quickly. That was new. She had always worn her emotions on the surface. Just what had the Verlanti court done to her?

It's what you've done to her.

The thought almost knocked the breath from his lungs.

"I see you're just as judgmental as ever."

"An answer, *my queen*," he sneered.

"He's working on himself, and he's working hard."

Arrik scoffed, his anger igniting in his chest. "Kalles has never worked a day in his life. All he does is drink, whore, and smoke his life away."

"He's trying to do better," she said tightly. "I imagine if you'd ever given him the time of day he might have tried much earlier on."

"You—"

Britta whimpered.

"No fighting," Cal warned.

Arrik wilted. He didn't want to scare the child. He

watched as the wee one curled onto Wren's lap for protection. That hurt Arrik more than he could ever say. This was *his* sanctuary, and now Wren had waltzed in and claimed everything as her own.

She was a bloody thief.

But that notion gave Arrik pause. Since when had this tiny island become a sanctuary rather than a prison? The revelation was shocking to him, but not in an unhappy way.

A beat of silence passed. Two. Three. Then Shane asked, "Any news from Verlanti? If you're here, then who's ruling the country?"

"Josenu," Wren said, a proud smile on her face. "He was the only, and the best, choice."

"You left our kingdom with him?" Arrik murmured in disbelief.

She met his stare. "My kingdom, yes."

He bristled but kept his sharp words to himself. The only way Josenu could be heir apparent was if Wren married him.

"How could you?" he said, tone icy cold.

"Do what?"

"Marry him."

Wren glanced between him and Shane, then burst into laughter. "Stars save me from dense men." She wiped her eyes and arched a brow. "Josenu has just as much royal blood as you do. He was the best option for the throne."

He crossed his arms and stared his wife down. That didn't explain everything. "You could have married anyone and kept the throne. It was the easiest path." His tone was gruffer than he'd have liked.

Wren held his gaze. "You know exactly why. Or at least you would if you'd read any of my letters."

Her words struck him like stones.

It was too much for him. Too much feeling.

There wasn't enough air.

Arrik abruptly stood up, his chair scraping across the stone floor. He nodded to Aileen. "Thank you for the meal." He refused to be disrespectful to the woman who'd been so kind to him.

She smiled at him and Arrik turned on his heel, striding out of the cottage.

He thundered down the stairs, registering the door opening behind him as he took off into the darkened moor.

"Go back inside," he growled, not looking over his shoulder. He couldn't look at her. Arrik couldn't deal with her.

"Stop running from me."

"That's not what I'm doing." He picked up his pace, trying to get away from the dragoness stalking him.

"Arrik, I'm sorry!" Wren yelled, when they were far enough away from the cottage that nobody could hear them.

That stopped him in his tracks and lit the fuse of his ire. Arrik spun around to face his wife, hands shaking. She stood several paces from him, palms out in supplication.

"I don't accept!" he roared. She stared up at him, unflinching and unwavering in the face of his anger. The way she'd always been with him. "You took away my life—you took away my kingdom!"

"I did it for your own good!" she fired back, stalking forward and invading his space. Wren was much smaller than

Arrik, but right now it felt as if they were screaming on level ground with each other.

She was too close.

"I don't need to hear your excuses," he hissed, turning to walk away. This conversation wouldn't be good for either of them.

But Wren was having none of it. She grabbed his arm, and dug in her heels as if to stop him.

"You have to try harder than that," he sneered. "Go back to the cottage. You're not wanted here."

One moment he was shaking off his lying queen, the next, his legs were swept out from beneath him and he was tackled to the ground.

Arrik let out a yell as he hit the earth, instinct causing him to pull Wren down with him and pin her beneath him. He glared down at her and slammed his palms against the dirt. "You must stop. Leave me be!"

"I've left you alone for long enough," Wren retorted, eyes blazing against his, her breath teasing his lips.

Arrik wanted to hate it. He wanted to loathe how wonderful it felt to have Wren beneath him. How *right* it was. How natural.

"I could kill you." He glowered. "I should."

"But you won't."

They both knew it. They had always known it.

"You're poison," he spat.

"And the balm for your soul."

He gritted his teeth and looked away. Staring down at her was too much. "You took everything that mattered to me. I sold my soul for the crown. It was my life's work. You destroyed my life."

"You're right."

That's not what he expected her to say. It took some of the wind out of his sails. "Why did you do it?" A deep breath. "Why didn't you trust me?" he asked raggedly.

Wren's eyes filled with tears. She raised her hand, tracing a finger along Arrik's jaw as carefully as she would a predator. He let her. His traitorous body wanted to lean into the sweet touch.

"I had to save you from becoming your father."

His lip curled. "I am nothing like him."

"Power has consumed you your whole life." She smiled wobbly up at him. "I know how much you've given up over the years but I could see how much the crown was changing you. It would never be enough. You'd give too much of yourself until you had become your father. I couldn't let that happen. You couldn't pull yourself out. You needed help from the people who loved you."

He wanted to say that she was wrong. That, together, he would have been a fair king, a just king. But the value of hindsight was that Arrik could plainly see the unforgivable compromises he had made as king. Working with Idril. Refusing to outright abolish slavery. Capturing a wife and keeping her bound to him. Not keeping his promises.

He felt sick.

Wren knew him better than he knew himself.

Without thought, he leaned into her touch like the weak fool he was.

"And besides," Wren whispered, "I trust you the most."

His voice cracked. "I don't see how. You kept everything from me."

She glanced in the direction of the cottage and then back to him. "That which is most valuable to me, I entrusted to your care."

He frowned and glanced at the cottage as Britta walked by the window. Understanding slammed into him and he sucked in a sharp breath. He stared for a long time. It felt as if Arrik had been struck by lightning. So much made sense now. *Wren* made sense, finally, for the first time since he'd laid eyes on her. Everything she had put up with. The torment. The pain. The suffering. She hadn't broken at any instance when anyone else would have. Arrik hadn't understood it, and now he did.

"She's your sister?" he said, turning back to his wife.

She nodded, studying his expression. "Yes. And the true heir to the isles."

He blinked slowly. "True heir?" He'd never heard of another princess.

"She was a closely guarded secret from the outside world. It was my parents' wishes and my own to protect her until she was older. *Britta is special.*"

"That she is," he murmured, turning over puzzle pieces in his mind.

The real heir to the Dragon Isles. Not Wren. Never Wren. All of Soren's scheming, and all of the despicable things Arrik had done in his father's name, had been squandered by the good and true and unbreakable bond between two sisters. The love of a family that understood what *family* meant, something which Arrik only now understood.

"You did this all for her."

Tears pooled in Wren's eyes. "Yes. She's been my purpose."

"And I the obstacle in your path."

She shook her head and cupped Arrik's cheeks. "And you the other half to my soul."

He shuddered and closed his eyes. "How can we move forward from this? We're so broken."

"Look at me."

Arrik opened his eyes as she glared up at him through her tears.

"We are not broken, my love, just a little roughed up and dented. A little fire, a little polishing and we'll shine again."

"You want me after all of this?" He needed to know.

Her fingers sank into his hair. "I refuse to live without you."

There were no more words that could relay how Arrik felt, or what he wanted to do. Words didn't matter anyway—actions did.

And right now there was only one action that mattered.

Arrik kissed his wife and it was the purest thing he'd ever done in his life. He lowered to his forearms and settled his weight against her body. The most natural thing in the world. Wren smiled into their kiss. "Why are you smiling?" he murmured between kisses.

"Because I've missed you and I can't believe I'm here."

Arrik pulled back and soaked in his queen's flushed face. "So you conquered and gave away a kingdom just to return into my arms?"

Her smile widened. "I did. I'm no longer the queen."

"That's where you're wrong. You will always be my dragon queen."

"And you my dearest villain."

He brushed his nose against hers. "We're not fixed."

"No, but it's a start."

He nipped her bottom lip. "It's everything."

CHAPTER 43

WREN

1 MONTH LATER

THINGS WEREN'T EASY.

Revealing the truth of their deceptions to each other hadn't been simple. The wounds were deep and would take time to heal for both of them.

Arrik was restless and haunted.

Wren was lost and withdrawn at time.

Communicating was difficult.

Their path forward was unclear.

Wren and Britta couldn't stay on Neamh.

Arrik couldn't leave.

Everyone thought him dead and if anyone were to find out otherwise... it could ruin everything. Plus, her people would never accept him after the atrocities he and his men had committed.

They were at a crossroads, and she didn't know which direction to go.

All of these troubling thoughts plagued her as Wren wandered toward the cottage, running her fingers over the long grass. Arrik and Britta were speaking and weeding, while Shane cleaned the fish he'd caught that day.

Britta glanced her way and smiled, revealing a missing front tooth. It was so goofy and endearing. Her sister abandoned her chores and ran toward Wren. Every time Wren left the cottage, she had to reassure Britta that she'd come home. It broke her heart that her sister thought she'd never come back.

Wren knelt and wrapped her sister in her arms and held Britta tight. "How has your afternoon been, sweet?"

"Good. The carrots are getting tall."

"That's good."

"Uncle says that we need to thin them out or they won't grow."

"That sounds wise," Wren said with a small smile as she inhaled the earthy scent of Britta's hair, before pulling back. "You ready to help surprise Uncle?"

Britta gave her a toothy grin. "Yes."

Wren shared her smile. "Go get him."

Her sister bounded off toward Arrik. She touched his shoulder and held her hand out. He paused his weeding and set down the spade.

Hook, line, and sinker.

No one could resist Britta's sweet face.

He climbed to his feet and took her hand. She led him out of the garden toward Wren and her breath caught. This was the future she wanted.

Her family together.

Arrik caught her look and cocked his head in question. She waved a hand at him as they approached and placed her hands on her hips.

"You ready for our walk?" she asked.

Britta bounced on her toes and held her other hand out to Wren. She took it and off they went.

They wandered the moors, collecting herbs and the stray flowers. Wren's nerves grew worse the closer they got to Pearl Bay. She'd never done anything like this before and she hoped Arrik would like it. They hadn't gotten to spend much time together away from Cal, Aileen, and Shane in the weeks prior and it was taking its toll.

Britta released their hands and raced over the hill, leaving Arrik clutching her flowers.

Wren smiled at him. "How pretty you look, sir."

Her husband gave her a devilish smirk that made her heart race. "Why thank you, my lady."

Almost shyly, he held out his large hand. Without hesitation, she slipped her own into his and gave it a squeeze. The scent of salt and the crash of waves reached them.

Here goes nothing.

They crested the hill and her pulse raced as her surprise was revealed.

A picnic.

Arrik slowed as he took in the scene.

It wasn't anything elaborate but she'd done her best.

Simple pillows surrounded an old quilt. She'd managed to get a bottle of good wine from Gunn and some fruit specific to Verlanti.

"What's all this?" Arrik asked roughly, emotion clogging his throat.

Wren faced him and took his hands. "You prepared a picnic for me to help me feel at home. And to show me your love. I know it's not the same...but I wanted to show you how much I love you." There, the words were out.

He grinned and before she could say another word, he pulled her to his chest and claimed her lips.

"If this is how I thought you'd react, I would have done this earlier," she managed between kisses.

Arrik lifted her off her feet and carried her to the blanket, carefully sitting down so she was straddling his thighs. He ran his lips down her neck and bit her collarbone, groaning.

"We have to behave," he huffed against her skin, causing Wren to shiver. "Britta is no doubt watching."

Wren glanced over her shoulder. Britta ran in the surf just a short distance away. The little one began singing at the top of her lungs, calling both Greeny as she liked to call the enormous emerald dragon and Trove. Shaking the water off his scales, Wren's mount clambered onto the rocks to sun himself. He was worse than a cat.

"You're right," she admitted and slid from Arrik's lap.

Arrik pulled her tightly to his side and wrapped his arm around her. She laid her head on his shoulder. "Is this the reason you've been quiet for the last few days?"

"Part of it."

"And the other part?"

This was the question she'd been dreading.

"I don't see a way forward," she rushed out. "I can't stay here forever and..."

"You can risk my appearance," he supplied.

Wren stared up at his strong jaw. "I don't want to leave you."

"I don't want that either."

"What do we do?" she whispered, feeling desperate.

"We do what we've always done. Fight for each other." He glanced down at her, blue eyes holding so much warmth and love that it made her want to cry. He lifted his left hand and touched the tip of her ears. "I've been thinking of a solution."

"What is that?"

"I'll go with you."

"They'll never accept you. I'm so sorry."

"Not as Arrik, they won't." He gave her a bittersweet smile. "We can clip my ears so they appear human."

Wren gasped in horror. "I would never, *never* ask you to do something like that. It's barbaric."

"I'm a barbarian." He shrugged. "I can handle pain and a few more scars." He fingered one of his braids. "Plus, I fancy a haircut and perhaps a change in color."

She scooted away and turned to face him. "You can't mean to do that. I can't allow you to sacrifice who you are. It's wrong."

He took her hand and laced their fingers, before kissing her wrist. "A few physical changes do not define me. Family, honor, and true love do. I refuse to be parted from you." His gaze turned to Britta. "And my family. She's my sister as much as she's yours now." He looked back at Wren. "I know we are still learning to trust each other. You put whatever document you need to in front of me to protect the Dragon Isle throne and I will sign it. It's taken me over a year to know that what I've been searching for my whole life is right here on this beach."

"Even Trove?" Wren joked; her voice thick.

Arrik leaned closer to place a gentle kiss on her lips. "Even the bloody dragon."

ALSO BY FROST KAY

THE AERMIAN FEUDS

(Dark Epic Fantasy)

Rebel's Blade

Crown's Shield

Siren's Lure

Enemy's Queen

King's Warrior

Warlord's Shadow

Spy's Mask

Court's Fool

Prince's Poison

THE TWISTED KINGDOMS

(Epic Fantasy/Fairytale Retelling)

The Hunt

The Rook

The Heir

The Beast

The Hood

The Wolf

DRAGON ISLE WARS

(Epic Fantasy)

Court of Dragons

Queen of Legends

Throne of Serpents

ABOUT THE AUTHOR

Thank you for reading
THRONE OF SERPENTS!
I hope you enjoyed it!

FROST KAY is a USA Today bestselling author and a certified book dragon with an excessive TBR.

She adores telling stories of strong women, diverse cultures, and epic fantasy worlds filled with relatable characters and true love. She lives in the United States and when not immersed in her newest book, you can find her free diving in her mermaid tail, rock climbing, camping, or soaking up the sun with her cat.

If you'd like to know more about Frost, her books, or to connect with Frost online, you can visit her webpage https://www.frostkay.net/ or join her facebook group FROST FIENDS!

Milton Keynes UK
Ingram Content Group UK Ltd.
UKHW012155091123
432302UK00016B/165/J

9 798892 389976